THE
DISMAL
SCIENCE

THE
DISMAL
SCIENCE

{a novel}

PETER MOUNTFORD

Tin House Books
Portland, Oregon & Brooklyn, New York

Mountford

Published by Tin House Books, Portland, Oregon, and Brooklyn, New York

Distributed to the trade by Publishers Group West, 1700 Fourth St.,
Berkeley, CA 94710, www.pgw.com

Library of Congress Cataloging-in-Publication Data

Mountford, Peter, 1976-
  The dismal science : a novel / Peter Mountford.—First U.S. edition.
    pages cm
  ISBN 978-1-935639-72-5 (pbk.)
  1. World Bank—Employees—Fiction. 2. Middle-aged men—Fiction. 3.
Widowers—Fiction. 4. Economists—Fiction. 5. Loss (Psychology)—
Fiction. 6. Identity (Psychology)—Fiction. 7. Washington Metropolitan
Area—Fiction. 8. Psychological fiction. I. Title.
PS3613.O865D57 2014
813'.6—dc23
                                2013026627

First U.S. edition 2014
Printed in the USA
Interior design by Diane Chonette
www.tinhouse.com

For my father

After such knowledge, what forgiveness? Think now
History has many cunning passages, contrived corridors
And issues, deceives with whispering ambitions,
Guides us by vanities.

—**T. S. ELIOT**, "Gerontion"

1

MEETINGS

The annual meetings had become a kind of rowdy reunion, bearing, increasingly, the muffled bonhomie of a great funeral. At the Omni's and the Sheraton's dueling bars, dignitaries—old friends and colleagues and rivals who'd been driven apart and together by the conflicting currents of their careers—gathered over strong drink and weak gossip. For most, the old ambition that had brought them together was now largely vacuumed away. Vincenzo planted himself at the Sheraton's superior bar, occasionally reading briefs in the comfortable chairs of the adjacent lobby, but otherwise holding to a tight orbit. There were fewer bilaterals this year, or at least he wasn't required to go to as many. The young attendees still passed around their business cards, as if there was some angle to be had, as if someone would remember in a week, as if it meant anything to be remembered.

This being 2005, it wasn't lost on them that there hadn't been a major economic catastrophe in five years. Except for

Argentina, and that didn't count, because their central bank was just too inept for words. So maybe everyone was starting to feel like they'd gotten it right after all. The medicine was taking. It was terrible about Iraq and Afghanistan and a lot of other things in the world were terrible, too, but really, it could've been so much worse. And so the proceedings seemed lifted by a calm buoyancy that had been absent before, especially during the troubled nineties when there began to be a lot of talk about hegemony, a word that hadn't really seemed to exist before, but suddenly became so ubiquitous as to be immediately exhausting. Everything had been fraught in the international aid community then—crises came huge and frequent, each more terrifying than the last. Executives sharing elevators would exchange wide-eyed looks, shaking their heads, quietly pining for a return to the relative sanity of the Cold War.

With this new calm, Vincenzo knew it was all the more important to remain vigilant. There was always, anyway, a lurking danger to DC's autumn months. The city's summer torpor lifted unevenly, erratically—especially for Vincenzo, from Milan, where the weather wasn't so dramatic. DC in fall was unpredictable in the same way that driving at dusk can be more dangerous than driving at night, because at least at night you know that you can't see, but at dusk the light is sneaking away and there are no headlights, no streetlights, nothing but long shadows and seductive gilded light streaming in from the horizon. In the fall, you'd leave your house in a winter coat, scarf, and gloves, scrape ice off the windshield, but by lunchtime you'd be rolling up your sleeves, turning up the air-conditioning. Everything was upside down. This was prime season for losing winter apparel—gloves left on a bar (after all, it felt like Caracas outside!).

The meetings were in late September, the most inconsistent month, when the trees in Rock Creek Park were still shrouded like attic furniture under blankets of vines. Once that bite came in, you knew the howling bugs in the trees were not long for this world, nor were the vines. Soon, the trees would be stripped bare and freezing rain would claw the heaps of soggy debris, decomposing into mud, down into storm drains, flush it all out into the Potomac.

Even with the chaos of September in the air, the meetings were fine. Everyone was fine. What else was there to say, after all? In Latin America, things were going well, more or less. The Bank's programs, in particular—Vincenzo deserved zero credit for it, truly—were going swimmingly. No one really deserved credit. Politics had matured, capitalism was working. Stability had taken hold and the emerging markets were now actually *emerging*.

"It's almost on autopilot," he said to halfhearted chuckles from the crowd.

His panel was in one of the larger halls in the basement of the Omni. Although it was in a way the more stately hotel, the Omni always felt a bit bereft by comparison to the hullabaloo up in the Sheraton; it was kind of slouching into the valley of Rock Creek Park. The chairs had been mostly empty when he convened the talk, but he'd been pleased to see people filing in over the first half hour. And then, during the Q&A portion, he glanced at the clock and saw that there were eight minutes left, and what had been said? Nothing. Nothing much was ever said, but they had *really* said nothing this time. People were listing drowsily in their chairs, glancing at their phones; at least one of the reporters up front was doodling in her steno. She was attractive, or maybe not. She was young and healthy, and that was attractive. And his recognition of the predictability of his anguish at her boredom was almost as painful as his anguish at her boredom itself. Could it be so ghastly and predictable? Yes, it could.

Afterward, he and his copanelists had a half-hour break before they were to reconvene in a boardroom upstairs for an hour-long closed-door session with delegates from the major Latin American economies, namely Argentina, Mexico, Peru, Chile, and Brazil, who all wanted to explore their evolving relationship with the wealthy countries that had for so many decades been either—depending on whom you asked—bailing them out of bad situations they got themselves into, or shoving them into bad situations and then charging them for a bailout. In any case, these countries were seeming less feeble by the day. Something had shifted underneath everyone's feet. It was time to have a frank conversation.

$$=$$

Vincenzo was leaving the first meeting when Cynthia, whom he hadn't seen in a decade, approached with that mischievous squinting grin. Maybe as an adolescent she had been embarrassed by her teeth, which were in fact a little crooked, but she always hid them with her lips. She'd left the World Bank for some forgettable leadership role at Inter-American Development Bank years ago. Now here she was, edging toward him with that self-conscious smirk, saying, "Oh my God, he's alive!"

Setting his briefcase down on the chair, he grabbed her by both shoulders and kissed her on her cheeks and then held her back, like a child he was appraising. "How the hell are you?" he said, and they hugged.

"I hate being back here," she said into his shoulder. "I can't walk ten feet without running into horrible old ghouls like you."

He grinned and they separated. "But you live here, right?"

"God *no*, I slid over to the UNDP and they put me in Brazil, hence—" and she waved vaguely at the room. The new job was, strictly speaking, a step down from the old one, which was probably why she hadn't broadcast the move. She'd gone meaty and middle-aged. A sexless pall had fallen over her, as it did most of them, as it had, no doubt, him. Back when they were sleeping together, when she was on mission in Peru, she had an impressive body for a mother of three in her forties, and her aura was distinctly sensual. She radiated low-frequency sexual enticement. Something in the body language, the way she sat down so slowly, how long she held your hand during a handshake, the overdetermined eye contact. Even her coy grin seemed dangerous. You just knew she was a pervert. Now she was—what?—probably in her late fifties. More battle horse than colt. That radiant carnality had dimmed. Or maybe it was still there, and his sensing mechanism was damaged. Worse still, maybe she just didn't turn the signal on for him anymore.

"Look, we should have a drink," he said. "I have another meeting." The last of the others were filing out of the room now.

"I'm going to be at that meeting."

"Oh—the one upstairs?"

"Yes. We'll go to the bar up at the Sheraton afterward?" she said.

He nodded.

She smiled a little, and then said, "If you're thinking what I think you're thinking, don't think that."

He snorted. And then he slowly drew a deep breath, shook his head, looked away.

Since he didn't deny it, she said, "Do you still want to have that drink?"

He paused for effect, looked her in the eye, and said, as unconvincingly as possible, "Of course I do."

She chuckled humorlessly, no doubt weary of men like him.

It was only once they were in the elevator going up that it dawned on him that this wasn't really a coincidence. She didn't really have a reason to be at either meeting. No, she was angling for something. Maybe a job.

They were not alone in the elevator, but he could smell Cynthia's perfume, too sweet, too conspicuous. So much honeysuckle; it brought back a sour stain of guilt, all the worse now that he'd lost the reason for that guilt.

Perhaps sensing where his mind was heading, she said, "How's your kid?"

He squinted at her. This not mentioning his wife—he didn't quite know what to make of it. Maybe she hadn't heard? Probably she had. Either way, he wouldn't bring it up. "She finished college and is in New York."

Cynthia nodded.

"A waitress. Tattoos."

She smiled in the repressed way that people do in crowded elevators, in the way she always did.

"Your husband?" he said.

"Fine," she said. "Great."

He nodded. But she wasn't wearing a wedding ring. There wasn't even a tan line.

≟

The problem was that Peru shouldn't have been invited to the closed-door meeting. Peru's development was still too gestational. As if to underscore this, their delegate was dour in a shapeless sports jacket and khakis, while everyone else in the room wore suits. But this was the era of inclusion, apparently. Eastern European countries were tumbling into the EU and the field was everywhere more open, more noisy and confusing.

Not long after they had settled in, the Peruvian delegate set forth with a question, a statement really, about the Bank's commitment to global emissions reductions. The question was odd and awkward for a variety of reasons, not least that a Peruvian delegate would take up this non-Peruvian issue so publicly.

Here it was, naked and crazed, the hobgoblin of their era: *fairness*. A muddleheaded man, the delegate also produced a subordinate question about the long-term viability of the petroleum-based successes, which could seem like a weird dig at Brazil. Or maybe he was parroting Ecuador's recent noise about the Yasuni-ITT initiative. Of course, he just wanted to show that he was formidable, but he came off as far too confrontational and obsessed with the hegemon. Anyway, he was on the wrong subject.

Pablo Rendón, deputy director of the environment direc-
torate at the IADB, and an old friend of Vincenzo's, had talked
about the environmental policy downstairs. Pablo had said
what was to be said, really. They were forging ahead despite the
maddening intransigence—Pablo had put it more politely—of
the USA. Bush had just made it clear that they wouldn't sign on
to Kyoto, and that was the end of that.

But the question was out now—he'd gone bold and there
weren't many people in the room, so they had to dignify it with
a proper response.

"Look," Vincenzo said, "I appreciate what you're saying,
but the point remains that the growth is real." Cynthia had
sat away from the table, at the back, against the wall, and
Vincenzo was distinctly aware of her presence. "Oil or no
oil," he went on, "those countries are buying time to develop
a more sophisticated economy, and they're using that time
well. That's my impression. Peru, also, your GDP comes from
minerals, so it's—"

"But I'm talking about values, sir," the man said.

"Values?" Vincenzo shrugged, as if amused, and scanned
the room incredulously, but no one met his gaze. Many of
them also looked bemused, even Cynthia. Pablo, an Argentine-
an who adored Scottish whisky—and was visibly hungover—
rolled his eyes and glanced out the window. The conference
room was on the fourth floor; the floor-to-ceiling windows
faced Rock Creek Park, the sloping grass and the twisting
roads, the tall trees, the band of forest snaking through the city.
Far on the other side, toward Dupont, Art Deco apartments
stood stately on the rim of the vale. It was hard not to stare out

the window. Noted for his pretty ice-blue eyes, Pablo was dull, had the suspicious languor of a lizard captured at midnight in the desert. Vincenzo waited another moment, hoping he'd wake up enough to put the delegate in his place, but apparently he'd already spent all his energy that morning.

So it fell to Vincenzo:

"Mister," he said, "the question is vague and we have a lot of business ahead, so I don't know why or how we would start—"

"I'm concerned about the indigenous communities in the Amazon basin."

"Because they have money now?" Vincenzo said. "That's what's destroying them? They have medicine and education and—"

"Have you even met these people?"

"No, why would I? I'm not a politician. I don't shake hands with people who work on oil rigs in the jungle. I'm not the pope or something."

People chuckled a little, but Vincenzo didn't like his own tone, didn't care for his own line of argument. It was true, and it wasn't true. A more important question was why the US delegates were more or less denying climate change and refusing to sign the Kyoto Protocol or contribute to the process. There were other valuable questions, too, about carbon swaps and so on.

From the corner of his eye, he saw Cynthia pick up her phone and start typing. Collecting himself, he went on: "These people in this forest, they want to be part of modern society to some extent. I know because they are showing up for work at these oil-drilling platforms. But you here, in this room"—he gestured at the glinting chandelier above—"you are going to decide that they should remain in loincloths eating rodents and dying of the common flu?"

"You're making a decision, too," the man pressed, "deciding that taking them from their community and putting them on oil rigs—you're saying this is good."

Vincenzo groaned. "Let's just—I know you haven't been in these meetings before, so maybe you can just let things transpire naturally." Again, he hated his own tone. He knew his condescending lines would be echoing in his head for days. "We should talk about this, but it's too complicated for today's meeting."

The man glared at Vincenzo. And still no one came to Vincenzo's defense. No one said anything. What were they afraid of? Cynthia was still typing on her phone. So, with a rising voice, he said, "I can't believe we're having this conversation now, instead of the meeting we planned, but if we must! Let me see—history!

"For many thousands of years, the world has been moving from being a barbaric and brutal place filled with people who roam the woods with blades and clubs, to a place where people pull four-course meals from their freezer and zap them in a microwave. Is this sad? Yes, it is sad. It is tragic! Really! We have lost our souls, and I believe this. Is it beautiful, too? Yes, it is beautiful. Babies don't die from simple illnesses, and that is good. We can talk face-to-face to people on the other side of the planet, we can fly from here to Europe in half a day. We live in a time of miracles. So these people in the Amazon are going to do horrible work for Exxon for a generation or two. They might ruin that part of the jungle. Yes. They might be

miserable. Yes. But they might not be miserable, too. It doesn't
matter. And yes, it *does* matter. We lose and we win. I don't
know what's right, but, uh"—he looked at Cynthia, who had
put down her phone, was biting back a grin.

"Look," he said, "this is capitalism. We happen to think it
works. We might be wrong, but we think it is the best option
available, and that's why we are here. We have hope that this
will work out."

He looked around the room, and there it was: *life*. People
were awake! Not just Cynthia, but the rest, too—everyone was
sitting up a bit straighter. For the first time all day, the first time
all week, they were listening; even Pablo seemed to have been
roused. Not that it mattered, really, it was just a bit of throat-
clearing before the real meeting began, but still: here they were,
all awake together for one wonderful moment in that gleaming
conference room.

≐

Two hours later, at the Sheraton's vast bar, he and Cynthia parked
on a pair of stools, the afternoon light gloaming at the distant
window, and she told him about Brazil, her residence, and so on.
She'd been pushed out of her last job, sort of, but her boss had
been a lunatic, so it'd been for the best. Neither of them mentioned their families. It was a full hour before she finally brought
up the thing that she had sought him out to discuss.

The Bank had tried a series of partnerships with mobile phone
companies throughout Latin America to get more cell towers
built in poor, underserved areas, but the companies had not been

incentivized properly and the rural customers hadn't understood how to partake. With no existing infrastructure, the phone companies hadn't been able to market the program, weren't even sure where to sell their products. Ultimately, it was still too expensive to figure it out. They'd hoped to get the Internet to tiny schools in the Amazon, mobile phones to doctors far from hospitals. It could have been great, but it wasn't great. The tranche was small and the debt soft, so Vincenzo had cut everyone's losses and killed it. In each country, the money was rolled into the general project fund—a bureaucratic purgatory for failed ideas.

Cynthia wanted to try it again in Brazil through the UNDP, but Vincenzo had been so adamant in mothballing it that no one, especially the mobile phone companies, would be interested in taking it up again. He'd done the same thing with a housing subsidy, and with a partnership between microbanks and water treatment companies. Elegantly drawn projects that he'd clipped. She wanted to revive all three grants in Brazil through her office. Thanks to her own nonperforming grants, she'd had budget overruns, and now it was clear that if she didn't allocate money by the end of the fiscal year, they'd cut her budget accordingly.

Fair enough, but no. It would be one thing if she had just wanted his leftovers. Instead, she wanted to plagiarize the Bank's work on the defunct programs and then contradict their assessment of the programs. And in order for her to do this, he'd have to publicly endorse her reinvention of these programs.

"I have ideas for how to fix them," she said. She had begun to lay out her ideas for how to fix them, when he stopped her.

The fact was that there was no way he'd agree. It was a nice idea, in theory, but it was unseemly on so many levels.

If it worked, the Bank would be drawing attention to the fact that the UNDP succeeded *exactly* where they'd failed. If it failed, they'd all look foolish to their Brazilian counterparts. In any case, he'd be letting a different organization plagiarize the Bank's work. Still, it was a nice idea, in theory. In a better world, maybe.

"Where are you staying while you're here?" he said.

"Vincenzo, I remarried."

"Then why aren't you wearing a ring?" he said and cast an eye at her hand.

"I could ask you the same."

He nodded.

$$=$$

Later, back at her hotel room, they had sex, and it was about as exciting as running on a treadmill before breakfast. She had put condoms on the bedside table, as if there were any danger of pregnancy, or STDs. They didn't use them, thank God. Still, his mind wandered as he stared at her body beneath him, her breasts spilling over her rib cage, sloshing like half-filled sacks of water. She had insisted on leaving the lights on, which was a terrible idea for people like them. Despite her best efforts, the whole thing was just carpentry. There had been more passion between them when they hugged earlier. But he had to see it through. Her milky belly, the familiar but foreign manner that she had with him, her feeble groans—he observed it all from the far side of a very great chasm. Eventually, just as he was about to fake an orgasm, something happened. The depleted hormones, or synapses—or was it a dormant part of the soul?—whatever had been absent so far came back to him, lit up all at once. He grabbed her hips and she squealed.

Finally, when he finished and collapsed beside her, panting, his pulse throbbing in his skull, she gasped, and burst out laughing. "Wow," she said. He grunted, nodding in agreement. "*That* was impressive," she said. He nodded again. It *was* impressive—life, again, had just been hiding somewhere, waiting for its invitation.

Afterward, once he had recovered, they put on the hotel bathrobes and opened a bottle of pinot grigio. There was little left to discuss.

She again talked about her career, now more philosophically. She talked about being a woman with power in Brazil, of all places. He kept waiting for her to suggest that she should come back to the Bank, but she didn't. And then she gave updates on her new husband, her old husband, and she even told him about her kids. She didn't, fortunately, show him any pictures. The marriage was in trouble, she admitted, but she thought they'd get through it.

Later, they embraced quietly and he breathed in her hair, the smell of that sugary perfume, her coconut shampoo. After a while, so much skin pressed together became uncomfortably warm, so he let go and got up to pee.

Sitting at the table by the window, he said, "Look, you know those tranches are dead for a reason. I understand you need to earmark that money, but I can't encourage something I know doesn't work. I made enemies closing those programs."

She stared at him for a long time. "They have potential."

"No. We have evidence that they're terrible. I have reports, I have so many reports, you won't believe. Look, I understand why you want to play Frankenstein, but why can't you try to revive your own corpses?"

"You killed them prematurely."

"And what if you succeed? What if you make them work? Can you imagine?"

"No one is watching, Vincenzo."

He shook his head, sighed. He wished he were home. Wished he weren't home, too. What he wished, in fact, was that he were in a different home, someone else's home, with someone else's life. "They failed," he repeated.

"Things change," she said.

He groaned. The half-finished bottle of wine was open on the table, losing its chill. They'd never finish it now.

"When are you going to retire?" she asked.

"I plan to die at my desk."

Then she said, "Your wife. I was sorry to hear—"

He nodded. No one ever liked to say it, so they left it incomplete. The absence of the absence. Maybe they thought it would sting him to speak of her death, but no, this was worse—everyone working together to erase her. And of course Cynthia had known. Everyone knew. There had been enough meetings by now, enough gatherings of this jet-lagged clan around hotel bars. By now, everyone knew.

He glanced over at her on the bed, arms crossed, ankles crossed, bulky hotel bathrobe constricted around her waist. Outside, downtown DC was barren at that hour, awash in the sickly orange light of thousands of old streetlights.

It was his turn to talk. He drew a deep breath. "It was . . . " he said and halted there, searching for the next word and nodding slowly in silence until, eventually, he stopped nodding.

$$=$$

The following morning, on CNN, there was too much to say, or maybe there was nothing to say. In any case, they did not seem equipped to explain what was happening in the world. Here, a dog appeared to be singing "Happy Birthday," while over there someone predicted that the prices of homes in the United States would rise indefinitely and, somewhere else, someone said they'd fall soon. Everyone was afraid of rogue waves, flu pandemics, texting while driving. Everyone said what they thought and everyone was wrong. Even the people who said they didn't know anything were wrong.

Then yet another day began: more sun streaming through the window. Everyone got up and tried again. Wrong again. There was nothing left to say, no option left but to keep talking. And so they did.

2

COMMUTER

The forecast spoke of a blizzard but only flurries decorated the air, so Vincenzo, Walter, and Leonora went for a walk after Thanksgiving dinner. They got all the way to the Brookville Market, where they hoped to buy ice cream to supplement the Safeway-brand pumpkin pie Walter had brought, but it was closed. Under the buzzing streetlight on that lonely, meager strip of retail, Walter looked pastier than normal, even sickly. A year or so ago a vein had risen under his left eye, and now it looked a little like a prison teardrop tattoo faded to an indigo blob.

Walter and Vincenzo had both made it through their forties looking and feeling not unlike they had in their thirties, but middle age was in full swing now, extracting stark tolls. They'd met twenty years earlier when Walter, a lifelong columnist for the *Washington Post*, had interviewed Vincenzo about some World Bank project, neither could remember what it was now, and Walter—also an avid chess player—had noticed the chess books on Vincenzo's bookshelf. Here, all these years later, Vincenzo was, needless to say, glad his old friend Walter had come over, especially considering the new awkwardness with Leonora. It was helpful to have a third. The awkwardness was such that she even went out to see her high school friends on Friday and Saturday, despite the fact that she couldn't stand those people. While stranded at home during the days, she'd stare at her father slightly askance, as if she were waiting for something else from him, or just realizing the real scope of his frailties—the weakness, the vanity, the fearfulness, and that somewhere along the way he must have made some calamitous decision. How else, after all, could someone end up with a life like that?

While they were walking back from the Brookville Market the snow started coming harder, spinning up miniature glittering cyclones in the air. At Connecticut Avenue, they stood and watched a herd of cars, yellow headlights igniting the blur of flakes. Everyone driving too fast. Leonora had a new prosthesis on and although she walked on it as if it were real, Vincenzo worried it might be loose and fall off if they ran. He grabbed her hand firmly and then, in a gap between barrages of traffic, they jogged across the slushy street.

Between the black road and the peach sky and white snow and blond streetlights, the world had gone both vivid and dreamlike. Other than the crunching snow and their loud breathing, it was quiet out there in Bethesda, and in the silence Vincenzo reminded himself to be thankful for Leonora and for Walter and for his house, and the rest, too.

A couple of blocks on, Vincenzo overheard Walter, beside Leonora a few paces ahead, say: "I'm impressed, Leonora, you've turned out to be quite a cool kid. I was a little worried there for a while!"

Leonora patted him on the back, faux-condescending, and said, "You've turned out okay, too, Walter." But then she squeezed his shoulder a little, like it wasn't just sarcasm, like there was something true, and Vincenzo knew Walter would appreciate that.

When you're raising a child, you sometimes get to see them do something that you didn't know they were capable of. It can be a stirring experience. This was one of those moments for Vincenzo. He stuffed his hands into his overpriced overcoat and knew, in a certain slanted way, that she was right about him: he'd made a bad, a *ruinous*, decision somewhere. Still, he'd scoured his life from the first half memory to this moment and found nothing to explain it, nothing but life itself, bathed, as it was, in muck and chaos, obese with very good luck and very bad luck, with household chores and uncontrollable laughter and breathtaking spells of disappointment and exhaustion and misery and unmitigated victory and bad traffic. That there had been any pivotal decisions at all within that twiggy, slushy morass seemed itself miraculous, and that there might have been one or two decisions that had mattered especially, well . . .

=

In the summer of 1981, when Vincenzo and Cristina arrived in DC, they had never experienced such humidity, such thunderstorms. The weather was openly hostile to humanity. Cicadas droned all night and Leonora, then a newborn, squalled nasally in reply. Days were delirious, malarial. They sweated always. Rome had been hot, obviously, but Rome had also cooled at night. The heat in DC bore down relentlessly, keeping them awake when they should've been sleeping, putting them to sleep when they should've been awake.

The World Bank was toward the end of a long expansion spearheaded by its then president Robert McNamara, and Vincenzo, hired as a junior economist, worked long hours in the pleasantly air-conditioned building.

Vincenzo spoke English fluently already. He'd spent a year in Denver on a high school exchange program, had forever since been fascinated by the Latinate versus Germanic roots of English words. After six years studying economics at MIT, he returned to Italy in his midtwenties now able to pass for American. But Cristina—who spent that first Bethesda summer sweating in the garden of their overlarge house, her newborn on a blanket nearby—struggled with the language's wooden Germanic notes. She joined a group of non-English-speaking wives of Bank-Fund staff who met weekly for tea, cookies, and English conversation in a small conference room on the International Monetary Fund's mezzanine level. A real sense of fluency came to Cristina only once Leonora started at the Woodley Academy, and Cristina could enunciate (if barely) the über-Germanic, "What kind of kindergarten gives its children homework?"

Over the next thirteen years, the three commuted together in the mornings. In the early years, Leonora would often be the only child on the train—most public-school children traveled by bus, most private-school children by car—and strangers would stare at her in a nakedly enchanted way. She had an intriguing kind of beauty: grimly dark hair and pale skin that contrasted with her wide, euphoric grins; she used her eyebrows to great effect, generating flirtatious and precocious facial expressions (she became accustomed, early, to being cooed at by strangers, and learned to transfix the attentions of potential admirers by making direct eye contact). The wiles of an only child. Her mother dressed her adorably, too, in trendy little outfits—a pastel polka-dot pattern in the lining of a jacket might be repeated in her headband. She even wore little sunglasses on bright days. Vanity was a hobby for everyone in the family. Arriving a shade or two too dapper for a party was, for Cristina and Vincenzo—and later Leonora—always the preference.

Vincenzo felt a bit monstrous next to his women—he'd gone bald in his thirties, had too-large eyes and had always thought his face avian, if not downright villainous: he was dagger-nosed and hollow-cheeked, with a wide thin mouth. So he gleaned a palpable spike of pleasure when he sat there on the train with his gorgeous wife and daughter in front of an admiring, if drowsy, audience of commuters.

Six stops in from Bethesda they'd arrive at Woodley Park-Zoo/Adams Morgan, nearest Leonora's school. Initially, Cristina would walk her to school, but after five years Leonora walked herself and Cristina stayed on the train for one more stop, alone with Vincenzo, before she got off at Dupont Circle, nearest the Brookings Institute, where she worked as an event planner and marketing coordinator. That trip from

Woodley to Dupont, all 120 seconds of it, was spent either in silence or talking about some business of the house, generally to do with Leonora. After Cristina got off, Vincenzo rode one more stop, to Farragut North, alone.

As soon as Leonora arrived at puberty, she began shutting out her parents, with the help of a bright-yellow Walkman.

Within a month, Cristina—probably panicked by the prospect of so much conversational time with her tense and unfamiliar husband—bought her own Walkman. Vincenzo, in a mild show of defiance to their headphones, started bringing the newspaper.

Then the summer before she started high school, Leonora's life was brutally upended. First, in June, her best friend jumped to her death off the Adams Morgan bridge. A month later, on Lake Garda, Leonora was floating in an inner tube when a speedboat piloted by a wealthy teenage boy drove over her legs. Vincenzo was at the market at the time, and her mother, on shore, carried Leonora—her legs hacked up by the blades, gushing blood onto the grass at the water's edge—up to a police car. They were able to spare her right leg, but her left leg had to be amputated below the knee. A decade later, thanks to the War on Terror, advances in prosthesis technology would make it possible for her to walk almost normally without a cane—you had to look for the limp to see it. Still, her days of wearing miniskirts were over before they started. For several years, the mention of sports was enough to make her cross her arms and blush. Whereas Leonora had been invisible, at worst, in middle school, she entered high school the object of the most vicious kind of fascination. Somehow she was simultaneously invisible and relentlessly noticeable.

Before long, she was wearing blackberry lipstick and dark eyeliner, making dozens of mixtapes, and smoking Marlboro reds. A psychologist Vincenzo and Cristina surreptitiously queried explained that she sounded no angrier than any teenager would be in her situation, but they should look for evidence of drug use and self-mutilation. She pierced her nose and her lip at the beginning of her senior year, but according to the psychologist, that didn't count. That year, the bathroom sink upstairs was stained a dimmer shade of whatever hue she had most recently applied to her hair. It went from mute pink to watery indigo to a sickly vermillion.

When Leonora went to Oberlin, Vincenzo and Cristina continued riding the Metro together. After several months, she put away her music. He put away his newspaper. Tentatively, they began talking again, but not in the same way. They started talking about Leonora as if she were not in their house, because she wasn't, and they talked about what they might do with the rest of their lives. They held hands once. A week later, they held hands again. She began kissing him on the forehead before she got out at Dupont.

Leonora was in her junior year at Oberlin when her mother, wearing noise-cancelling earphones with a new no-skip CD player, stepped out into Massachusetts Avenue during her lunch break and was struck down by a truck full of shovels.

The trauma team at George Washington did its best, but by the time Leonora's flight landed at National, her mother's body had been moved to the morgue. Vincenzo picked Leonora up from the airport and they stopped in a turnout on the GW Parkway to sob and hug across the bulky center console. They almost made it to the hospital, but stopped short, went instead to the Uno in Georgetown and ate bad pizza, weeping while they chewed. He didn't want to see the body, he said, but if she did—and she just shook her head. They were exhausted already, and there was a long way to go.

Vincenzo had seen Cristina in the emergency room shortly after her heart stopped. Her blood was warm still and she almost looked alive, except that her mouth was open in a dreadful way, lip curled in an expression she'd never made alive. He opted for a closed casket, thinking he was sparing himself some agony. Only later did he realize that it was quite the reverse—that he'd be glimpsing her out of the corner of his eye for years to come; a quick double take and he'd see that it was just another woman of about the same height, with similar hair and posture.

He accepted the two weeks off, but once Leonora had returned to Oberlin he found he couldn't stand being alone at the house, so he went back to work early. He ended up working longer hours, up to twelve or fourteen a day, six or seven days a week. At night, he saw Walter often for chess and dinner. He played chess with strangers online, too.

All of the work paid off. In less than a year, he was promoted to vice president of Latin America and the Caribbean.

That was when he began driving to the office. His new position came with a parking spot on the red level, reserved for the most senior staff, and though Vincenzo wasn't overly interested in the status boost that came with being the one in the elevator who said, "Could you please press the button for the red level?" he did find that continuing to ride the Metro twice daily alone was more than he could bear.

＝

This Monday would, in fact, be the first day since the promotion that he took the Metro to work. The previous night, over Korean takeout, Leonora—living in New York since she'd graduated from college last year, and visiting for Thanksgiving—had insisted on taking public transportation, because Vincenzo's Mercedes had eight cylinders and was not, strictly speaking, eco-friendly. Maybe it was the cumulative effect of her repeated and early exposure to the unequivocal brutality and fragility of mortal existence, but she had mellowed prematurely, had become quietly persuasive, rather than brash. Whereas similarly aged children of Vincenzo's colleagues were often petulant, Leonora expressed her displeasure subtly, calmly.

"That car—I know you love it—but it's kind of crass, Dad." That was how she phrased it, but she grinned warmly at him when she said it.

"It's just comfortable."

"I know, but let's take the Metro. For old time's sake."

He nodded.

The following morning, Vincenzo awoke an hour earlier than normal, took a shower, and knocked on Leonora's door. Downstairs, he fetched the newspapers from the stoop, put coffee on, and opened the refrigerator. Yesterday, they had abandoned their three-day campaign to consume the Thanksgiving leftovers and had ordered the takeout; the aluminum trays were stacked up in the refrigerator beside the bowls of vegan stuffing, vegan cranberry sauce, and (not so vegan) whipped potatoes—Leonora, newly dairy-free, had managed to convince herself that what tasted like butter and cream in the potatoes was actually just olive oil.

Vincenzo cracked only two eggs into the new skillet, because apparently vegans didn't eat eggs either. When Leonora finally showed up, he had already finished his breakfast and was reading about the Bolivian election in the *Journal.* She poured herself a mug of coffee from the new coffeemaker.

She opened the refrigerator, pulled out a box of rice milk, and said, "Did I mention that the Rainforest Coalition is going to be at the Bank today?"

"You did, yes—thank you. They do incredible protests."

"You know them?"

"Of course—the last time they came, I had to park in Georgetown and walk. I wore blue jeans and a T-shirt so that I could get through, but they had heard that we do that, so they all wore suits. You couldn't believe it! Thousands of hippies in suits—it was *amazing*. That afternoon I went to their website and donated one hundred dollars out of respect for their techniques. The message, I'm afraid, is a little tiresome."

She rolled her eyes, put some granola into a bowl, and filled it with rice milk. She sat at the kitchen table, looking at him earnestly. "The thing is, Dad, I was thinking of stopping by before I catch the train."

"Oh?" Vincenzo shrugged. He'd suspected that that was what she was thinking about, but still it stung. Hoping to put the issue down lightly, he said, "I don't know if I like that, but I suppose I could just tell the police to aim their fire hoses at the girl with the lip ring."

She mustered a dutiful smile, then said, "You wouldn't really mind, would you?"

He shrugged, looked out the window at the collapsing fence in the backyard. "Maybe, I—I don't know." It seemed remarkable that she didn't know that he'd really mind. And it seemed remarkable that she could take his breath away like that. He put two slices of bread into the new electric toaster, pressed the button, and watched the slices slowly descend.

"It's nothing personal," she said.

"Oh?" Wishing he could resist, but finding himself unable, he said, "Well, yes, it is something personal." He shrugged again. It had become a favorite gesture for him, the shrug. It was versatile, the implication open to interpretation. "My work means a lot to me." He stared at the glowing wires inside the toaster.

"You really don't want me to be there."

As if thinking about this, he squinted and looked out the back window again, then said, "Could you come in for lunch?"

"That would sort of defeat the purpose. You know, if halfway through the day, I put down my sign and went inside for a veggie burger with Dad."

"I see."

"Do you? I think you're taking it personally. This isn't about you."

"You think?"

"Yes." She stared at him, unblinking. After a moment, she pressed her lips into the tense smile that she used to indicate that she was ready to drop the subject, but was nonetheless sure that she was right, anyway. Then, seeing that his certitude

matched hers, she said, "You know, there will be no other children of Bank employees out there today."

This seemed to support his argument. "Because they know
better," he said.

"No—my point is that this isn't something children do to
get even with their parents. If it was, there'd be dozens of us.
This *really* isn't about you."

He just nodded slowly, and continued looking at her intently.

At last, she said, "I'll just go back to New York."

This was when he was supposed to assure her that it was fine
for her to attend the protest, but he couldn't bring himself to do
that. So he said nothing. She sighed. He looked at the toaster.

"I like the new kitchen supplies," she eventually said in order to squash the blooming awkwardness.

"Thank you," he said.

"Why did you buy it all?"

He shrugged. "It was just a shopping spree," he said.

She nodded. Did she really believe him? Did she not know
him any better than that? No, probably not. How would she? He
turned back to the toaster. He could hear the wires buzzing inside.

=

The shopping spree had taken place on a Sunday, a day that
had begun innocuously enough: over a slow brunch at the
Four Seasons in Georgetown, he read an inch or so of the
Sunday *Times*. Then he drove home the long way, along the
canal, his window open, cold air numbing his ears. It was
a bracing morning, autumn at its dazzling zenith, the oaks

a nearly industrial yellow, while the maples ran fuchsia and
the poplars deepened to dirty umber. Down in the woods
by the canal he caught the faintest traces of smoke from the
fireplaces burning the season's first fires. He cruised up Ne-
braska and crossed over to Western, and saw the great white
facades of Mazza Gallerie. Soon, he was corkscrewing too fast
through the concrete tunnel and screeching onto the lowest
level of the parking garage where he parked near the elevators,
the only car that had ventured so low. Up at Neiman Marcus,
he spent $461.08 on a pair of burgundy pajamas and calfskin
house slippers. It was an odd whim for a man who, in spite
of his vanity, had always been as frugal as any economist. But
this was fun in a surprising, almost explosive, way—in a way
that he hadn't felt in a long time. Like being drunk and care-
less when everyone else was still sipping their way carefully
through the cocktail party.

Strolling through the mall afterward, he decided to stop in
at Williams-Sonoma, where he browsed for a while and three
women, all of them attractive and in their thirties or forties,
approached him separately to ask if he wanted anything. He
felt like telling them that he did want something, he definitely
did—but he just shook his head. They had spotted his Neiman
Marcus bag, of course, and thought he was in a buying mood,
which he was.

Everything in the store was pristine, just so—exactly like
the catalog. He liked that about it. He liked it all a lot. He
went back to one of the women, a voluptuous one with the
wary expression of someone acquainted with the kind of loss
that can disfigure a person.

She asked if he had changed his mind, and he told her that he had.

"Let me help you then," she said and he was struck by the urge to kiss her, right there and then, but he resisted. She was just doing her job, after all.

It took half an hour to decide that he would like a set of Belgian copper cookware; two Le Creuset cast-iron pots; an array of stoneware serving dishes and mixing bowls; a hand-carved olive-wood salad bowl; a full set of bubbly lime-green Biot glassware; eight full settings of dinnerware; designer pot holders; an unremarkable coffeemaker and an attractive toaster; a mighty roasting pan; an industrial-strength blender; a full set of Wüsthof knives; and a diamond-dusted sharpener. Taken together, the items presented a fearsome, if improbable, arsenal of blades and blunt instruments. The other saleswomen watched on, wide-eyed, as he kept going, kept picking up more and more things and the boxes started to pile up in the space beside the checkout counter. Eventually, it stopped. The grimacing woman spent a long time tallying it all and once she finally finished she seemed apologetic and flustered when she said that the total was $6,107.21. She worked on commission, no doubt, and he had just made her month, so he stared at her for too long, wanting to find some lightning bolt of connection, some paroxysm of uninhibited humanity to slap them both awake. But it was not forthcoming and—though she was clearly being as polite as she was able—he eventually looked away.

With the help of a second saleswoman, she and Vincenzo hauled everything down to his car in two trips.

Back at the house he spent hours replacing the old with the new. He unloaded the new supplies onto the counters and floors, took all of the old supplies and loaded them into the Williams-Sonoma bags, and carried them out to the car. Then he started unpacking the new things and putting them in their places. It was hard work, hauling it all to and fro, and by the time he was done it was three in the afternoon and he was exhausted. It was the most manual labor he'd done in years.

Styrofoam peanuts and pills had escaped and touched down on the floor gingerly and now dashed away from him when he hurried past to fill one of his new glasses with water. He called Walter, his closest, if not to say only, friend. They met occasionally for lunch and lightning rounds of chess in the pocket park beside the World Bank, the café on the Bank's mezzanine when the weather was hostile to chess. Walter had never stocked up the kitchen of his post-divorce apartment; he ate cereal out of his disintegrating Teflon sauté pan in the morning, drank everything out of the three mugs he'd picked up at recent conferences. The open maw of the baking soda container at the back of Walter's refrigerator appeared, to Vincenzo, to be cackling at the overlit emptiness.

"Walter," Vincenzo said, "I have something in my car that I think you will want. Will you be there in half an hour?"

"Half an hour?" Walter said and moaned slightly under his breath. "I'm trawling chess chat rooms for single women. It's safe to say I'll be here for the rest of my life."

=

The city's Metro system was built by forward-thinking people
and had barely changed since the 1970s. Nor had many of its
passengers, apparently. When Vincenzo and Leonora boarded
the southbound red line at Bethesda that morning, he saw a
number of familiar faces. Some glanced at him and smiled
weakly before averting their eyes. He and Leonora stood in
silence until Dupont Circle, where Cristina would have debarked. The doors opened and some people got off, a few
others boarded. The doors chimed twice and slid shut. Vincenzo watched this intently. He was wondering if he'd ever
see it again when Leonora leaned over and whispered, "Hey
Dad?"

"Yes." He swallowed the lump in his throat, looked at
their feet.

"Will you do me a favor?"

"Of course."

"Will you tell Paul Wolfowitz to go fuck himself?" she said,
and laughed exactly like her mother, slightly too loud for the
setting, which shattered something else he'd been guarding.

"I don't think Paul would like that," he whispered, and
made himself chuckle. He looked up at her. No one spoke on
the train except for them, and it was crowded enough that,
whispering or not, people could overhear. He wondered if any
of them were Bank employees.

"Do you think he cares?" she said.

"Oh," Vincenzo said. He shrugged. "Yes, definitely. He's
not *inhuman*."

A woman he did not recognize looked up, stared blankly at
him, as if he weren't even there, and then looked down again.

They said nothing else until the train pulled into Farragut North. Metro Center was next and if she got off there, she could walk to the protest and he'd never know.

He leaned in, kissed her on both cheeks. "*Stammi bene cara. Mi chiamerai presto?*"

"*Sì Papi. Ciao.*" She squeezed his arm and he felt the lump return to his throat.

The doors parted and he was swept up in the current rushing toward the escalators.

Once on the escalator, the pace slowed and he rose steadily toward the day, listening to the baritone sax. The musician had been there for fifteen years and his dreadlocks were like long tubes of cigar ash—Vincenzo's hair, what was left of it, had also gone gray. The nakedness of the musician's emotion as he played there every morning provided an amazing contrast to the waves of commuters who rushed past him. Most people who emerged from the K Street exit at Farragut North were in the thrall of their professional mission, whatever that might be.

When they moved to the United States, Cristina didn't have any trouble learning the word "commuter," which she employed often, teasingly, to describe her husband. The word was only a few letters away from the Italian *commutatore* (commutator), but bore no resemblance to their word for someone who traveled a great distance to and from work: *pendolare*, from their word for pendulum. Still, "commuter" seemed amusingly inapt to them. It turned out that the usage emerged in the 1800s. Before that, to "commute" simply meant to change or substitute one thing for another; often it implied substituting a penalty for one less onerous. In the nineteenth century, people used "commutation tickets," good for multiple rides on the railway. And, for a brief time, the people themselves were called "commuted," as in: "I'm commuted; my ticket is worth ten rides." Maybe it was the passivity of that construction, or its criminal hues, but by the early 1860s the word was "commuter."

As he walked down K Street amid the swarm, he thought about an article he had seen in the *Wall Street Journal* that morning. According to a new poll, Evo Morales was all but certain to win the Bolivian presidential election. Evo was the antithesis of these people crowding downtown DC, and the opposite of most politicians. Although Vincenzo had been an economist at the World Bank for most of his adult life, he considered himself an outsider, too, and empathized with Evo. The election was still weeks away, but, according to the *Journal*, Evo had a double-digit lead. A former coca farmer, he was a charming and handsome bachelor who never wore suits or ties, seemed gleefully oblivious to such things. His complexion was like desert clay after a rain, his hair full and ebony. He was, it seemed, never photographed without a guileless grin on his upturned face.

Once elected, the article said, Evo would be a hero of the new populists—a saner Hugo Chavez, a younger Fidel Castro. Pundits were surely already talking, Vincenzo guessed, about a new kind of domino effect whereby formerly friendly Third World states followed Bolivia's example and elected leaders who were openly hostile to the interests of the United States. Brazil was already halfway there with Lula. They were right to be afraid, Vincenzo thought, and he was also sure this movement was, all in all, a good thing for the world. The stonier think tanks would say that George W. Bush had been too quick to embrace democracy as the cornerstone of his version of post–Cold War policy. The Chinese had the right idea, they would say: capitalism needed to precede democracy.

Vincenzo knew he would hear about the results of the poll at work. The American executive director, William Hamilton, would want to know if Vincenzo intended to cut Bolivian aid in response to Morales's policies.

The protestors from the Rainforest Coalition were gathering on Nineteenth Street, between the IMF and the Bank. The Bank had installed a temporary security kiosk by the service entrance for the cafeteria in the back on Seventeenth, so Vincenzo entered that way. He could smell bacon and chlorine coming from the kitchen as he rushed down the hall toward the elevators.

In his office, he removed his Armani overcoat and put it on the hanger behind the door, was about to settle in at his desk when he noticed the pink Post-it on his new flat-screen monitor. With dread, he leaned in to look at it:

Can you meet me at the IMF's cafeteria for breakfast?
—W. Hamilton
8:27 AM

Less than ten minutes ago. That time stamp indicated that he, Hamilton, was at work already and Vincenzo was not. Not that they were competing for any professional territory, but the number implied something about their differing degrees of enthusiasm.

Hamilton had already spoken to his bosses at the State Department, no doubt. The board's annual review of Bolivia had come and gone without incident recently—Hamilton had not said a single word during the entire meeting—and the Bank's policy in Bolivia wouldn't be up for review by the executive board for another ten months. In the meantime, Vincenzo was the only person who could change Bank policy toward Bolivia.

The best thing to do would be to pretend he hadn't gotten the note in time. But he wasn't going to hide today or be subtextually prodded about his work ethic. He pictured Leonora striding across the platform at Metro Center, dragging her wheeled pink-and-black checkered carry-on bag, one of her boots touching the ground a little unnaturally, as she debarked the southbound train and boarded the northbound; he could see her dragging the bag down K Street from Farragut North toward the warm mob outside his office. He saw her wearing her headphones, stomping along in her crazy green boots, off to battle, clutching a cup of coffee in a fingerless-gloved hand.

Setting his briefcase down on his desk, he opened his closet and checked himself in the long mirror on the inner door. Gravity was having its way with his face now, dragging sacks down beneath his eyes, tugging jowls out of his cheeks. He looked like an Italian politician—some ghostly cousin of Berlusconi. Finding nothing improvable in the mirror, he shut the door and marched off, back in the direction of the elevators.

3

OFF TO BATTLE

Rumor had it that breakfast at the World Bank's cafeteria wasn't
as good as breakfast at the International Monetary Fund's cafeteria, even though both were made by Marriot from identical
recipes and identical ingredients. The debate was, of course, not
about breakfast at all; it was about the participants in the debate, a select group in the twin organizations, where breakfast
wasn't a popular meal to begin with, since most people took it at
home *before* they came to work. By joining the debate, a person
could indicate that he was prepared to take at least two of his
three daily meals at the office, which implied ambition. Too, he
was signaling his eagerness for a special kind of staid jocularity
that was de rigueur among the number-crunching economists
who filled the two buildings. William Hamilton, the United
States' executive director at the World Bank, had pioneered the
breakfast argument. Hamilton claimed, in a memo circulated
among the executive directors and senior management of both

organizations, that he had conducted a blind taste test of both cafeterias' biscuits 'n' gravy, a dish he chose because "it requires the most skill to pull off well." He concluded, "Unfortunately, the Fund's cafeteria kicked our behinds!"

At the time of Hamilton's memo, Paul Wolfowitz was only half a year into his term as president of the World Bank. So far, Wolfowitz had supposedly never had breakfast at either cafeteria; nonetheless, he circulated the only response to Hamilton's memo, in which he jokingly called Hamilton a "turncoat," and said that "any good economist knows how to read the data in a way to get a favorable result!"

The fraternal ribbing was intended, doubtlessly, to be taken as evidence of the close relationship between the two, who, prior to joining the Bank, had worked together in the Pentagon. After the memo exchange, Hamilton made a daily show of going across the street to the Fund's cafeteria for his breakfast. Wolfowitz, meanwhile, continued to forgo the meal.

On days like the one in question, when there were protests on Nineteenth, Hamilton would use the tunnel connecting the two buildings' parking garages. Due to the low attendance at breakfast and the odd arrangement of the Fund's cafeteria—a labyrinthine warren of interconnected and irregularly shaped rooms, none of which had windows—Hamilton often had a room to himself.

According to rumor, he ate two eggs, two sausages, and an English muffin, but Tuesday was salmon cake day and he always treated himself to one.

"Oh yes. It's definitely better," he said, when Vincenzo sat down and asked if it was really that much different. "But my cholesterol, I don't even want to think about it." Hamilton was a stout man, physically conspicuous but not obese. Though he was mostly bald, a blond cirrus adorned the peak of his shiny dome. He had jovial eyes, an affable way, and looking at him up close, this early, Vincenzo felt his antagonism dim a little.

Still, he wanted to limit the banter; he was considering calling Leonora on her cell phone. If she answered and he heard crowds, he'd know she had gone to the protests. If he heard the clacking and caterwauling of a train, he'd know she'd left. If she didn't answer, he'd have to decide what to believe. It shouldn't have mattered, but it did. "You wanted to talk to me about something?" he said.

"I wanted to talk about Bolivia. You heard about the poll?" He forked salmon cake into his mouth and chewed slowly.

Vincenzo nodded. "I did. So, why did you want to see me?" Of course, he knew why and was just being difficult.

Hamilton had been asked by the State Department, no doubt, to persuade the World Bank's management—namely Vincenzo—to cut off aid to Bolivia in the event that Morales made good on his campaign promises. Common wisdom held that appeasement didn't work with men like Morales. Coercion was better, but coercion was not discreet. Unless they could quietly strip away Bolivian aid, a great deal of which originated, in one form or another, at the Bank.

"You do know that he intends to expropriate foreign-owned gas refineries?" Hamilton snorted. "He's going to kick out all the foreign investors, and he wants to increase the production of coca. It's going to be their number one crop."

"Isn't it already their—" Vincenzo interjected, but Hamilton pressed on.

"And he'll kick out the oil companies, he'll kick out the telephone companies, he'll cut off gas to Brazil and Argentina. It'd be a disaster for the entire continent."

"Cut off Brazilian gas? Why would he do that?"

"Well—he'll spike the price."

"They pay market right now, and if the price drifted up a few cents, that would have no real effect on BOP, right? Anyway, they could afford to pay a little more." Vincenzo didn't actually believe that this was a nonissue, and he knew several good arguments against his own argument, but the argument served his purpose.

Hamilton's eyes widened. He had apparently used a dull razor that morning; his skin was speckled with bloody razor burn, and the droplets had stained the ridge of his starched white collar a rusty brown. "I'm just asking what you plan to do if Evo enacts these policies."

"Well, I . . ." Vincenzo shrugged.

"You're going to cut back on aid, right? Don't be an idiot, Vincenzo."

Pleased that he'd managed to get a rise out of this enthusiastic and cheerful American, he said, "I'm not sure. I don't see how any of this is the Bank's problem. It's out of our jurisdiction. This sounds like a political issue more than an economic one, so I don't think I'd do anything." He was playing with semantics now, the last refuge of an ill-equipped debater. "If you think we need to change our policy then you should put it to the executive board." Vincenzo knew full well that the board would not be discussing Bolivia again for another ten months, and that Hamilton might not be able to gather enough votes to pass a punitive measure, especially if Morales were to win some friends in Europe.

"Morales is talking about kicking out foreign gas companies and seizing their operations. It's theft. We can't wait for the board. You're the only one who can do it now."

"If I cut Bolivia off, I will have to cut off Venezuela, too—because they're just as bad. Are you saying you would have no problem if the Bank took action against Venezuela, one of the main oil-producing nations in the hemisphere?"

Hamilton shook his head. "Damn it, Vincenzo, of course that's different! Venezuela is a completely different case."

"What's different about Bolivia, except that they don't have much oil? The policies are not different, just the size of the revenue."

"Their fiscal—" Hamilton started and then shut up, spotting the trap. He folded his paper napkin neatly and then threw it onto the table. "Okay, fuck this. Let's just let it go." His lips pressed shut, white with pressure. Vincenzo knew that Hamilton, despite his vulgarity, was more or less within his purview—not quite, but he wasn't exactly demanding action from Vincenzo. But he couldn't help himself.

Then, in an unfortunate step in the direction of absolutes, Hamilton—who was evidently no expert at hostile negotiation—said, "As I interpret it, you're not going to touch Bolivia no matter what Evo Morales does. If he confiscates the savings of foreign nationals, you'll do nothing. Is that correct?"

"Don't be ludicrous, he's not going to confiscate anyone's savings. My position is that if you and the board vote to change the Bank policy in Bolivia—"

"In ten fucking months!"

"Yes, if—in ten fucking months—you can get enough votes to change the Bank's policy, I will enact the new policy, but I don't think that this man Morales's plan demonstrates the kind of *egregious malfeasance*"—he made a point of using a phrase directly from the Bank's written policy—"or corruption that would require an intrusion from my office. My position is that this sounds like a political matter, and I wouldn't feel—"

"You axed an eighty-million-dollar tranche in Brazil last month!"

"Completely different!" Vincenzo snapped. "That was a failed subsidy!" He paused and took a breath. He was becoming truly angry, too, now, too angry to continue, and too angry not to continue. "I cut the subsidy because it was poorly designed, I didn't cut it because the president of Brazil was saying George W. Bush is an asshole. Personally, I don't think the Bank should become an instrument for Condoleezza Rice to coerce or bribe favorable policies from poor countries."

And, although this had seemed like just another jagged point to score in an already jagged argument, when Vincenzo looked back on the conversation later, he would see that this particular statement marked a key transition. They'd strayed far outside the implicit boundaries of these conversations, and he'd led them there.

When Hamilton put his fork down and said, "You better watch yourself," Vincenzo knew the conversation was approaching its endgame. Almost all of the major decisions had been made.

"Are you threatening me?" Vincenzo hoped he came off amused, not furious.

Hamilton shrugged, had a sip of coffee. He raised an eyebrow in a way that didn't indicate anything at all.

"If Wolfowitz calls me about this I will go directly to the *Washington Post*," Vincenzo said, which was rash, irrevocable, and signaled a definitive transition into endgame.

Vincenzo had been playing chess with Walter at least three days a week for ten years and he'd found that the mid-game was the key to speed chess. At that pace, the opening was all reflex and the endgames were often averted either by a forfeit or time running out, so all the real strategy took place in the middle. One player usually made a fatal mistake in the middle, some apparently innocuous move. And if conversations were most like speed chess in that they were a rapid-fire negotiation of surprising, changing terms, with formalities up front and closing remarks at the end, then the outcomes of conversations—especially argumentative ones—were also determined by the decisions made in the middle.

Hamilton took a bite of wheat toast with raspberry jam and chewed it, nodding. Vincenzo could hear his own pulse in his head now—the conversation had its own direction, its own momentum, and he was just filling in the blanks. He wiped his palms on his trouser legs.

"Well," Hamilton said, "if you do that, you'll lose your job."

"And you'll lose yours."

"That might be true and it might not. Would it be a consolation?"

"Yes, it would," Vincenzo said. He could back down, now, he knew, but he didn't really want to. Stalemate was just that:

stale. "I have worked here for twenty-four years," he said. "They will push me into early retirement. What about you? How old are you, forty-five? If this thing breaks, you will be done. You will be working as an adjunct at some tiny think tank. If you're lucky, you get to be an associate professor at a university in Ohio."

"That's bullshit." Hamilton's eyes darted away and then returned. The gesture was small, but in it Vincenzo saw doubt, and judged that he had the initiative.

He looked around, no one else was in the room, so he said, "If Wolfowitz contacts me about this, I will call the *Post* immediately. I swear."

There was a pause. The threat was unprecedented. There existed hallowed, if unwritten, agreements about the sanctity of these kinds of conversations, and talking to the press about them was completely out of the question. The pause extended until the awkwardness dissolved and then continued until it became uncomfortable again. By then, the rage that was driving Vincenzo had given way to reason once again.

In a five-minute game of chess you can't always consider the permutations of every move, but must try to work entirely on a broad strategy. This move of his had been a straightforward gambit. In the famous Queen's Gambit, which Vincenzo used rarely against a strong opponent like Walter but often against a weaker player, white opened with a defenseless pawn on the queen's side. If black took the pawn, white could move to gain initiative and take control of the center of the board.

"Is it worth this much to you to make me look like a fool?"

"I don't care about you, William. That is the truth."

"Jesus—you came here looking for a fight, didn't you? What the fuck is wrong with you?"

"I don't care about you, William," Vincenzo repeated.

"And you don't care about yourself either?" Hamilton said.

"There are worse things than being forced into early retirement."

"Such as?"

Vincenzo shook his head, stood up. He buttoned his suit jacket. He lingered for a half moment and then unbuttoned it again. "I'm telling you that I can live with this. I *want* to live with it. My wife and I bought a farm in Italy six years ago and I haven't been there since she died. The house needs a lot of work! I would love to go work on it." Hamilton's mouth twitched slightly when Vincenzo mentioned Cristina. It was clear now that Hamilton really did want him to back off, that Hamilton was afraid of what violence Vincenzo might inflict on them, but Vincenzo couldn't bring himself to retreat from this precipice. The decision was made. He would not recant, and he would not hesitate.

And so, at that moment—standing and staring down at William Hamilton in the IMF's subterranean cafeteria— Vincenzo's life pivoted, and hundreds of other lives pivoted with him.

4

KAMIKAZE

On whether it was better to be loved or feared, Machiavelli wrote, "One would like to be both the one and the other, but because it is difficult to combine them, it is far better to be feared than loved." His reasoning: "The bond of love is one which men break when it is to their advantage to do so; but fear is strengthened by a dread of punishment, which is always effective." Vincenzo, who set out to pursue a degree in classical Italian literature and wallowed for too long in the texts of Machiavelli before coming to his senses, didn't think that love was actually more breakable than fear. But as a general approach to statecraft, as a way of thinking, Machiavelli's book was, undeniably, worth reading. *The Prince* was not a self-help book for world leaders—it was a map for self-preservation.

In 1944, when Europe had been freshly demolished, the Allies decided not to stick the losers with the bill once again. Not this time. Recent history had provided a stark example of how it wouldn't be in their self-interest to foist further hardship onto the Axis, which would only become more politically unstable as their economies were ravaged. So, in 1944, before the first atom bomb had fallen on Japan, the Allies convened in Bretton Woods, New Hampshire, and created the World Bank and International Monetary Fund in order to finance the rebuilding of Europe. Within a few years it became clear that the institutions could play a global role preventing economic disasters, too. More to the point, the kind of economic debacle that made it possible for a Hitler to win a presidential election could happen anywhere.

In a smart but controversial essay published in *Foreign Policy*, William Hamilton wrote that the spark that lit the Holocaust was not to be found in "Hitler's warped mind, but in the flawed calculus of the Reichsbank's president's notebook, circa 1923, which created space for Nazism. The target of the Nazis' ire was, not surprisingly, the ethnicity most associated, by crude stereotype, with the banking sector." Hamilton continued: "If Rudolf Havenstein [the German finance minister in the 1920s] had pursued a rational policy, Hitler would have been just another deranged, failed painter. Likewise, if the average Rwandan made a living wage in 1993, there would not have been genocide there."

William Hamilton didn't play chess, though, and neither had Machiavelli. Chess is, counterintuitively, a game that requires extraordinary creativity, even emotionality; it demands a person capable of recognizing the cold realities of a given strategic landscape, but that person must also be able to make surprising and apparently self-destructive moves—to offer the throat of his queen, if need be, and to feel that loss for what it is. Why else do our most advanced computers—machines capable of untangling a thing as complex as our very genome—find themselves struggling to outwit a tubby Russian in this game of logic?

=

As he walked through the fluorescent-lit tunnel connecting the IMF's parking garage and the World Bank's garage, Vincenzo knew that while his job was interesting enough, in the event that this confrontation with Hamilton marked the end of his career, it wouldn't be so bad. Not really. Despite a gut aversion to the scenario, he knew, logically, it was fine. He could just as easily pass the rest of his life rereading the Russian masters and firing off the occasional angry letter to the editor of the *Financial Times*. More than anything, it was clear to him, as it had been for a while, that he had little left to keep him in DC. His daughter lived in New York, and his friends had mostly moved away. Those who remained in DC were really Cristina's friends, and despite their generosity, he never felt entirely comfortable with them. They were forever sighing when he was around. They wanted to talk about her, or didn't—either way it felt wrong. While he still saw them once a month or so, he found that they squinted at him often, as though he were out of focus. *Do I just remind them of her?* he had wondered. *And, if so, how sad—because they just remind me of her.*

Now, waiting for the elevator in the World Bank's basement, Vincenzo returned his attention to the conversation with Hamilton. Both of them had made mistakes, had overplayed their positions.

Over the long weekend, Leonora had said that she thought the World Bank was "basically run by the US government," which had bothered Vincenzo more than he could explain. It had kept him up at night formulating and editing counter-arguments, which he'd never used, because the subject hadn't come up again. But now, this morning, witnessing Hamilton's swagger at breakfast—Vincenzo was more than a little dismayed by the way it dovetailed with her comment.

They would not fire him, he knew, because to do so would only exacerbate whatever PR problems his conversation with the press would cause. The management would, instead, offer a large severance. Not that money was an issue anymore. This was one of the sadder things about hitting his middle fifties as a widower: suddenly the debts were all gone and the investments were pulling record returns, the house in Bethesda was worth five times what he and Cristina had paid. And yet, apart from his dinosaurian nest egg, he had no significant use for this money. He had begun eating osetra caviar casually, and drinking Barolo with his carryout from Obelisk. He had bought that stupid Mercedes-Benz and the new kitchen supplies. It was a mirage, of course, the shimmering apparition of newness. What he wanted was sad and predictable: a younger woman, not too much younger, but enough to be truly beautiful, with whom he could settle at his farm in Piedmont and pass his remaining years in peace, tending to the olive trees. He wouldn't ask much from her, certainly not that she adopt the same pace of life. If she went out and didn't return until late, he could live with that. Maybe he'd even feel okay if she had boyfriends. In theory, he could live with all that. He just wanted the company of someone beautiful and lively and carefree. During his free time, he could play chess, read, write, and pick up the other hobbies of the educated and indolent: gardening, watercolors, tennis, cycling, cooking, all the rest of that.

Vincenzo stood in the elevator alone. Above the doors, the numbers lit one by one as he ascended.

He grasped the wooden railing and stared at his blurry face, bisected by the crack in the brass doors. There were always finger smudges on the doors, he'd noticed, especially near the black space in the middle, as though someone had been trying to pry them open. Sometimes there were more smudges and sometimes there were fewer, but they were always there.

He passed the rest of his morning anxiously, repeatedly checking his e-mail, waiting for the message from Wolfowitz requesting that he come in for a talk. The phone rang twice, but neither call had anything to do with the confrontation with Hamilton.

When it rang a third time, Vincenzo saw from the caller ID it was Wolfowitz himself. He let it ring three times. He readied himself, and picked up. "Hello."

"Hello, Vincenzo, how are you?" He sounded light and friendly, even unaware.

"Fine, fine." He processed Paul's tone and decided to move cautiously. "What can I do for you?"

"It's the protestors. I've invited their leader up to talk to you. Their complaint involves our Latin America program, and while it's essentially meritless, it's in our interest to meet with them briefly. Don't spend a lot of time on it. I thought you'd be the man to talk to. His name is, let's see—um . . . Jonathan

Paris. Economics degree from Yale—good for him. *2002!*
Wow, he's a child. Okay, let's see: magna cum laude—and, well,
you get the idea. A frisky guy, altogether, so I thought we'd try
to mollify. Carrot is better than stick with these people; they
live for the stick."

Vincenzo had spoken only a few times to Wolfowitz and
didn't know whether he was joking or not. Standing there,
he pictured the face: jug ears and gnomish features, squinting
eyes. Paul really wasn't as bad as they said, but he was also hard
to understand at times. And this was one of those times. Did
this have to do with his conversation with Hamilton? It seemed
likely. "Did you really invite him up to my office?" he said.

"Absolutely. I've met with a number of protestors so far.
With these ones—look, they're just kids. You have kids?"

"A daughter, twenty-four years old."

"So you understand. This is not as big a deal as people think
it is. At the Pentagon, Don had a policy against even acknowl-
edging protestors, but I always felt that if it'll stop them spray-
ing us with pigs' blood every time we step outside, let's hear
them out. They'll feel like they achieved something and we can
get back to work."

"Well, Paul, I'll let you know what this boy says."

"Good. Thanks. Please feel free to call me whenever." And,
with that, Paul hung up.

Vincenzo barely had time to recover from the surreal phone
call when Jonathan Paris himself, escorted by a lanky North
African security guard, knocked on his open door. Vincenzo
stood, told the guard he could leave, and beckoned the young
man inside. Jonathan had a freshly shaved face and an ill-fitting

suit, possibly on loan from his father. He was maybe about Leonora's age—out of college, but not yet acquiescing to the realities of full-blown adulthood. He shook Vincenzo's hand and flashed a future-politician's smile, toothy and hollow and curiously beguiling.

"What can I do for you?" Vincenzo motioned for him to sit.

Jonathan ignored the chair. He turned and walked to the window, put his hands behind his back—it was an affected gesture, but Vincenzo sympathized. He often interviewed young men like this for positions at the Bank. They were often handsome and boasted fresh degrees from legendary institutions; they felt, in short, like destiny was in their favor, but they were always the most conspicuously insecure candidates. Jonathan Paris wore his nervousness a little proudly, as if the reticence were itself a product of his morally superior position.

"You can't hear us from up here," he observed glumly. He leaned toward the glass, peering down. "You can't even see us, can you?"

Vincenzo squinted, put his fingers into a steeple, as if this were a very weighty matter.

While sitting at the desk he had occupied since the promotion, he could see the corner of the International Monetary Fund's top floor and a tidy rhombus-shaped swath of sky. "If you were a block away, I could see you when I stood at the window," he explained. "If you rented a hot air balloon, I could see you when I sat at my desk, but I'm guessing that the propane isn't"— he shrugged, winced—"it doesn't burn very clean, does it?"

Jonathan turned and smiled at Vincenzo, but kept his hands still latched together behind his back. There was a confidence—affected or not—that felt off-putting in someone so young. Vincenzo was tempted to ask if Jonathan had seen his Leonora down there. Any green combat boots? He had pictures of her in frames on the shelf. But no, it wouldn't be appropriate.

"Do you want a cappuccino?" Vincenzo said, wanting to make him feel more at ease. "We have a coffee shop on the mezzanine level. We could talk there."

Jonathan nodded.

In the elevator on the way down, Vincenzo talked about Leonora. He explained that she had tattoos covering her arms, and that she supported the Rainforest Coalition. He said that she was beautiful and bright, that she lived in New York. He managed to resist the urge to say that she might be out there. He didn't know why he was able to manage that one piece of self-control, but gave so much on other fronts. She had majored in something called media studies at Oberlin, he explained. When they arrived at the mezzanine level, he realized it sounded like he was trying to set Jonathan Paris up with his daughter. And then, walking across the buffed travertine lobby, he realized he *was* trying to set Jonathan Paris up with his daughter.

"Oberlin is a good school," Jonathan said.

"Well, yes."

They arrived at the café and Vincenzo glanced around but saw no one he knew. "Oberlin is also an expensive school," he said. "And I told her that if she went to a state school, I'd give her the difference. That is, I would give her the money that I saved."

Jonathan shook his head, amused. "Well, you're definitely an economist."

"True. But she could have made a hundred thousand dollars if she'd gone to Maryland. She said no. What does that tell you?"

A small pause. "It tells me that people have a difficult time seeing the long-term consequences of their actions. We prefer to burn our resources now, deal with the consequences tomorrow." He smiled at Vincenzo, understandably satisfied.

Vincenzo smiled back. "That was nicely done," he said, and patted the boy on the shoulder. "That wasn't what I had in mind, but it was nicely done." Since they were apparently switching from banter to business, he said, "I think the Bank understands quite well the long-term consequences of its actions. What would you like to drink, Jon?"

Jonathan did not try to refuse when Vincenzo offered to pay for their coffees. They sat at a table in the corner, and Vincenzo listened to Jonathan talk about the problem of prioritizing short-term economic growth over the long-term welfare of the planet. He could not have done it better himself, and enjoyed especially Jonathan's ability to whip himself into an emotional climax that corresponded with the sharpest points of his argument. Not quite Bill Clinton, but definitely impressive. This part of the conversation was painstakingly choreographed, he knew. The edginess from before, when their conversation had been improvised, was replaced by a frosty certainty.

Vincenzo wasn't really up for a battle, though it probably would have been easy enough to hand the boy his own head. Instead, he offered a few halfhearted counterexamples, because it would be unseemly not to. Jonathan's argument was sound, in a sense, although it hinged on a critical misunderstanding of the World Bank's role. It was like critiquing the rules of a game, or not understanding the rules . . . To Jonathan, the World Bank wasn't *fair*, as if being fair was something they set out to be.

Still, doing his part, Vincenzo said that the Bank welcomed new ideas. He then went on to explain that they were continually adapting their policies; specifically, he said, they had been *softening* their policies since the seventies. He deliberately used that word, softening, although it wasn't politic to do so. Then, rushing toward his conclusion, he said, "We are gravely concerned about the deforestation in the Amazon and elsewhere, and we are doing what we can to address that, but we also have a population there that is desperately poor. Our principal goal, at this point, has to be to alleviate the human suffering."

"Brazil is one of the richest countries in Latin America, by your measure," Jonathan said.

"There are persistent problems with inequality."

"Are you trying to fix that? Are you pushing for fiscal reform? Are you asking for an increase in taxes on the rich?" Jonathan was hitting his stride now.

"That kind of thing is really a domestic political issue. At best, it is a question for the IMF territory, but I don't think they would want to insert themselves that deeply into a country's fiscal policy," Vincenzo said. The truth was more complicated, but there was no point in trying to explore it with Jonathan Paris. He had finished his cappuccino and was eager to get back to his office to await any fallout from his argument with Hamilton, or maybe there had been a message from Leonora. When he was at his computer, he sometimes hit *refresh* on his e-mail again and again and again, as if trying to draw up something new that couldn't be drawn up. "Anyway," Vincenzo said, aiming to deal out a quick coup de grâce, "I thought your position was that we should interfere less in their governance?"

Jonathan shook his head and pursed his lips. "Where did you learn how to make a conversation into a game of dodgeball? *God*—is there a special school for people like you?"

"Yes, there is." Vincenzo stood up. "I think you went there."

=

When Vincenzo called Wolfowitz's office the assistant patched him through.

"Vincenzo," Wolfowitz said, "did you talk to the kid from that rainforest group?"

"I did."

"And what was his position? That we shouldn't favor development over ecology?"

"More or less."

"But we're the World Bank, not the World Rainforest Preservation Organization."

"That's what I said."

"Good," he chirped.

A pause. Vincenzo looked at his vanilla pudding phone, the butterscotch pudding console. It was awful how little a person had to be concerned, how little a person had to awaken before the whole event—what was now underway—was understood to be useless. As a rule, it was all useless. Every conceivable way of being upset, that was useless, too. Every form of sorrow, confusion, fury—each one a small thing pretending to be something big, each masquerading as another feeling. But life was more astonishing and terrestrial than the great gestures that seemed to be occurring here.

"By the way," Vincenzo said, sensing with some certainty now that this mission he'd been sent on had been a cover for something else, something to do with Hamilton. It was too convenient a coincidence. So instead of playing the innocent, he thought he'd put Wolfowitz on the spot with a direct question. "Have you spoken to William Hamilton today?"

"No. Why do you ask?" That sounded honest and Paul wasn't going to lie, after all, not like that. And this was not what Vincenzo expected.

Moreover, Paul's question was framed with a distinct forward momentum, which demanded a true and clear answer, so Vincenzo made room, saying, "We had breakfast today." Then he added, "He wanted to talk about Bolivia." And by now he was starting to wonder if he shouldn't have just kept his mouth shut.

"Bolivia?" Wolfowitz sounded circumspect. "Did he want to know whether we would be cutting aid in response to Morales's election?"

"Yes."

"And you told him to get lost?"

"That is exactly what I did."

"Well done." Neither of them said anything for a while. Vincenzo was baffled. Was Paul not so friendly with Hamilton, after all, or was he just not going to put that friendship in front of his duties? Vincenzo, having lost sight of his understanding of what was happening here, said nothing for a moment. So Paul said, "Is that it?"

"Yes, that's it," Vincenzo said, and then he saw that it would be better to clarify this all with Paul now than let Hamilton, who now *would* be roped into the conversation, do the clarifying, so he added, "Except that I told him that if he managed to get me fired over this, I'd go to the press. I said I'd talk to the *Washington Post*."

"You did?" A firm pause. "Why did you say *that?*"

"I was concerned about my job." This was how things disintegrated.

"Well. Then let me be clear: Bill Hamilton has absolutely no control over your job. None at all. But for you to threaten to go to the press—that's not very sportsmanlike. I appreciate your position, he was trying to bully you, but I hope you don't feel like talking to the press about sensitive issues is a parachute for you. It's not going to save you. If anything, it's got more in common with a kamikaze's strategy."

"I understand." He looked at the phone, aware that something was shifting in the conversation, and in his understanding of his situation. This wasn't new information, it was old information seen anew. "But you are saying you support me in this?" he clarified, although already he sensed that Wolfowitz wasn't interested in working out détente.

"I support you as long as you don't make a goddamn scandal out of it, yes," Wolfowitz said. "Hamilton is a friend of mine, but he had no place threatening your job."

≡

Half an hour later, Vincenzo called Walter and told him that
he wanted to go on the record about something that had happened that day at the Bank.

Walter was silent for a moment, then cleared his throat.
"You aren't trying to put me into a difficult position, are you?"

"No," Vincenzo said. "But I am serious." If the moment
he'd made the decision had to be pinpointed, he'd say it happened while he was talking to Paul. Or maybe just after. Or
there was no specific moment, really, just the entire circum-
stance, just everything about the year, too, and the year before,
and the one before that. It was time to drive the boat ashore.
In case Walter was still vacillating, he added, "I'm just going on
the record about something."

"You're kidding?"

"Not at all."

Walter laughed nervously and then sighed. A little silence
ensued while Walter thought it through. "Is this something
where I have to weigh your interests against my interests? That's
not something I want to do." He was a barker on the phone,
unnecessarily loud all the time. Even in person, he tended to be
argumentative and brash and unnecessarily loud.

"No, we have the same interests."

"Oh, I doubt that." There was another long pause while
Walter groaned, mulling it over. Walter verbalized, perhaps
unknowingly, his harsher emotions: groaning under his breath
(but nonetheless audibly) at boring people, sighing loudly
at exasperating conversations and also, evidently, at friends

steering themselves into the weeds. At last, he said, "Fuck it. Okay. Go on."

Much of the rest of the conversation was a blur, as are most of the truly important moments in life. Those great events always seemed to be formalized in interactions that, when recalled, appeared bright and blurry—like an iridescent watercolor left out in a rainstorm. The memory of his proposal to Cristina was like that, as was the conversation when she told him that she was pregnant. Leonora's birth: the only remaining image was of the thick dark blood seeping slowly from the freshly cut umbilical cord—and later, in Italy, when Leonora lost her leg, he remembered only huddling with Cristina, her nails digging deep into his wrist, while the electric saw screamed in the next room. Of the conversation with the doctor who told him that Cristina was dead, he remembered nothing whatsoever, just a hand on his shoulder. And, of this latest incident, telling Walter about the conversation with William Hamilton, Vincenzo would remember mainly that Walter offered him several opportunities to back out, but he continued.

At one point, Walter even said. "God! Have you talked to Wolfowitz, because I bet he'll take your side."

"I actually did talk to him. And you're right. He took my side."

"So, what's the point?" Walter shot back with unusually stark emotion in his voice. Like so many of the old guard in the DC press, Walter was a wan and debauched preppy— blond and fond of seersucker in the summer, tasseled loafers whenever; he was Buckley-esque. Still, his mind was a ferocious instrument dulled only around the periphery by years of monomania and heroic boozing. That his ex-wife had endured nineteen years with him, sans children, only spoke to her own delicious kind of madness, and his infuriating magnetism. But he was clipped now. That ballooning vein beside his eye was a newer development, and it did, Vincenzo thought, almost irreparable damage to his roguish authority.

"I don't know." Vincenzo had started going through the drawers of his desk and putting anything he wanted to keep in a plastic garbage bag. Things he kept included several pens he'd picked up at annual meetings, pictures, a dull rock he'd found on a hill in Scotland while on holiday with Cristina, some foreign currency, unread mail from the credit union and from other official organizations—then he got up and started shoveling files, his crucial outgoing correspondence, into the bag. Things he didn't keep: everything else. He didn't keep four other drawers of documents, including letters of recommendation that he'd written and all the contracts. He put the painting by his daughter into the bag, along with several of the books on his shelf, but left the rest, which he didn't care about anymore, or not enough to take it past the threshold.

"Vincenzo, do you have any idea what you're doing?"

By now, he was winded. So he paused. The easiest explanation was what Wolfowitz had alluded to, that this was the kamikaze's strategy. It had an appealingly straightforward quality: he resented the Bank and he despised himself for participating in its work, so he torpedoed himself into the Bank. Unfortunately, that wasn't the truth. Yes, he was exhausted by the Bank's bloated ineptitude and inefficiency, its inertia, but this wouldn't change any of that. William Hamilton was only as cunning as his job required him to be and his request, in retrospect, wasn't even that inappropriate. Vincenzo had seen worse.

And, contrary to what many onlookers would inevitably assume, it wasn't about ideology, either. The fact that Vincenzo, and more or less everyone else who was paying attention, detested George W. Bush was, in the end, beside the point. Actually, as he saw it, the kind of policies that Evo Morales was proposing made very reasonable grounds for at least a partial suspension of Bolivian aid.

Although even he had trouble understanding why he was doing it, he knew with an immaculate, blank certainty that he wouldn't regret this. Or, alternatively, he knew that it was the right decision, even if he did regret it. This was a problem to be sorted out later. There was an opportunity here, today, and there might never be another. The time to act was now. The way to act was this.

After reconfirming, yet again, that they were going to talk on the record, Walter recorded the conversation. He said that he couldn't wait much later than five or six before the story was a lock for the next day.

Vincenzo told him not to wait at all, but Walter insisted. He said, "If I don't hear from you by then, it's a go. Is that okay?" he was barking especially firmly, evidence of the degree of his concern. There would be an initial short piece, he said, which would be followed by a feature, and maybe more, depending on how his editor responded.

Vincenzo stopped rummaging through his things for a minute. He'd already filled one and a half plastic bags with garbage. He drew a deep breath. Exhaled slowly. "This is the start of something good for me, I think." He walked over to the window. "It's—" he shrugged. He leaned forward. Standing there, he could almost hear the crowd below. With his face right next to the glass he could almost see them, but not quite.

5

SCANDAL

The following morning Vincenzo—who had slept more or less normally, surprisingly enough—donned his mustard corduroy slacks, a too-large Redskins hooded sweatshirt he'd been given years ago but hadn't yet worn, his camel hair greatcoat, his gardening loafers, and his daughter's white crocheted skullcap to protect his bald dome, and then, looking like a homeless man who'd had his way with a Neiman Marcus freight container, stomped off in search of a *Washington Post*. In Los Angeles, in Chicago, such an outfit would be merely eccentric, but in straitlaced DC he looked genuinely insane, a fugitive from reality. Still, amazingly, disappointingly, the man behind the counter at the Brookville Market didn't appear to be surprised. The man was black, young, plainly fed up with the cheerful white suburbanites who traipsed to and fro, fragrant with exotic perfumes, within the shop. But this was Vincenzo's moment, the first evidence of his undoing, such as it was, and he wouldn't have minded a little recognition from the clerk. It wasn't to be. Instead, he was just an oddity, some well-off old guy with a madman's fashion sense.

On his way home he stopped, despite the lacerating wind, and set the newspaper down on the hood of someone's Jeep. He hadn't seen the article on the front page, so he checked inside, feeling both mildly panicked and relieved that it might not have been published at all. But then, on page three, he saw a small picture of his face beside the large headline: WORLD BANK VP QUESTIONS U.S. ROLE. The article was prominently displayed. It encompassed almost the entire right column.

He read:

WASHINGTON — A veteran economist and vice president of the World Bank abruptly resigned yesterday, offering an unusually frank critique of the United States' influence on World Bank policies.

Vincenzo D'Orsi, who had been with the Bank for twenty-four years, indicated that he'd witnessed a long-standing pattern of diplomatic pressure from the United States toward senior members of Bank management. "This pressure comes in regarding issues that are not related in any way to World Bank programs, but are rooted in political disagreements," D'Orsi said.

Specifically, D'Orsi cited an incident that occurred yesterday, when he said the United States' chief representative at the Bank, William Hamilton, attempted to pressure D'Orsi into reducing Bolivian aid if Evo Morales, a Bolivian presidential candidate who opposes U.S. influence in the region, is elected in next month's presidential election. "Aid

programs are not intended to be awarded or withdrawn
based on the outcome of an election," D'Orsi stated.

Reached at his office yesterday, Hamilton declined to
comment. The World Bank's director of communications,
Vera Gallash, stated that she had no knowledge of any
disagreement between D'Orsi and Hamilton and had not
received a letter of resignation yet from D'Orsi.

The World Bank, the largest international aid provider . . .

Vincenzo folded the paper back up, pulled out his mobile
phone, and called Vikki, his assistant. She wasn't there, of course.
It was far too early. He left a message: "Vikki, I'm not going
to be in. You probably know why. Or, if you don't know"—he
stopped, beginning, for the first time, to feel the true weight of
this shift—"you can take a look at today's *Post*. I—" He drew
a breath, looked up from the newspaper and saw a neighbor's
house, grand and symmetrical, well tended to. Every year, they
pressure-washed their driveway. They had a tremendous lawn.
The lights were on and he could see a child in a puffy black coat
casting his head back, exasperated by something someone else in
the house was doing or saying. "I just wanted—I don't know if
I'm going to be back," he continued, "but I wanted to say that
I really enjoyed working with you and if I can be of any help in
the future . . . well"— at which point he started to choke up, his
eyes stung. He tucked the paper under his arm. "I just—um,
well . . . just give me a call, if you want."

He hung up and drew a sharp breath, the icy air scorching
his lungs. He wiped away his tears with his sleeve, sniffled, then
stuffed his hands in his pockets and headed home.

Reading the article was one of the more surreal experiences of his life. To begin with, the tidiness of the narrative that Walter had arranged was bizarre beyond measure, especially when contrasted against the altogether more complicated and confusing reality of what had happened. Equally surreal, on a separate level, was how strange it was that Vincenzo's complaining to a friend on the phone about his job had become a prominent story in a major newspaper. Of course, it wasn't about him—not at all.

His ego was set straight once and for all when he read the comments in the online version, in which people didn't seem remotely aware of his particulars.

There were fifteen comments so far. He read the first few:

> RRFavallin:
> oh man now what if the rest of them would do it too

> Tina_The_Irish_1122:
> I for one think that its about time everyone sees the World bank is a big waste of tax dollars. No more! Especially when we cant afford things we need at home! Are we going to keep the world's "pan handlers" living the good life while our own middle class is starves. Why do we have to pay for these other countrys lives? This is F-ing stupid!!!

> SrMixALotsaDrinks:
> Amen, RRFavallin, one at a time, like lemmings.

MuchaMadHatter:

All I know is that all you grumpy fistdowners should just leave well enough alone about this. I love the cojones on this chap. Face it, dude is the badassest mother f*cker on his country-club's golf course for the next year. All I gotta say is "Jeeves, hurry along and get that man another gin and tonic."

He closed the browser.

Standing in the kitchen and feeling wholly enveloped by what he'd done in the worst way imaginable—or, in ways worse than he could have imagined—he blushed at the sickeningly public nature of it. He tried to steer his mind into benign territory—pondering, to start with, the things he could do with his extra time. There were tasks, so many tasks! He glanced back at the computer, half tempted by, but too panic-stricken to face, the other comments. No—better to focus on the tasks.

For example:

The garage had been overtaken with huge empty cardboard boxes and blocks of Styrofoam from his buying blitz at Williams-Sonoma and from maybe a dozen other large and less large objects he'd bought over the years. Those boxes and their ice-floe-sized hunks of Styrofoam never fit into his garbage can. Life was sieve-like with trash: sooner or later, all that was left was the oversized flotsam. Vincenzo had ceded the garage to clutter long enough ago that he felt sure that Cristina had a hand in letting it happen. So he could haul that to the dump, or maybe some of it could go to Goodwill. That was one thing. The attic, likewise, had two decades of things that they had not wanted to think about. Who had time for those things? Well, he did, now.

Then there were the gutters, which needed cleaning: he'd seen a huge tropical epiphyte sprouting in his rear gutter at the end of the summer. The asphalt on his walkway was cracking and countless eager weeds and mosses were only making matters worse. The sink in the basement, the one beside the washer, drained slowly enough that whenever he ran a load the water filled the basin nearly to the rim; he was still paying a gym membership at a gym he hadn't set foot in for two years. And this was only the local clutter—he really needed to figure out what he was going to do with his house in Italy, which was probably completely overrun with ivy and mold and God knows what else by now. The mortar was disintegrating inside the chimney there, had been since they bought it. And there'd been termites—someone had seen termites a year ago.

This list was perilous: once you started to populate it, dozens of uninvited deeds popped up. He needed to get a new career going, for example. Yes, he would not merely tend the garden for his remaining decades. And there were other things, too. Like women. He could start dating women.

His phone rang—strange at that hour, so he picked up. "Hello?"

"Vincenzo D'Orsi?"

"Yes, this is Vincenzo."

"Good morning, I'm Matthew Hastings with the *Financial Times*, and I was wondering if you have a minute to talk."

"I don't think so. How did you get my phone number?"

"You're listed."

Vincenzo groaned.

"It'd just be a minute of your time." When Vincenzo didn't speak, the reporter said, "For what it's worth, it's really not that hard to find someone's phone number." He was trying to nudge things along with his jaunty attitude.

Vincenzo sat down at the island in the kitchen. It was raining outside now, lightly pattering on the deck, dribbling down the window. The fence out back was collapsing into the neighbor's garden and needed to be repaired. It'd been that way for a year, another thing he could fix.

"Am I the first to call?" the reporter said.

"Yes." It hadn't occurred to him yet that other journalists would call. But, of course they would. He grunted involuntarily.

"Can you talk?"

"Oh—" he said and then sighed. He wasn't used to dealing with journalists. "I think so."

"Was this the first time Mr. Hamilton tried to pressure you over a country?"

"Oh," he said again, caught off guard by the directness. The question was simple enough on one level, but also impossible to answer without being controversial in one way or another. "I would rather not answer this right now."

"Really?" He sounded surprised. "Why? You don't work there anymore, do you?"

"No, I think I—" Vincenzo hadn't officially resigned yet, he also hadn't officially been fired, so he did still work there, legally speaking. "Let me—can you call me back in a couple hours?" he said.

"Should I give you my number?"

"No, just call me again in two hours." Vincenzo hung up on him.

He quickly checked his e-mail and saw that there were eight messages. None of the names of the authors were familiar. He felt sick as he began to see that this scandal—his scandal—was unfolding in such a conspicuous way. It was horribly public. Strangers were contacting him before dawn. There'd been occasional e-mails before, and he'd been quoted in articles, but nothing like this. And, to his surprise, it was incredibly embarrassing. It wasn't exciting, it was mortifying. He'd sort of imagined liking a flare of celebrity, but he couldn't help wonder what his coworkers were thinking—all of the thousands of people he'd worked with. Would they all be disappointed in him? *Yes, all of them.*

He got up and made himself another espresso, banging the black puck of old grinds out into his kitchen can, rinsing the silver cup, and pitching in a few more spoonfuls of the fair-trade stuff that he'd purchased for his daughter's benefit. On the kitchen clock that Cristina had bought but hated, one of the few old things left in the kitchen, he saw that it wasn't even eight yet. More than anything, he wanted to take it back—or at least to do it differently, less dramatically. This was too much. Way too much.

No sooner had he drawn the espresso than he sat down and forwarded the article to his daughter. He wrote and erased several different messages to her, but couldn't find the right tone. Everything he tried came out with accidental subtexts: "What have I done??" and its many incarnations sounded too regretful; "Look what I did!" was weirdly childish; "What do you think?" was much too offhand. No message at all would be peculiarly inexpressive.

At last, he collected himself—the phone was ringing again—and wrote:

I made this decision quickly, and I hope it was right. We
should talk soon.
Love, Papi

He clicked *send.*

Then he got up and looked at the caller ID: *Unidentified Number.* He grabbed his coat and went out for a brisk walk through the neighborhood—pondering the chaos he'd wrought, turning it over and looking at it from different angles, searching for a way to comprehend it.

He was home again, a little after nine, when the woman from human resources called.

The conversation was mercifully straightforward. After some formalities, she said: "I'm sure you're not surprised, but I wanted to offer you early retirement."

"Right, yes, that makes sense," he said.

"We were hoping you'd be willing to accept a severance of two years full salary with most of the same benefits."

"You—" he started, but stopped because he was shocked by the generosity of the offer. He withheld for a moment. If it seemed too good to be true, it was. "I'm wondering about the state of my pension."

"Nothing has changed with your pension. You're retiring early. You'll receive two years of pay and benefits as if you were an employee. In twenty-four months, you receive the package that you would have received had you retired then."

This still didn't compute. "What do you want from me?" he said.

"We would also like you to sign an agreement that clarifies the scope and amplifies the terms of your existing nondisclosure agreement."

He snorted and said, "I will not sign a gag clause."

"I know, which is why we're not proposing that. You're free to speak or write about the Bank, as you please, but there will be limitations on what you're able to discuss. Basically, you'll be prevented from discussing specifics. I can fax over the agreement. We need you to avoid speaking to any more press until you've seen the contract. If you don't agree, the entire package is void, and you'll be fired."

He was glad that he'd cut off that interview with the *Financial Times*. "I don't have a fax machine," he said.

"We'll messenger it over. You'll have it by noon. Call me once you've read it. The deadline is five o'clock today. In the meantime, don't say anything to the press."

=

When Leonora called fifteen minutes later, she was rapturous, beginning: "Oh my fucking God, Dad, what did you do?!" He hadn't heard her sound so pleased with him in years. In fact, he couldn't remember a time that she'd sounded so pleased with him.

He laughed and said, "I made some enemies."

"Fuuuuuuck!" she drawled and then laughed, before saying, "Wow, Dad, you are a badass! Wow. *Wow.* Really, I can't believe you." This almost made the whole thing worthwhile.

"I just couldn't—I couldn't let him be like that," he said, ebullient and struggling with his false modesty.

She groaned in the way she did when she was impressed by something she had heard from one of her friends. "Jesus," she said again. And then a certain stiltedness entered the proceedings, he could feel it, even in the silence—there was a stilted something, maybe just because she was so excited, but what did this burst of glee say about how she'd felt before? She exhaled. She laughed, sort of, and he sort of laughed too, but the moment was spoiling quickly from something that he couldn't quite see. Really, he didn't think it was funny at all, and maybe she knew that, maybe that's why her joy was failing so quickly. Still, as misinterpretations went, this was one he was prepared to accept.

"I should go," he said.

"I love you," she said.

"I love you, too," he said and then hung up before it got any worse.

=

The waves of shame came and went, interspersed by successful and semisuccessful campaigns to assure himself that he'd done an honorable thing for Bolivia, for the Bank, a thing that would, in the long run, also benefit his life enormously. He'd obliterated one version of his life, yes, one that had endured for a long time, yes, but in so doing had created space for something else. Something better than his previous occupation. He paced, didn't answer the phone. He forced himself to stop reading the e-mails, reading the comments on the article. At the crescendo of one particularly bad wave of shame, he found himself groaning aloud, his heart racing, while the phone rang and rang and rang.

=

Once it arrived, he read the agreement through as carefully as he was able, but his mind was addled by the panic and he found it too opaque to comprehend, so he called Eleanor Griffin, a lawyer who'd been close with Cristina—one of the few friends of hers he'd genuinely liked—and asked if he could drive it over to her office for a rush appraisal.

Vincenzo explained the circumstances, broadly, and then Eleanor glanced through and told him that his interpretation of the document seemed to be correct. He could not speak or write about any specific individuals or particular conversations that he had held in his professional capacity, but was free to talk generally about his impressions of the Bank. There could be no tell-all memoir, but there could, in theory, be a lecture tour about the Bank's rotten structures, she said. Eleanor was short, her head surmounted by a gigantic black mass of curls, which didn't add height so much as draw a black mark over her shortness; her skin was waxy and pure white—she was a bit bloated from forever sitting in large comfortable leather chairs and peering at documents on her colossal desk. Despite her deathly appearance, she was a gloriously uncensored person, mordant and gaffe-prone, but smart enough to make it all quite winning, at least to Vincenzo's tastes. The kind of person who could be counted on to blurt out an expletive far too loudly during a funeral, which is exactly what she did during the service for Cristina. And while she'd seemed mortified at the time, Vincenzo had always wanted to thank her and assure her that it was hilarious, really, even if he hadn't found it in himself to laugh about it at the time.

With two hours left before the contract was void, Eleanor let him use the Wi-Fi in her office. His laptop gaping up at him, he checked his e-mail one last time, just in case—saw, with a considerable dollop of dread, that there were thirty-seven new messages. None of the messages, at a glance, looked relevant to the issue at hand, so, with an hour and forty minutes left, he called up the article online and found that there were 209 comments. He groaned.

"You good?" Eleanor said.

"Yes," he said initially. "Not really," he then admitted. He clapped his laptop shut and stuffed it in its nylon carrying case.

"You'll let me know if I can do anything else."

He kissed Eleanor on her baby-soft cheek before hurrying out to the elevator.

=

Arriving at the World Bank headquarters, he parked in his spot on the red level and marched briskly over to the elevator. In the blurry brass doors, he could see how bizarrely his yellow trousers clashed with his sweatshirt and his coat, and he almost managed to feel embarrassed about that, too.

Teresa, the human resources woman he'd talked to earlier, stood when he entered. "Thank you for coming," she said wearily, her thin-fingered hand extended. She had frosty blue eyes, long flaxen hair, and a feline languor in her movements. A tremendous scar ran the length of her jaw, as if to preemptively quash any doubts about her battle-readiness.

She offered him a seat, but he just pulled the signed document out from his bag and extended it to her.

"Thank you," she said and sat down. She put the document on her desk and he stood there while she flipped through the boilerplate, scanning for addendums, he guessed. Then, seeing his signature on the last page, she looked up at him, said, "Well—we appreciate your understanding."

She signed, in duplicate, and gave him one copy.

Then she stood up and they shook hands again. He was about to leave when she said, "We'll need your badge, actually."

"Oh—of course." He unclipped it from his breast pocket and handed it over.

She smiled a little drowsily, smugly, blinking too slowly, and looking at her grinning face, lovely as it was maimed, he wanted to punch her out.

"Fuck you," he blurted, incapable of stopping himself.

She was taken aback, at first, and then her expression returned to where it was before as she apprehended, no doubt, that this was just who he was: it was why he'd done what he'd done. And it all made sense to her now, which only made him hate her more. She shook her head and did one of those oily smiles where the sides of her mouth were downturned, like a frown. She was enjoying this, in a way.

"No really, fuck you," he said again.

She appeared startled, and he could see that he'd disrupted her day, at last. "Uh—" she stammered.

He shook his head, at once satisfied and sick with himself, then turned and left.

=

Vincenzo spent the better part of five hours poring over the e-mails, erasing the dreck, which came mostly from wacky fanatics. He glanced at the comment section of the article, but didn't venture too deeply into it. No denomination of political preference came off as particularly more sensible; only a few, fortunately, seemed genuinely insane. The frothy-mouthed ones left messages anonymously, and the passionate but reasonable sent e-mails. Most of the rest occupied that great succulent midsection of misconception that had assembled the impression that he thought the World Bank was rotten and should be abolished. Most of them agreed wholeheartedly with him.

At its most basic, the allure of fundamentalism, whether religious or ideological, liberal or conservative, is that it provides an appealing order to things that are actually disorderly. As a bonus, one that shouldn't be underestimated, members of an ideological camp, especially one exclusive enough to sit well outside the mainstream, come to feel a strong sense of belonging. "Circle dancing is magic," wrote Kundera in *The Book of Laughter and Forgetting,* and he then went on to describe a group bound together by ideology joining hands and dancing and laughing until they ascend heavenward. Cristina had adored Kundera's novels, and Vincenzo had always been jealous of whatever part of her embraced the sensuality of his stories. It was worse than infidelity, it was as if he had simply never met that part of her. Still, he read the books, each one, once she was done with them, always searching the pages for dog-ears and any trace of where she had lingered.

For Kundera in *Laughter*, all spiritual and ideological movements are circle dancing and the circle, crucially, is a *closed* shape, one that creates magical love between members, but if you leave the circle it will close behind you. Whereas, if you leave a row, you can return to it, because it isn't a closed shape, but a row isn't *magic*, does not induce levitation or love, does not solve the problem of not belonging.

Of course, to the great inconvenience of everyone, few issues in life are actually as straightforward as circles—so skilled at killing loneliness, but not good for much else. In the end there is no vast conspiracy. Most people are too disorganized and insufficiently odious, in the necessarily horrifying way, to mount large-scale conspiracies. The reality is brutally humdrum. There are just a bunch of people, each one as helpless and baffled as the next, most battling against loneliness by swearing allegiance to vivid gods and vivid ideologies, and assembling—hands joined—in churches and outside office buildings, to dance in unison. In a passage that Vincenzo would have asked his daughter to memorize if she'd been capable of hearing it clearly, Kundera wrote: "The best of all possible progressive ideas is the one which is provocative enough so its supporters can feel proud of being different, but popular enough so the risk of isolation is precluded by cheering crowds confident of victory."

=

Vincenzo saved twenty-some e-mails, mainly from journalists wanting to talk to him, including two producers from cable news shows. The rest were from friends or acquaintances inquiring after his well-being.

Among the e-mails from people he knew, most just said some version of, "Wow, I can't believe you did that!" but there was one that stuck out. Colin, who'd left the Bank eleven years before for a job at Lehman Brothers, hadn't been in touch in eons. But Colin wrote: *You're stepping out? Hope you'll visit us. I'd love to talk about your plans. If this is of interest, I can arrange to bring you up to NY for a talk.*

He hadn't expected any overtures from the private sector. It especially hadn't occurred to him that a company like Lehman would come calling, let alone so aggressively. They did that for outgoing chief economists, he knew—such people were poached actively—but he hadn't been an intellectual icon at the Bank; he'd been a career bureaucrat. After a minute, he determined it was a superb idea at least to explore that opportunity. If nothing else, the trip would give him an excuse to visit Leonora.

He wrote: *This sounds good. I'm on my way up there soon to see my daughter.*

6

MENDING FENCES

The following morning, there were two dozen more e-mails, including one from someone he'd never met with the subject line *You decapitated yourself?* And another from Cynthia, and one from Jonathan Paris, the boy from the Rainforest Coalition. He read them all, more or less, erased most of them, and replied to a couple, but not Paris's. Cynthia kindly didn't ask any questions, perhaps she knew he would be overwhelmed with questions. Instead, she wrote: *That Peruvian delegate will be proud of you. (:* Meanwhile, someone had anonymously, creepily, left a vase of flowers outside of his house with the note: *Well done!* Vincenzo set the flowers on the kitchen table along with the paper. He made his oatmeal and stirred in the raspberries, made his coffee, and then went upstairs, put on jeans and a sweater. In the garage, he collected several metal brackets, a hammer, a pocketful of woodscrews, and the power screwdriver. Everything was garlanded with cobwebs and powdered with dust. Wearing his new overcoat and a cashmere sweater, along with his ratty and paint-splattered loafers, he stomped into his cold backyard. He went down to the stand of dogwoods at the back of his simple lot, a miniature forest that carried on into the more commanding swath of jungle in his rear neighbor's impressive yard.

There, he took stock of the fallen fence, not sure where to begin. Walking across the face of the fence, he entered his neighbor's yard and then turned and reassessed it. He tried to hoist it up, but it was too heavy. He'd thought to pin it to his next-door neighbor's sturdy new fence with the brackets, but now he grasped that it was too warped and rotten to be salvaged. He tried to hoist it up once more, digging his loafered feet into the leafy ground. Nothing moved.

Thinking he might break it up and cart the broken sections away, he jumped up and down on the fence, but it just jiggled.

Taking the claw hammer from his pocket, he tried to pry apart the braces from the slats, but he couldn't get the claw into the gap, and anyway, he wasn't strong enough for that task. Finally, a little winded and starting to sweat, he drew a long breath and swung the hammer at the brace nearest him. The hammer thocked against the wood, shooting a bolt of pain up through his arm, but leaving only a small dent. Furious, he swung again and hit it hard, gripping the hammer harder. That felt better. So he swung again. And again. He hoped this would somehow produce visible results, but the wood was too moist and pliable. He swung twice more and his arm, now plangent with ache, compelled him to release the hammer. He bit back the urge to scream.

Appraising the fence again, he realized that he could, at least, break the slats. Or, at least, he could break the pointed tips, above the upper brace. Picking up the hammer, he swung for one tip and heard a crack as the old wood snapped at the nail. He swung again and the loosened tip snapped off the top of the fence and spun to the ground.

It wasn't very satisfying, but it would do. He swung for the middle of the same slat, thinking it might be weakened, but it was like hitting a tire.

Not willing to just head back inside, not after all this effort, he swung again at the next fence tip, which also snapped. He drew a lungful of that scalding cold air and swung at the next, but it didn't crack. He swung much harder and it snapped off completely and spun into the brush. He swung at the next tip, even harder.

When Walter came around the side of the house an hour later, Vincenzo paused to catch his breath—he'd forgotten Walter was on his way over and was a little embarrassed to be caught smashing the fence. One of the flying shards of wood had hit him in the face and cut him slightly. Hot sweat beaded on the top of his bald dome; he could feel it steaming in the cold air.

"Well, I rang the doorbell but there was no answer. I thought you might have done something rash."

Breathing heavily, Vincenzo shook his head. He wiped sweat from his forehead with his forearm.

Walter frowned, pointed at him, and said, "Your cheek is bleeding."

"A piece of wood hit me."

Walter smiled. "It hit *you*? Vicious wood."

Vincenzo just grunted.

Walter kept smiling. "How's retirement otherwise?"

Vincenzo was down to his mucky loafers and jeans and his white T-shirt—his coat and sweater had been flung onto the fallen fence. He had broken at least twenty of the fence's tips. He put the hammer down and rubbed the stubble on his jaw. "It's fine. I'm okay."

"Good. Well—try not to fall apart. I don't want that on my conscience."

"There is nothing wrong. I came out here to fix this fence. It has been like this for a year. And this is a problem. Do you agree?"

"I agree it's a problem." And then, smiling again, he added, "And you're fixing it!"

"No, I'm breaking it up so that I can take it away!" He swung and broke another tip, to demonstrate it, and then he held the hammer up to Walter and said, "Do you want to try?"

Walter looked at the hammer and frowned, unconvinced. For all his bluster, Walter wasn't a very emotionally available person, or not expressive, anyway, and probably needed to smash some fence tips fairly badly, whether he knew it or not. "Thanks," he said, "but not just now. I think I'm going to go inside for some coffee. I have no coffee at home."

Vincenzo inhaled deeply, felt the cold air like shards of glass in his lungs. "Make enough for me. I'll be inside soon."

=

Twenty minutes later, Vincenzo settled in at the kitchen table while Walter refilled his mug, though the initial volley of coffee seemed to have done the job of sparking all available synapses to life. Walter's small expressive hands whipped up the storm, conducting the torrent of his own monologue. Vincenzo, in his dirty jeans and T-shirt, sipped from his mug and scanned his raft of e-mails, sometimes shooting off a short response, while Walter sat opposite, his right foot slapping against the kitchen floor's tiles. At cocktail parties, Walter liked to face off against taller men, especially, braying up at them with his shoulders hunched and his normally active hands tame at his sides—a maestro baiting the orchestra by refusing to pick up his baton. Vincenzo had watched this often. Once his interlocutor finally took the bait, Walter would be on him with the savagery of a wolverine trying to fell a bison, dismantling every point the man had made since they met. "Should've been a litigator," he'd said more than once, while basking in the glow of a particularly gruesome bout. It was, understandably, exactly what his ex-wife had loved and hated most about him: his over-energetic intellect and how that mind laid asunder every conversation they tried to have. This morning, the subject of his focus was nothing combative, only Vincenzo's "astonishing" options:

"You've got Lehman Brothers attempting to pull you into bed over here, and the fucking think tanks"—Vincenzo had received an offer to come visit Tellus Institute, and according to Walter other liberal think tanks would have, by now, realized that he might make a good mascot for their causes, too—"and God knows what else." No doubt Walter's enthusiasm was, at least in part, a way of sublimating any lingering guilt he felt over his part in Vincenzo's flameout. Under no ordinary circumstances would he express enthusiasm for what was clearly a questionable decision; only guilt could elicit such an outpouring of optimism.

"I should draw them out more," Vincenzo said.

"You've got a month, I think, to make a move. If you play it right, you could be more influential in retirement than you were at the Bank. You could become an Italian Stiglitz, but maybe less of an esteemed idea person and more of a regular commentator on NPR. You have a great face for radio. And in the event that you do end up on TV, you look as comfortable in a suit as any politician I've seen."

Vincenzo thought about the possibility that he might become a personality in that way and said, "There's a lot I do want to say. The most frustrating thing for the last many years has been the way people misunderstand these things we work on." He paused, realizing he had forgotten to put that in the past tense. "And there are so many idiots on the talk shows. If I—"

"Exactly," Walter said, "but don't commit to anything. You're baiting them—best to chum the water a little, wait until it's frothing with silvery fins, and then harpoon the living shit out of them!" He smiled grandly.

"Ha!" Vincenzo was not aware of having a profile that might attract people in such a way, but what Walter said made a kind of sense. A good gambit is a trap that takes a while to mature; if you're impatient, and try to strike back too soon after your sacrifice, you threaten to diminish the gathering power of your loss.

There were other possibilities developing, too. He'd received an e-mail from a woman in Evo Morales's office and he thought that maybe there was something there. She was Evo's press attaché. She'd said that she and Evo appreciated what he'd done and hoped to meet him someday. "I could give the story a little extra fuel," he said.

Walter's eyes narrowed and he stared at Vincenzo. "How would you do that?"

"Go to Bolivia. Visit Evo Morales, and you could tag along and cover the story."

Walter rolled his eyes at the dig, but nodded in approval at the idea. "Who would we contact in Bolivia?"

"I've already been contacted by someone in Evo's office."

At this, Walter perked up. "Who?"

Vincenzo showed Walter the message from Evo's press liaison, Lenka Villarobles. After reading it, Walter appropriated Vincenzo's laptop and opened a blank document and started drafting a response. They applied to the letter all the vim they could summon. Twenty minutes later they had a page, but agreed it could be more charming.

In broken Spanish, they'd agreed to let Evo host a reception for them the night before Evo's inauguration in January. The party had been Villarobles's idea, but they expanded on it, saying they'd come to La Paz, do a series of interviews. Walter would write another piece or two for the *Post* along the way.

Walter got up to use the bathroom and once he was out of the room, Vincenzo sent the message, flaws and all.

Walter returned a little later, and said, "Can you print out a copy for me, and I'll look it over later today?"

"Yes, but I already sent it," Vincenzo said. He was cleaning up the coffee machine now.

"You did?"

Vincenzo nodded but kept washing and didn't look up.

"Why on earth did you do that? We could have improved it!"

"It was fine in that condition," Vincenzo said.

$$=$$

Later, while Walter was outside with the hammer snapping a few tips off the fallen fence—from the kitchen, Vincenzo could see that he wasn't putting nearly enough heart into it for it to be satisfying—Vincenzo wrote a quick e-mail to Colin at Lehman and said he was coming up in the next couple of days and would be happy to meet.

His official reason for fleeing DC, the one he told Leonora, was that he wanted to escape the sudden bright glare of celebrity—"My fifteen minutes," he declared at one point on the phone, and indeed it was just that. But, really, he was also alarmed and enticed by the dangling possibilities; frustrated, too, at finding himself with only Walter to keep him company during his molting from caterpillar to—well, something else. So he said that he had to go to New York. He said he was annoyed with the paparazzi, even though there had been only one news van outside his house (for a Latin American television station) on the first night and none thereafter. He did, to be fair, receive a crushing amount of e-mail and he had been invited onto *Democracy Now!*, but Larry King was not exactly banging down his door.

The people most interested in his case lived in Latin America, particularly Bolivia, so the calls were mostly from Spanish-speaking journalists, which was awkward, because he didn't speak Spanish well. When he tried to reply in Italian, they generally gave up.

Professionally, he'd only had the e-mails from Tellus and from Colin at Lehman. Lenka Villarobles had written to say that she was thrilled that he and Walter had suggested coming to Bolivia for a function hosted by Evo. She was going to talk to Evo about it, she said, and already Vincenzo regretted bringing it up at all. She wrote that she and Evo wanted to thank them for outing Hamilton's plot to coerce the Bolivian leadership. That Vincenzo hadn't intended strictly speaking to save Morales's hide gave him pause. Still, it was so, of course. Vincenzo had put such a bright spotlight on the Bank's Bolivia policy that it would be difficult, if not impossible, for the Bank or any other aid organization to withdraw aid to Bolivia for a while unless there was a very good reason to do so. Vincenzo had given Bolivia immunity, for the time being.

Her message had been vague, though, and left room for some interpretation. She hadn't, for example, tried to hammer down a date, so he was optimistic that the whole thing might go away, if left unbothered.

The more important question was whether, in the next month, he could decide what he'd be doing with the rest of his useful years. For the first time in his life, he was something like a minor celebrity, and so Walter's point made sense, that if Vincenzo wanted to do something substantial, he needed to act while the glow was still upon him. That he couldn't be both a fellow at Tellus, which was as strenuously lefty a think tank as existed, and a consultant to Lehman Brothers at the same time was clear. But he'd already been hasty, so he decided to defer the decision for the time being, see what happened.

=

"Why do you really want to come, Dad?" Leonora said when he called to tell her that he was fleeing the media onslaught.

"I'll stay out of your way," he said. "I'll be miles away from Brooklyn. I plan to stay at the W Hotel in Midtown. Do you know the one? I hear it's nice."

"Don't be weird, Dad," she said. "I can't wait to see you. It'll be fun. And really I'm so thrilled that you've quit. I've been telling all my friends and they're so impressed. They're like: 'That was your dad?' because they've heard about it and they can't believe you're so punk rock."

"Punk rock?!" he said and laughed.

"Yes, *punk rock!*" she yelped, in her unfortunately effete imitation of his voice, and then she laughed hysterically, because he was still just her dorky dad, the unhip bald man in a dark suit and expensive neckwear, the man whose most casual look was when he wore a button-down shirt tucked into pleated slacks. And then, settling into a more serious tone, she said, "I just don't want you to be shocked by the fact that I'm living with Sam."

She had told him about this new arrangement over the Thanksgiving weekend, and he'd been quietly trying to assure himself since then that it was less than completely true. Maybe she was there for a while because rent was so expensive? That

made sense. It was temporary. But the demise of her relationship with Sam had been imminent for a year in his mind, and
he had to admit it was starting to seem a little less preordained
than he had hoped. He was surprised that the thought of her
moving in with Sam had filled him with such dread. It wasn't
that he was a prude, or believed his daughter to be sexless. He'd
seen how she could lose herself in other people—her mother,
her friends—how easily she could put miles between him and
her, and he was terrified of losing her, too.

Still, Vincenzo refused to intervene. It was her life—he believed that adamantly. "I'm not shocked," he said. "You're a
grown-up. People live together. It's normal."

"But you hate Sam."

"No, no, how could I hate him? He's a little annoying, but
I like him. Or, I don't hate him. There's nothing there to hate."

"Thanks Dad, that's really nice," she said. Like her hair-
dyeing, which was also supposed to be a phase, she still hadn't
managed to outgrow this habit of flinging sarcasm around
whenever she was displeased.

"No, really, I like Sam. He's interesting." He was on his
third glass of wine, a perk (and danger, he could see) of the
unemployed life, and he was tempted to say too much, but
resisted. Instead, he said, "I'm glad you care about him and that
he cares about you, but you are young."

"Dad. I'm older than you were when you married Mom."

"No. Is that true?" he said, although it obviously was.

Vincenzo thought of Sam primarily in metaphors that insinuated a kind of comforting wisdom, but were also pleasantly
abstract: Sam was an apartment his daughter would rent for a

few years when she was in her early twenties and look back on fondly; he was training wheels on her bicycle; he was a summer job at Denny's.

The first and only time Vincenzo met Sam was a few months ago, when she brought him down to DC for a weekend. Vincenzo took them to dinner at Tosca that Friday. Sam spoke with a Bob Dylan affectation, and looked like an unhappy rodent, with his wispy beard, upturned nostrils, and squirrelly overbite. Genetics had denied him a chin, and his fingers, which pawed Leonora casually, constantly, were stained ochre by the unfiltered cigarettes he smoked. At times he seemed folded in on himself, legs crossed, arms crossed, head bowed. A nostalgia addict, he claimed to be a playwright, listened to old records, was fond of Camus, Brecht, Stravinsky—everyone he admired was long dead. Sam was also a self-described "activist," which seemed to mean that he was able to formulate strong positions on issues that he did not understand. In his hazy grasp of these things, for example, the World Bank was in some kind of insidious collusion with the George W. Bush administration. He said as much at that dinner at Tosca.

"Well, no, that's not how it works," Vincenzo had explained. Leonora looked at him intently and he knew she doubted him, which was ludicrous—like taking the advice of a witch doctor about your heart arrhythmia when your father is a cardiologist.

"They have veto power, though, right?" Leonora had said, tentatively. She had rarely attempted to discuss these matters with her father. At dinner she wore a long-sleeved top, in order to hide her tattoos. The tattoos were—Vincenzo had to admit to himself, if not her—quite beautiful, though he was terrified of what they'd look like in twenty years. Her skirt was long, too, to hide her leg. So, apart from her raven hair, streaked with strips of crimson, and her dramatic eyeliner and her facial piercings, she looked strangely modest, as if the head of a punk had been transplanted onto the body of a Mormon.

"The US has veto power on many decisions, yes. So does Europe. So does the Third World. A lot of things are decided by committees or teams of people. A small fraction of my coworkers are from the US, and apart from the American executive director, none have any kind of relationship with your government."

"That's what they say," Sam said, as if Vincenzo didn't know how these things worked. Like any good fundamentalist, his outrage was not dimmed in the least by his ignorance.

Vincenzo made himself cough; he sipped his wine, as if to clear his throat. "Do either of you have room for dessert?"

It was no good. They persisted.

Finally, when he could take no more, Vincenzo said, "You don't seem to grasp how, or to what end, the World Bank functions."

"You've been brainwashed!" Leonora said, and the irony was so rich that Vincenzo was rendered mute with awe.

"I'm going for a cigarette," Sam said and stood. Leonora followed him out.

Despite its steep prices, Tosca did not have the best Italian food in DC. Still, it was his favorite restaurant in the city. It was serene and elegant, the service far warmer than at other high-end restaurants in DC. He used to take Cristina there every year on their anniversary, and continued to take Leonora there every time she returned home.

The maître d', a lanky Frenchman named Denis, came around and folded the napkins that had been tossed onto the chairs. He replaced them beside the bread plates. "How is your dinner?" he asked, in heavily accented Italian.

"Wonderful, thank you. My daughter, she has her mother's temper," he said, in case Denis had overheard. But when he said this, it reminded him of the times when Cristina had hissed angrily at him in restaurants, including Tosca, and how he would try to get her to be quieter because her rage embarrassed him. And when he thought of that he felt a pinch of pain in his chest—that dull hollow ache that comes from wanting something impossible for too long. Sometimes, he was self-conscious about the feeling, and how quickly tears came to his eyes, and he wondered if people could see how heavily the dead were with him.

"I'm sorry for the disturbance," he said to Denis.

Denis smiled warmly. "It's not a problem, Mr. D'Orsi."

＝

An inveterate dilettante, Leonora was very interested in art, literature, sustainable ecology, music, knitting, natural and locally sourced foods—all of which shared only one common denominator: they were pursuits that weren't likely to result in a gainful career. If she'd been casually interested in computer programming, he'd be less worried, but she did not seem especially interested in making a living. He blamed Cristina for this. Cristina had nudged Leonora into summer classes, summer camps, a lot of enriching, but not especially difficult, summertime activities. Then again, he blamed himself for not pursuing the issue, for not demanding that Leonora get a job, for not choking off her cash supply. To her, money was boring. It came and it went and it didn't matter, really. What mattered were things like yoga and art. That she couldn't understand that yoga and art were also about money, that summer camp was about money, that every aspect of her life was about money—he blamed himself for that, and he blamed Cristina, too.

Having graduated from one of the most mind-bogglingly pricey colleges in the world, Leonora waited tables at an over-priced diner in Brooklyn, where she took the graveyard shift. She was vexed, above all else, by loiterers, inebriated batches of *hipsters*—as she called them—seeking a few hours of coffee and conversation late at night, maybe some fried eggs, before they wandered homeward. During their phone calls this was what she talked about: loiterers and their illegible tip tallies, their splashing vomit, and the time she watched a famous musician doze off and urinate in his jeans after a long tour and too much heroin.

Of course, everyone talks too much about their job, regardless of how uninteresting it is, and now Vincenzo, abruptly deprived of this cornerstone of conversation, found himself having to work harder at small talk in general. The thought of this void, the void he'd created, filled him with terror, something that he felt in his chest, a constriction.

While Leonora was just about to begin learning how much money would matter in her life, in his case, money wouldn't be a concern again. Per his agreement with the World Bank, he'd be coasting indefinitely. Coasting, though—that word harried him, the lifelessness implied. Coasters were cork pads upon which people rested their moist drinks. To "coast" was to idle, which was one thing when you had a car full of brilliant people to keep you company, but quite another if you were alone.

By the time Walter finally returned from attacking the fence, Vincenzo had determined that he needed to start researching his options. The Tellus Institute's website had been unhelpful: a healthy and reassuringly sane blue predominated and the slogan "For a Great Transition" sounded either invitingly apropos, or menacing. So he surfed away, started reading more online articles about his case. The *Wall Street Journal* had something short. So did *Bloomberg*. Unfortunately, his life was forever abbreviated by the same dependant clause, "a vice president and twenty-four-year veteran of the Bank," which was deployed, in one form or another, in almost all of them, as in: *Mr. D'Orsi, a vice president, and twenty-four-year veteran of the Bank, has no plans but looks forward to coasting in the approximate direction of oblivion.*

Walter proceeded directly through to the kitchen, saying, "You Italians, you really do a better job of even making pasta. How is that? I put pasta into boiling water, you put pasta into boiling water, but yours is better."

"Will you check in on the house while I'm away?" Vincenzo said.

"I can invite women over and tell them that it's my house?"

Vincenzo nodded. "Wear my suits, too. Or, maybe I'll leave my passport and you can simply take over."

Walter frowned sharply at the thought, and then slopped a herculean portion of pasta into what was meant to be a serving bowl. Walter had the metabolism of a hummingbird, and seemed immune to the deleterious effects of excess carbohydrates, lipids, salts. Energy crackled like an electric field around his body. He sat down at the kitchen table and began forking the rigatoni into his mouth and shaking his head in admiration.

"Are we really going to go to Bolivia?" Vincenzo said. The more he thought about it, the less he liked the idea.

"Don't wilt, Vincenzo—that woman's serious. For Christ's sake, *we* suggested it." He laughed a little, eyes widening, as he did when excited about something he was going to say, some point he was making. "You can't decline an invitation to your own party!"

"I am not wilting, Walter. I'm wondering if it's a good idea."

"Of course it's a good idea!" Walter turned the kitchen television on and started flipping channels, marching toward CNN. Whenever he was over, he relentlessly flipped between CNN and Fox News, a two-step channel dance he referred to as "taking the temperature." So that, if they were watching a film and Vincenzo paused to open some wine, Walter would ask if he could quickly "take the temperature." Once he settled on CNN, he glanced over at Vincenzo. "How would it be bad? Bad, like, it might annoy your new friends at the Cato Institute?"

"Cato hasn't contacted me," Vincenzo said although Walter had nicely pinpointed the issue: he might alienate someone who could otherwise offer him a bridge out of this void.

"They haven't contacted you *yet*! Avoid Bolivia and they'll send you roses." Walter gazed at Vincenzo, wide eyes expressing something between dismay and a sincere curiosity about whether Vincenzo might actually be interested in such an offer.

When Vincenzo didn't speak, Walter went on: "Look, eventually you're going to have to decide who you want to be friends with and who you can live without." Vincenzo had already gleaned as much and that was precisely why he wanted to proceed cautiously. "For better or worse, this world you're entering isn't as sweetly nondenominational as the one you're leaving. Not that the Bank was exactly a pillar of independence, obviously, but at least there was a pretense. That pretense doesn't count for much out here."

Vincenzo sighed and sat down. On the TV he saw footage of a snowstorm in the Midwest; it was advancing eastward, wreaking havoc on Christmas shoppers and commuters. He watched footage of cars parked on the side of the highway, their headlights shining in the direction of nowhere through the muffling torrent. They cut back to the studio briefly, then to President Bush on a military base somewhere shaking hands with a leathery general in dusty-hued camouflage. The president was pinkened with sunburn.

Walter turned the volume up a couple of notches, but it still wasn't audible. "Say hello to Leonora for me," he said. "I must say, she really has turned out quite well balanced, all things considered. It's a real testament to human resilience."

Vincenzo picked up a fork and eyed the pasta, hoping to restrain himself from overeating. "Testament to human resilience? Is that an insult?"

"No, you seem like a fine dad, at least from the perspective of someone who hasn't been a parent before, but for a while there I thought she was going to go over the deep end. The tattoos, the hair, that boyfriend."

"Yes, well, he's still around. So are the tattoos."

"But she's turned out to be pretty sensible, hasn't she?" CNN moved to a sports update and Walter hit the mute button.

Vincenzo gave in and skewered several tubes of rigatoni with his fork, pushed them into his mouth. "My food is better because I make it with care. That's the only difference."

Walter scowled.

Vincenzo smiled, got up, and went to the bookshelf to fetch the chessboard. Walter pushed his bowl aside to make room.

7

PENDULUM

As the train pulled out of Union Station, Vincenzo read over the details of his pension agreement, which was complicated. He had to decide if he wanted euros or dollars, for one thing, and he was entitled to an array of payment plans, and there were various tax implications. Because the Bank was an international institution, he had never needed to have a green card to work there, and he hadn't paid any income tax. In ninety days he would become, to the INS, an illegal alien. And, no matter where he lived, he would have to pay taxes on his pension.

In Italian, the word *pensione* had two distinct meanings: "pension" and "boardinghouse." The root *pend* signified "weight," a retiree's pension implied a weighing out hence, and was the etymological sibling of both "pendulum" and "pensive." Such were Vincenzo's thoughts as he gazed intermittently on the scrolling scenes of DC's slums, which soon gave way to sparser and still poorer areas, and then, at last, to farmland.

Rows of plowed mud, frozen stiff, zipped by, a pure blur in the foreground, making an orderly fan of lines farther back. White-barked birches rose on hedges near a stretch of forest, their naked branches like bones against the dark backdrop. The only birds left were a few blackbirds that gathered to peck their way through the crust of ice over puddles in the fields and drink the muddy water beneath.

A nap.

The train was pulling into a station somewhere in southern Jersey when he awoke again. Grudgingly, he took out the pension agreement and finished picking his way through the byzantine thicket of legalese, and finally, although it felt like gambling, made a couple of decisions. Then he opened the latest issue of the *Economist*, a magazine he had been receiving, if not quite reading, for twenty years. Before Cristina died, the magazine would be stacked neatly on the console by the door until, at the end of each year, she threw them all out, via wheelbarrow, and the process started again. In the last few years, however, he'd found he had more than enough time to read the magazines as they arrived, and the stack was now on her bedside table—all issues that he'd finished.

In this latest issue, there was a brief mention up front about the fiasco at the World Bank involving the Italian ex-vice president in charge of Latin America, who had quit his job over a scuffle regarding Bolivia. "The other party involved, William Hamilton, the U.S. executive director, has not yet tendered his resignation," the unnamed author wrote, cheekily, as if it were just a matter of course that his resignation was due.

Vincenzo arrived at Penn Station in the late afternoon and ate dinner alone in the hotel's restaurant. He noticed that there were an unusual number of other graying gentlemen in shirt-sleeves eating alone. They all had reading material. They all drank wine, mostly red. They all passed on dessert.

=

According to Elisabeth Kübler-Ross's infamous stage system for bereavement, the "phases" to mourning were: denial, anger, bargaining, depression, and—finally—acceptance, the littlest of consolations. The system did at least offer an attractive order, a reassuringly straightforward shape to the disordered experience, so it was hard not to think about it once in a while. Still, he wondered why there was no space for bafflement. Maybe it fell under the rubric of "denial." But, if so, why did it persist through subsequent phases? And anger, smuggled in the middle, didn't it burn its way through other emotions? Couldn't even lofty acceptance, couldn't it be embraced balefully? Maybe his was just an unusual case. In thinking about Cristina's death Vincenzo had noticed that there were actually an array of discrete losses. Maybe it was only because the loss was so sudden. Because a bomb lands on a village and yes, the blast itself is tragic, the people it kills, but the subordinate tragedies also ricochet away from the initial blast: a brilliant child goes deaf and loses his way in life, resulting in a troubling burden for his sister; or the wife of a man rendered chronically impotent by his injury enters into an affair, which results in a daughter, whom the impotent husband rears with as much love as he can muster, but it's always a qualified . . . et cetera, et cetera. And in this way the aftershocks ripple through history itself.

In the case of Cristina's death, there were at least a dozen serious subsidiary losses for Vincenzo. Enormous plans that needed to be unwound, countless relationships that unraveled. The worst of all had to be the damage to his relationship with Leonora, who had been closer to her mother to begin with. Still, the family had been triangular, the sturdiest shape known, and when one of the points was wiped out, the remaining two formed a line, which stretched in search of some new formal identity.

So, because there were actually many different waves of mourning, the stages might be muddled. If so, might they achieve synchronicity at some point? And, if not, would he always be at the mercy of those separate waves raking across his soul, each tide perpetually chasing the last?

He had quit his job in the midst of what, from a clinical angle, must have been some grand wash of resignation. But it was much too late in the process for resignation. Years had passed. Surely he had to have arrived at acceptance by now. Up close, he might have looked to be tinged with a bit of lingering guilt, but he saw it all as a yellowy bath of acceptance. Because this was the end of the line. It just had to be.

=

At dawn, Vincenzo put on running clothes and went down to the hotel gym, which was almost completely empty. He lifted some weights, spent some time on the stationary bicycle, reading subtitles on CNN and glancing often at the young bodies dancing two screens over on MTV. Vincenzo had been captain of the World Bank's soccer team for a few years about a decade ago, but had given up for no worthwhile reason, and was pretty badly out of shape now. The fifteen pounds he'd put on felt normal. Every year his physician said, "You should lose about ten pounds, but otherwise you're still surprisingly well preserved." The joke that never got old.

Now that he was a retiree, Vincenzo decided he'd lose that weight—why not? He had the time. In fact, he'd do better, he'd lose twenty pounds. By the time the cherry blossoms were out, he'd be back to 165. The gym was fun. It felt good to get the blood pumping again, it felt good to sweat and push his body until his mind was finally forced to shut the hell up. Afterward, he showered and ate a healthy breakfast (black coffee, fruit, muesli), and went for a little walk around Midtown. He felt euphoric, giddy, and overly energetic when he returned, as if he could feel the stretching out of unidentified possibilities. While walking, he'd put his mind to his professional options. The following morning he was meeting Colin at Lehman Brothers' Midtown office. There must have been something appealing about that world other than the money, because he knew at least a dozen brilliant economists who'd left top jobs at the Bank and Fund for permanent careers at investment banks. Then again, if he worked at a think tank, he could focus on ideas and policies, and he could speak to an audience, could shape the discussion in his own way for the first time in his life.

The idea of consulting at one of the aid institutions—the Caribbean Development Bank, or the Inter-American Development Bank, or the UNDP—came and went while he waited for a light to change. Nothing about returning to that community appealed to him.

Back at the hotel, he winked thanks at the cute female concierge when she told him the names of some good restaurants, and she—to his surprise—smiled bashfully, as if flattered.

Upstairs, he checked his e-mail and saw a message from Lenka. He opened it with a little dread: he didn't really want to go there, after all, he thought. It was too much.

If he was available, she wrote, Evo's political party would host a party on December 30 at the National Museum. That would put it less than two weeks before Evo's inauguration. It was the very end of Vincenzo's grace period. If he aspired to be anything more than furniture, he would, by then, have had to declare allegiance to someone or other.

Leonora arrived at noon and they walked to Central Park. There was a cold front bearing down and the air was so icy the bones in his hands hurt, so he kept them in his pockets. Already the city was festooned with Christmas regalia: crimson bows on lampposts, vast plastic wreaths in windows, strings of impatient lights flickering in apartment windows, each casting its own golden-spoke halo. Salvation Army bells tinkled faintly, and the odor of roasting chestnuts snaked through the windswept streets. Holidays were awful, post-Cristina, some grim interminable party he'd agreed to attend before realizing he'd rather do anything else. Leonora treated the season similarly, with dutiful resolve.

She asked what he planned to do next.

He might, he said, get a consulting job at a financial institution in New York.

"Really?" She winced.

He resisted the urge to ask if she was more displeased about the prospect of him working for an investment bank or of him living in New York.

=

For lunch, they went to the eighth-floor café at Saks Fifth Avenue and ate at the counter. Both had fourteen-dollar Caesar salads. They shared a half bottle of Pouilly-Fuissé and an appetizer of taramosalata. Then he bought himself an absurdly long, many-hued Paul Smith scarf and, for his daughter, a snowy hand-crocheted angora sweater. While the items were being gift wrapped, he told Leonora that he'd put them under a little plastic tree in his hotel room and they could open them on Christmas Day.

Her face registered stifled shock. "You're not going to stay until Christmas, are you?"

"Of course." He laughed. "I'm not sure that I ever want to go back to DC."

"But I—I don't know if I'm going to be here." She looked at the ground, her face going red. Then she dropped her voice and said, "Can we go back to the café and talk?"

He leaned down and signed the receipt, picked up the bag, and followed her back to the café. They sat, once again, at the bar. He was aware of a dread in his stomach when she reached out and gripped his hand, earnestly, looked him in the eye, and told him that she was going to spend Christmas with Sam's family. She said that they would spend the next Christmas with him in DC. "We want to trade off. One year with them, one year with you. You know? It's only fair. I did Thanksgiving with you this year. So we'll do it with them next year. It's like— doesn't that make sense?"

Vincenzo blinked. The news was so unexpected that he had no idea how to respond. They'd never been apart for Christmas. He struggled to think about something else, anything at all, anything neutral, he thought about salt and pepper (what's the profit margin on those?), then laminate, paper, and angora, the concept of fashion itself, but none of it was any good, he was nodding at her, chewing on his lower lip, and warm tears were already falling out of his eyes.

"I'm sorry, Dad," she was saying. "I didn't realize you were going to quit your job." She was saying things like that.

The bartender approached but then stopped, no doubt seeing Vincenzo's face, and turned away.

"You have nothing to be sorry about," Vincenzo said. "It just caught me off guard." He said that he needed to find a bathroom. He stood up. He said that he'd be back in a second, and could she guard the bags?

She just stared at him, tears in her eyes now, too. He turned and walked toward the restrooms.

The summer Leonora lost her leg on Lake Garda, before they left for Italy, her friend Greta jumped off the Adams Morgan bridge. She left a note addressed to Leonora: *Tell my parents that I get it that they meant well, and I hope this doesn't hurt them too badly.*

Her parents shared the note with Vincenzo and Cristina, who decided to let Leonora read it, too. After she'd read the note, Vincenzo grabbed Leonora, who was already weeping, by the shoulders and fixed her with his gaze, told her that if she killed herself, she would also be murdering him. "I will die. Do you understand?"

She'd stared at him in mute horror, her lip trembling, and he wanted to slap her in the face, make her understand him, but Cristina had grabbed him by the shoulder.

"What do you think you are doing?" Cristina hissed, in Italian.

He shook his head, looked back at his daughter, who was too freshly traumatized even to speak. He looked back at Cristina. "I know you don't agree, but I happen to know that there is no God, no heaven. She must know this."

With that, Leonora ran out of the room.

Then, a month later, an Italian doctor drove a mechanical saw through Leonora's leg.

Life was so geometrical at times, the pieces fit so neatly that it was hard not to imagine that there were gods orchestrating the show. That is what Vincenzo thought when he sat in a marbled stall in the bathroom at Saks Fifth Avenue and wept as quietly as possible, biting the heel of his thumb. Eventually, the torrent loosened. He blew his nose twice. Flushed. He washed his face with cold water. He dried off and, looking at himself in the mirror, his giant eyes and his long narrow nose both reddened, was amazed by the intensity of his reaction. It wasn't like him to emote so nakedly: that had always been Cristina's turf. He was the stoic one, the one who tried to dampen arguments and apply cold reason to her outbursts. Maybe he'd acquired some of her heat when she left. Maybe that was how it worked.

In any event, this Christmas issue would be fine. He could do any number of things. He could, for example, spend the holiday in Piedmont working on the house. The space would do him good. *Jesus*, he could even stay in New York alone. Maybe Colin would have a little project for him to do for Lehman—if not, he could just stay at a hotel and start exercising and catching up on his reading. Or, of course, he could consent to his own Bolivia proposal and head off there with Walter. Yes, maybe it would do him good to get some space to think about things.

That—the simple act of considering his options—was how he realized that Leonora's rejection was not as straightforward as it had seemed at first. There were options, now. He'd been on a few dates, hoping to see in Cristina's absence that kind of array of possibilities—*oh, the women he could have!*—but it hadn't worked out like that. The whole thing had been soaked in awkwardness, as if the women knew he was a new widower without him needing to say so. Now, though, he felt truly free of that. Not in a metaphysical sense, but in a simple and concrete way; logistically, he was free. He had no responsibilities.

When he sat down in the café again, Leonora, who had seen him break down often enough since her mother died, looked like she had recovered from her own minor sadness and was now mainly concerned about him.

"Maybe I can change my plans," she said weakly.

"No. You go see Sam's family. That will be nice for you. I apologize for my reaction. I have been emotional ever since I quit the job, you know? It is a very difficult thing, the transition"—he said this, but it meant nothing, he was doing a press conference—"because my professional life is more or less finished, and even though it's my own doing, it's a surprise to me. Still, I know this is a chance for me to get away and do something else."

"You going to go to Piedmont?" she said.

"No, no, no, no, that place would kill me. I might even sell that house. It's too much! Reminds me of your mother. I might sell the house in Bethesda. I don't know. I'll stay here for a few days, I think. Then, I'll go"—he shrugged, pushed out his lower lip—"I'll go somewhere."

"I've heard Australia is nice this time of year," she said.

"That doesn't interest me at all." He found her suggestion inane and he did nothing to hide that impression.

"Well. I'm just trying to—"

"No need to explain. I might be going to Bolivia, actually."

She appeared puzzled. "What's in Bolivia?"

Was she feigning obliviousness? He said nothing, and she didn't either. "Do you want to call Sam?" he said. "I've made reservations for three, but they can be changed if he's busy."

"He'll be there, Dad. Are you okay? You seem weird."

"I *am* weird! You should know that about me!" He chuckled, with some difficulty. Then he looked away, shook his head.

"That's not what I mean."

"Then say what you mean."

"You seem, I don't know, you seem cold."

"Oh." He nodded. He understood, and it made sense—after all, there was something like an icicle driven through his torso. "I'll recover," he said and smiled. "So, I'd like to swing by the Met, if possible. I gather they rehanged the nineteenth century, and I want to see it. We have time, right? Two hours is plenty."

She put her eyebrows into an emotive arch, something her mother would do. It was condescending and infuriating. "Are you okay?"

He paused, shrugged. "I haven't felt this good in years." He had never deliberately hurt her before in that way and it felt awful.

Leonora's pain was clear in her face. It was as if she could tell he had never felt so little love for her. From that theory of the stages of mourning he had harvested one idea that, he thought, stood up to scrutiny: some emotions must occur, almost by definition, separately. So, although he loved Leonora—loved her far more than any other living being—he could still hate her at times, too; and when he hated her, he *just* hated her.

She wanted to stay and say more, this much was clear. She wanted to talk it out and dispel the horrible feeling right away, but he was already standing up, already going for his coat, saying, "You ready?" and, "Don't forget the bag."

8

FINALE

Vincenzo had been the middle of seven children whose father had lapsed, decisively, from the Catholic Church. Despite being docile in so many regards, his father, Geomar, had refused to attend any of his children's baptisms or confirmations. This wasn't something that they talked about in the house.

Occasionally, when drunk enough, his father ranted against the Church and the absurdity of the notion of God, but these soliloquies were rarely intelligible and, anyway, he said a lot of things when he was drunk. His father had held great promise once—he was an assistant manager of a leather factory at age nineteen, and everyone supposedly believed he would end up a tycoon—but his mind was addled by his time as an infantryman during the war. A shell had burst against the hull of a nearby tank during the Allied invasion of Sicily and his face was scarred from the shrapnel.

After the war, he couldn't return to the leather factory, found the work too grisly, and took a job instead working for the city as a gardener. Some years later, he was moved to sanitation, and helped keep the streets clean. He drank a liter of homemade grappa daily, but was never violent or angry—was simply gone, muttering to himself and making facial expressions as if carrying on a conversation. His mind and his liver deteriorated in tandem, withering soggily, together, until they brought down the rest of him. Death came precipitously, as it often does even in the supposedly slow cases. It was the sixties and Vincenzo was in his first year of university. He was back in Milan after spending a riotous year in Denver—aswim in blond girls—as an exchange student. Now he was starting to wonder if he'd made a mistake choosing to turn himself over to the frustratingly pious and otherworldly study of the classical Italian literature. Admiring, in his roundabout way, his father's dedication to the soil and the earth of the present, Vincenzo had started pining after something more terrestrial and something as far from Milan's working-class doldrums as Denver had been.

Vincenzo, who adored his father perhaps more than did any of his siblings, had lapsed early, too, shortly after his confirmation. But, when his father was on his deathbed, his mother summoned a priest, insisting that his father had implied, somehow, with his hands, rising in a circular motion, like smoke from incense, perhaps (by this point he could no longer speak) that he was looking for absolution. And though his father was mute, the priest claimed to somehow take his confession. The priest administered his last rites. If his father had been cognizant enough to know what was happening—that, after he'd spent decades rejecting the Church, his wife was shoving him back into the fold in his final hours—he would have been,

Vincenzo knew, sickened. At the time, it seemed an incomprehensibly brutal form of betrayal.

Outraged by his mother's actions that day, young Vincenzo got drunk by himself during the funeral and showed up at the post-funeral wake intending to set his mother straight in front of everyone. During the ensuing fiasco, of which he would, mercifully, remember very little, he reportedly yelled at his mother and the priest, claiming they were in some obscene and diabolical union, stealing helpless souls. His brothers intervened, pulling him out to the garden, but not before he destroyed at least one vase of flowers. Once outside, he managed to punch his eldest brother out before he was expelled from the grounds and left to stumble through the streets alone.

Two days later, Vincenzo apologized to his mother, but he couldn't quite bring himself to retract it all, because much of it had been true. She assured him that she forgave him, as did some of his siblings, but subsequent history would reveal that it had been one of those moments for a family—one of those breaks that wouldn't ever be fully mended.

Before long, he was in Massachusetts for university, and then Rome for work, then to Washington with the World Bank. Along the way, he missed all but two of his siblings' weddings. He stopped keeping track of their avalanche of children while he was still in Rome.

As a junior economist at the Italian central bank in the seventies, he met and fell in love with Cristina, who was then a student at Sapienza, and was as Catholic as anyone else in Rome. By then, he was not only atheist, but had a kind of worldly American air about him, too, in a way that Italian women found intensely sexy.

Early on, he told her that he would never attend church with her, and if she was going to make an issue of it, they couldn't see each other. Within two months, she had stopped attending church altogether. That had seemed like it was the end of the subject, but, of course, nothing is so simple.

For some years, he and Cristina sent each of his siblings and his mother a Christmas card. Then even that became difficult to sustain.

The one time he saw the whole family after moving to DC, during a business trip to Milan in the early nineties, everyone was cordial. Everyone seemed happy to see him. He took them all to a good restaurant. They were impressed by how far he'd come—he was the most accomplished person in the family, already, although he still hadn't even really bloomed at the Bank. Woozy with the wine he'd bought them, his siblings and mother hugged him firmly at the end of the night, told him that they should do a better job of keeping in touch. No one mentioned his father. No one mentioned the funeral. No one called or sent any cards for a year.

When his mother finally died, in 1998, he sent flowers, but was unable to find time to make it over for the funeral.

And when Cristina died, he received cards from only two of his siblings. He hadn't called any of them and had no idea how they'd found out.

=

A blizzard crept in overnight and when Vincenzo opened his hotel room blinds in the morning he peered at the dim but nonetheless blinding glare of a hundred million snowflakes, each glowing with just enough of the hidden sun to reflect its own little light, so that the air itself was a swirling frenzy of radiance. His muscles ached from his workout the day before—already, his enthusiasm for the new lifestyle was under threat.

Then he turned on the news and went to brush his teeth.

Sitting at the efficient little desk, he ate in-room-dining breakfast and sorted through his now ebbing flow of e-mail. There was another message from Jonathan Paris, which struck a casual tone. As with the first e-mail, he said he was excited about the news, and was wondering how Vincenzo was doing; he suggested they meet up next time Vincenzo was in New York. Once again, Vincenzo didn't answer.

He returned to the message from Lenka Villarobles in which she'd suggested a date for the party in Bolivia. After his horrible day with Leonora, he couldn't manage to think about Lenka's proposal.

He called Walter. "Did you get the message I forwarded from that woman in Bolivia?"

"I did, in fact. We should book flights soon, I think—there are not a lot of itineraries available. You can go through Miami or Houston and I—I think that's it. Not a very popular tourist destination!"

"So you think we should do it?"

"Oh God, are you still worried about alienating people? Jesus, Vincenzo—"

"I've got a meeting this morning with someone from Lehman Brothers, so I don't want to be rash."

"They probably wouldn't even notice."

"They will notice."

"Well, maybe, but it's hardly a reason to not go."

"Don't oversell, Walter. Please."

"Fair enough, but I do think it'd be fun. For what it's worth. I've been often, and I always like it."

After they'd hung up, Vincenzo read the rest of his messages. He closed the browser once the e-mail was read.

He leaned back and had another sip of the already tepid coffee. He looked around. What now? In that visit with the HR woman, when she'd asked for his badge, he'd puffed his chest and forged ahead, but looking back, he saw how deeply frightening that moment should have been—he was forfeiting his means of entrance into the building he'd been visiting daily for most of his adult life. Of course, he was ready to move on, or that had been the idea—but everything about it seemed less easy when he was sitting in his cramped hotel room staring at the dancing snowflakes outside, with no unread messages in his inbox.

To begin with, he was not accustomed to being unproductive.

But that wasn't even it. He'd been unproductive before. What he'd never done was stop advancing himself, steadily, gradually, upward within the architecture of the Bank. Now he was supposed to put that energy toward some other thing. The great second act. Or was he onto his third act, now? Alas, it was probably the third act. The finale.

He needed new fire, a fresh purpose to his days. Instead, he had a hissing heater by the window of his well-appointed hotel room. And he had those massive snowflakes, too, a hundred million delicate and crystalline lattices suspended peacefully between gusts, like a sea of glowing spirits floating aimlessly between waves—but then they'd all spin wildly away from the window as if gathering for a tsunami.

=

Vincenzo had been to investment banks before, but they'd all been ensconced in steely towers planted firmly into lower Manhattan. Only Lehman lived in Midtown, in the decidedly un-suave and un-somber Times Square. The building wore a belt of LED screens around its lower floors, in keeping with the flashiness of Times Square, as if it were just another wacky tourist attraction. The snowstorm had slowed, for the time being, and when he got out of the taxi and looked up, he found the building cut an impressive figure, glassy and glinting—tickers spinning maniacally around it. Wall Street was having a bad day, as it happened, so all of the tickers were running red.

In the queerly long and narrow lobby, he found a few guards clustered together behind an absurdly long table, maybe fifty meters, against the wall. He approached them and said he was there to see Colin Donnell. A portly black man put together a show of diligence and told him what he already knew, that Colin was on the twenty-sixth floor, office B-2664.

Vincenzo had assumed there would have been some security. Apparently not.

At the twenty-sixth floor, he entered a space that looked like any office building anywhere in America, the elevator banks opening out onto a row of cubicles. Quants and assistants and other younger people, mostly men, sat in shirtsleeves within their taupe cubbies. It was, somewhat surprisingly, rather less charming than the World Bank offices.

He walked around the cubicles, over to the window on one side, near a hallway going to the staircase, and saw the crowd seething on the street below, yellow cabs shoving their way through—there was little sign of the snow from up there. No sound came through the thick windows. All he heard was the quietly hissing heating vents and a faint whirring from the state-of-the-art elevators. Looking for his own visage in the glass, he caught his shimmering outline and checked that his tie was right, his collar. He tugged his jacket taut at his sides. He hadn't been nervous to talk to anyone in ages, at least since he talked to Wolfowitz about the possibility of a promotion. He checked his watch and saw he was three minutes late, just right.

He looked at the numbers on the offices ringing the periphery and saw they were ascending, so he started walking.

When he came to Colin's office, he found the door was open. He knocked anyway.

Colin, on the phone, waved Vincenzo in. The office was a shoe box, with a view to the Hudson and the hazy and snowy shores of New Jersey.

Colin hunched forward, visibly strained by whatever he was dealing with, and spoke into the phone: "—which is why we're monitoring them." Vincenzo sat in the chair and looked at the desk. It was quite neat. There were only a few bookshelves: no room, really, for many books. There were two armchairs and a table, too, but it was so cramped he couldn't imagine anyone wanting to sit there. "My belief, to reiterate,"

Colin went on, "is that the spreads will be widening as the Street mulls the figures. The balance sheets are just not as favorable as Mikhail suggested—and the near-term debt, in particular, is poorly priced." He paused, listening. "Fine. That's okay. I'll do that. But I don't want to have to walk you through this again and again. We've been through it already and you're still asking for more, but it takes me time to put it together and we're—"

He leaned even farther over his desk, so his face was poised over the phone's receiver. "Exactly. Look. I've got to go, so why don't we just meet at two and we'll go through it then—are you free at two?"

A brief pause.

"Two thirty?"

Another. His eyes wide with exasperation.

"Three it is." He hung up, rolled his eyes, said, "I report to children." Standing, he extended his hand to Vincenzo.

"Sounds like fun," Vincenzo said flatly and shook the hand.

Colin chuckled, flopped back down in his chair. "Would you believe me if I told you that it actually is tremendously fun?"

Vincenzo shrugged. "I believe anything these days."

"Come with me." Colin stood and led the way out. On the way to the elevators, Colin hashed out the basic biographical updates: a kid at Penn State, another doing a medical residency, neither married. He, meanwhile, was living with a woman named Gillian, who recently finished her MFA in video art at the New School. She made hilarious and absurd self-portrait films nightly, in which she rattled off improvised monologues. Afterward, she did extensive editing on each fragment, he explained, and it was clear he admired her art, in a way, but was mostly baffled. Some of these, he said, showed at a tiny gallery in Chinatown.

Colin's former wife had been a ghoulish fixture of the city's society magazines, a boozy heiress whose droopy face was forever slathered in makeup. The new girlfriend, bubbly and mercurial and—although Colin didn't say so, Vincenzo deduced it from what wasn't said—not terribly smart, was, not surprisingly, the opposite of his ex-wife in every way. His children, meanwhile, found his reincarnation repulsive in the most predictable ways, but they were grown, so they weren't—to be perfectly blunt about it—his top priority anymore. "They wish I'd stayed with Sandra in Cleveland Park so that they could cart their screaming toddlers over at Thanksgiving and everyone could rest assured that everything had worked out according to plan. But whose plan was that?"

"Your plan, I suppose," Vincenzo said, although he sympathized completely with Colin.

"So, I should've just stayed the course? Forced a smile and pressed on?"

"No, no, I didn't mean that." They stopped at the elevators and Colin pressed the *up* button. "Was it hard to leave?" Vincenzo asked.

Colin turned and looked at him knowingly, as if Vincenzo had intended for there to be extra subtext in the question. "It was the single hardest thing I've ever done," he replied, still staring at Vincenzo in that knowing way. "And I was afraid I'd made a mistake—it's not easy to dismantle such a complex and fully constructed identity: the house, the wife, the job—to leave all of that." He turned away at last and pressed the button again. Standing there, Vincenzo could hear the elevators whirring inside their tubes, thrusting air out of vents. "I guess you would know, too, in a different way."

Vincenzo shrugged, unhappy with where that fragment of conversation had gone, and said, "No, I don't know."

Misinterpreting his reticence, Colin said, "People scoff at the midlife crisis, as if it's just this trite masturbatory phase dumb men go through, just more poor male impulse control."

"But we know better," Vincenzo said, and they both laughed.

They entered an elevator and Colin jammed his thumb against the button for the thirty-second floor, the top floor, labeled *Club Floor*. "No, really, it was the most difficult and honest move I've ever made." Vincenzo thought about his own great move, tried to assess the difficulty and honesty of it, but found himself unable to measure it on such terms. As far as that tautology of an "honest move," Vincenzo had nothing to say—honesty was as extraneous here as it always had been. Hindsight would validate or repudiate the decision, but finally, the logic of these momentous decisions was no more certain than a pair of tumbling dice.

In the elevator, Colin continued, "I looked at my life and I could see it clearly, could see where it was going, and I said, 'I don't like this. I don't want this to be the rest of my years.' And it was scary to give up everything I'd spent the last three decades building, but it got better. Other things come along."

"Like beautiful art students?" Probably unfair, but it needed to be said.

"Make fun if you want, but if you'd like to see what I left behind, go visit Sandra someday. Go there for an hour—she's

still at our house. Have some tea with her and look around.
Imagine that's your life. It'll make sense."

"It already makes sense."

The doors opened onto a serene little foyer, adorned with a
preening team of outrageously ornate orchids; it was as lavish
as the entrance of a five-star restaurant. Bold orange leather
upholstery fronted the maître d's console. The place sounded
like handmade shoes brushing against handmade rugs. It was
where, Vincenzo gathered, Lehman employees took people
whom they wanted to impress into submission. The maître
d', a severe young woman with a flamboyant coppery nest
of curls sprouting from her head, marched them through a
hallway—past smaller and larger rooms within which an as-
sortment of other people were being wooed—before she de-
posited them in a small room with a view toward Brooklyn.
On a nearby table, a bowl of olives and some unidentifiable
amuse-bouches were being kept company by a half bottle of
Burgundy. The maître d' opened the wine and filled a glass
for each of them while Colin, not missing a beat, continued
talking.

Already, the hopeful cast of Vincenzo's imagination had
taken hold, offering visions of weekends with Leonora (Sam
conveniently absent) and himself—he now dating a witty divorcée, perhaps, in her early forties—drinking wine just like
that, but maybe in warmer environs. He and this divorcée
would go to the opera and take very long vacations. On weekends, he and Leonora would go to the movies, to museums,
they'd meet for coffee and—*whatx?* Life, maybe, but done
satisfactorily, and all the time.

Feeding a fresh morsel to Vincenzo's fantasy, Colin presented what he did at Lehman in this way:

"I get a request—something like, 'What do you think about the sovereign debt situation in such-and-such country.' I look at the numbers, write a couple pages and then someone, maybe wanting to seem smart, might ask some follow-up questions, so I'll explain a little further. There's also a team, which if you come on board, you'd be on. We're dispatched, not unlike a Bank mission, to do a complete diagnostic on the quality of the sovereign debt, or do a sector analysis—so it's very narrow in its focus. There are a handful of us and everyone's incredibly smart. It's fascinating work, bracingly clear, and there are absolutely no bureaucratic horrors, no incompetent governmental ministers to deal with. You can be completely candid. It's exhilarating to be so unfettered, so unburdened by organizational boundaries."

Vincenzo glanced around the room. There was a stark postmodern vase on a stand in the corner with corkscrewing branches shooting out in organized, attractive chaos. Vincenzo thought of the young quants who'd been wooed in that room and wondered if they had rooms with different motifs. Would there be a hip room in which candidates received microbrewed beer and vegan canapés, where the art was less dour and contemplative and more splashy and exciting?

"But you report to children," Vincenzo reminded him. Ever since Colin had said that, Vincenzo had been thinking indirectly of Jonathan Paris, and what it'd be like to report to someone like him.

"I complain, but he just wanted to clarify the source of my position. It's due diligence—his ass is on the line, not mine.

The bank is limber and there's real honesty here, which you'll find refreshing. If Egypt's balance sheet is a wreck, you don't have to write some fucking sixty-page report on the findings of your autopsy, you write an e-mail, 'Be advised that Egypt's balance sheet is fucked beyond all recognition.' And, often, that's the end of it."

This was, Colin knew well, a kind of pornography of efficiency for someone, like Vincenzo, who'd spent his adult life negotiating the internal politics and exasperating organizational minutiae of an institution like the World Bank. "It sounds exquisite," he admitted. Looking at the miniature bottle of wine with its chaotic label, the timeworn nuances of its pedigree stamped, in code, cluttering it with the details of vintage, vintner, cru, appellation. That was how it worked: despite the allure of the new, eventually, if you stayed around long enough, you'd be so encrusted with the stamps of your stations, your positions, ranks, that the sum of those emblems would become the armor that defended you, defined you. That, he had to admit, was his own lot. "Everything about it sounds wonderful," he said.

Although it was definitely a bad idea, he wondered briefly what Cristina might think of this. She hadn't ever warmed to New York, had found it too *ossessivo*—she'd spat the word out whenever New York came up. Now, sitting across from Colin, he tried to imagine her face, tried to imagine her talking to him about this—but his memory and his imagination were cutting crosscurrents and instead of the pricklier, more honest woman that she'd grown into, he envisioned the more pliant and encouraging woman of their first decade together. That

Cristina would have endorsed it because he seemed to want it. It was the same Cristina who agreed to move to DC, maybe the most ruinous decision of her life. Later, when she became more blunt, she also became less predictable. So he really had no idea what she would have thought of this dream of a life in *ossessivo* New York, where he worked for an investment bank, slept with a younger woman. It would be easy to assume that she would object to a world in which the photos of her were all stripped from their frames and relegated to a box underneath the bed, but somehow, he thought she would endorse this life, and all the more for the fact that she would not have to be around while it occurred.

The waiter, a pudgy and exhausted-looking Asian man in horn-rimmed glasses, entered and explained the menu, enunciating everything between long breaths, as if reluctantly. There was a choice, he said. Beef or halibut. He went on to describe another choice: Gorgonzola and potato croquettes or chanterelle and pea risotto. Sparking or still? Whole grain or sourdough?

While they ordered, the waiter kept glancing up, out the window at the spectacular views.

An hour later, when the meal was over, Colin said, "Let me know, and I'll pass along your CV whenever. Frankly, it'd just be a formality, though. You'll be on my team to start, and then, after a trial period, you'd have your own team. But we'd be working together."

Vincenzo looked back at the twisting black branches sprouting from the vase, back at the almost empty half bottle of wine, back at the window, so much like his last window, the same hissing vents, and said, "Why are you doing this?"

Caught off guard, Colin replied, helplessly, "I want you here. I think you'd be a good addition to the team." He reached out and divided the rest of the half bottle between their glasses. "And it'd be fun to work with you again."

Vincenzo saw a lot happening, so far, there, but he didn't see much fun. The word caught his attention. "Your coworkers—they're not so . . ." He shrugged.

Colin bobbled his head, looking at nothing in particular in a way that revealed that though he wished it weren't so, this was, in fact, the very point of this whole conversation: the banality of his coworkers bothered him enough to go headhunting on his own. "They're not, uh—you know, by and large, as interesting as the kind of people you work with at the Bank. It's a different culture, which has its benefits and its—um—" He tried to think of a non-pejorative word for this, and then gave up. Looking at Vincenzo again, he leaned in, almost whispering. "There's a lack of nuance, I guess you could call it. That's the only downside here."

Vincenzo attempted to imagine what it would be like to work with so many dullards, and if it would be so bad. It was very hard to imagine. Even now, having seen the place firsthand, he was at a loss. To test Colin's enthusiasm, he said, "I've been approached by some other people. A think tank, and I'm probably going to be making a speech in Bolivia."

Colin winced, shook his head, much as Vincenzo had feared he would. "What kind of speech?" he asked.

"It'd be a little event hosted by Evo Morales."

"Oh, don't do that."

"Why not?"

"Your exit from the Bank looks, to the informed, like a momentary lapse of judgment. You were sick of the bureaucracy and the nonsense there and had an episode, but only because you'd been there too long. That was how I presented it to my colleagues and it made sense. If the very next thing you do is make some speech on behalf of Evo Morales in Bolivia it looks very much like you're an antiglobalization zealot. A double-agent type. And no one likes that."

"Wouldn't that impression depend on what I said during my speech?"

Colin was not quite convinced. "I guess, and it'd depend on how much traction the story had. If it brings this story to life again, then you'd need to be out front with quotes about how you think democracy is great, but Evo Morales doesn't understand economics, and so on."

"I see," Vincenzo said.

—

The sky was clearing up and the views to lower Manhattan were majestic. Leonora would surely disapprove. But she was living quite squalidly now, coping with the harsher realities of a small paycheck, and maybe her once-swift dismissal of such a career, such a lifestyle, had been tempered. The same girl who had immediately refused a payout to attend an in-state university, had also—once she had arrived a few years deeper into adulthood—happily scampered into Saks Fifth Avenue in search of new clothes. She wasn't a material girl, of course, but the matter of her father's paychecks and the role of those pay-

checks in her life couldn't possibly seem irrelevant. Back at his
hotel room later that afternoon, he wrote an e-mail to Colin
thanking him for inviting him to New York and saying that he
was absolutely interested in working at Lehman, but he needed
a little time to organize his affairs. He'd try to keep the press at
bay while in Bolivia, he promised.

Then he wrote an e-mail to Lenka Villarobles, and cc'd
Walter:

> This sounds fantastic. I talked to Walter (cc'd) and we
> think this would be a great event. I'm looking forward to
> it. Let us know when you want us there and any other
> details.

Afterward, he wrote a separate e-mail to Walter, saying:

> Talked to friend at Lehman and it sounds great. While
> we're in Bolivia, I need to be on good behavior. No more
> wailing against the system in the press.

And he wrote an e-mail to his daughter:

> I'm busy tonight. Can we meet tomorrow morning?

Then he called down to in-room dining and ordered a glass
of champagne.

"Just one glass?" the operator said.

"Just one," he replied tersely. "Is that acceptable?"

"Oh—I'm sorry," the person stammered.

"It's fine." He hung up.

Screw them all! Yes! Goddamn it! He felt good—no, *great!* Fuck them all—he was having champagne in his heavenly hotel room that evening while the snow whirled again out his window under the swiftly darkening sky.

9

BEN

Vincenzo awoke to a faint knocking at his door and was confused because he didn't quite understand where he was at first—he'd just been lifting Cristina out of the icy shallows of a mossy and black sea cave. She was, incredibly, still alive—everyone else inside the cave where he lived had thought she was dead, but Vincenzo had known otherwise and had gone looking for her, and he had found her out in the sea somewhere, bobbing in the black waves, and then he had dragged her limp body back to the cave, and now here she was, standing, face of a corpse but evidently alive, gurgling nonsense as water dribbled from her mouth. Her lungs, he knew, were sodden as a sponge at the bottom of a lake, and she was dead but not dead, but he was just so relieved to have her back. Her eyes were pale, blind, and he thought he might be able—

But then there was this knocking and what was happening broke away into that empty black limbo between dreaming and waking and then he was winded with the fresh notion, as devastating now as it was on the first collision, that he was, in fact, in a hotel and that she wasn't there—he was in New York, and there had been no sea, no cave.

But someone was, in fact, really knocking on his door, so he called out, "I'm in here!" It would have to be housekeeping or somebody from the hotel. But wasn't it early for that? He thought of his wife's mouth, the water dribbling out, the fact that it had just been a dream—"I'm sleeping!" he yelled, because they kept knocking. He sat up and reached for his glasses. "Jesus, I'm sleeping!" Was the hotel overly soundproofed? The clock informed him it was six fifteen, which was either bad or annoying, because urgent and unexpected news was never, or almost never, happy news. He went to the door and opened it slightly.

"What can I do for you?" he said, squinting out at the person who had done this to his dream, but it didn't look like a representative of the hotel; it was a handsome black man with a cleanly shaved head and a cleanly shaved face. A man in a perfect white shirt that was freshly pressed, open lavishly at the neck, a blazer, khakis—he was dressed for DC, and a different season. He was what Leonora called, with a degree of contempt that Vincenzo never quite understood, a "preppie."

"Sorry to wake you up," he said and extended his hand. "I'm Ben." The tone of voice was so precisely calibrated that it didn't seem calibrated at all: it just landed nicely in the stilldream-addled consciousness of the listener, a voice confident that its offhand apology for waking the listener would suffice. It landed like drops of water on an already wet stone.

"What can I do for you?" Vincenzo shook his hand, allow-ing the door to open more because he wanted to be sure to imply to this black man that he wasn't afraid of him, because what kind of person was afraid of—

"Can I come in?" this man who was named Ben said, but the question was nullified or belated because he was already entering and Vincenzo, who had intentionally blocked the door with his body, was now giving way to this man who had somehow insinuated himself, physically, into the inch between Vincenzo's shoulder and the door, prying at that space with so disarmingly casual a feat of body language, fast and slow at once, that the breach was complete before Vincenzo had time to gather that there had been a breach at all. That Vincenzo was wearing his pajamas and barely awake and that he didn't know Ben was, to judge from the body language, not the kind of thing people should get uptight about.

Which was how Vincenzo found himself standing there in his hotel room, the door closed, with a man named Ben offering him a seat on the very bed in which he'd just awoken, as if they were in Ben's office; and Vincenzo, still trying to catch up with the tumbling shape of the interaction, the social jujitsu under-way, was now mainly aware that, without question, he was in the presence of someone who did this kind of thing often. Ben sat down and said, with all the nonchalance of an old pal encoun-tered, by chance, at a bar, "How's the city treating you?"

Why did Ben not have a coat? This was what Vincenzo wondered. There was a snowstorm outside, after all. He had never met a black man named Ben, for that matter—there was something especially askew here.

"You don't have a coat," Vincenzo said aloud.

Ben looked puzzled, which was strange since he was the one who was responsible for the puzzling aspect of this interaction.

"Who sent you here?" Vincenzo said, and as soon as he sent this forth he found the statement itself, the drama of it, called to mind some dexterously executed scenario from a spy novel in which the bookish bureaucrat ends up hanged to death by his own socks in the closet of his hotel room in what would be described—in the deliberately ambiguous lingo used in movies, if rarely in life—as an "apparent suicide." And so was this the disarming face of a CIA assassin? He looked somewhat like the black valedictorian of Leonora's graduating class at Oberlin, but that guy had been gay and an aspiring urban planner. Still, this guy was, Vincenzo gathered, someone who could charm his way through a room—any room. He'd cut through a party like an ocean liner. He could work a crowd of people—any people—and that was a special skill. Everything was balanced perfectly. The only hint of fury could be felt in the over-energetic handshake. Vincenzo had met the valedictorian at his daughter's graduation; that man's accomplishments were maybe just slightly too vigorously achieved. He had risen above his classmates so unequivocally that there needed to be a kind of furious accelerant there, some—

"Why are you in my room?" Vincenzo said.

"I'm here to talk about your plans."

"I have a phone." Vincenzo looked at the phone and Ben looked at it, too. Vincenzo felt that he shared the swelling anger in his own way. Now, he wanted to punch Ben in the face, but he also didn't want to die there.

"I wanted to talk to you in private," Ben said.

"The phone is private."

Ben smiled.

"What do you want with me?" Vincenzo pressed.

"You're in a peculiar place—you've got to make some decisions, and I wanted to discuss your options."

This man was like Jonathan Paris's more dangerous double, his dapper doppelgänger. Vincenzo stood, feeling the need to urinate immediately—he gestured toward the bathroom. Ben waved him along and leaned back, glanced around the room. Peeing with the door open, Vincenzo tried to think of what he should say next, tried to think about the moves available, the strategy. If it were chess, he'd want to control the center of the board, but there was no center on this board. There was no objective, except autonomy, survival. He flushed, washed his hands, considered himself in the mirror: the expensive pajamas hanging loose on his wilted torso; he considered his sagging face, hooked nose, intense dark eyebrows flecked with white, the mottled dome. It was extraordinary to think that *now* that he was an unemployed widower in late middle age he was finally worthy of a talking to by the CIA.

Returning, he said, "Were you in the military?"

Ben smiled. "Marine Corps. How'd you know?"

"You people often come from military backgrounds."

"Black people?" He had one eyebrow up, neatly arriving somewhere between incredulous and amused.

"I meant the CIA—or whatever you are."

Ben chuckled and crossed one ankle over his other knee; he was wearing argyle socks, those awful inexpensive black square-toed shoes. "It's not like that. You didn't ever serve, did you?"

"In the CIA?" Vincenzo said, hoping to be funny, and Ben obliged with another almost-smile. Then Vincenzo, wanting to continue steering for a while, disposed of subtext and said, "Do you kill people and, if so, is this how you do it—do you just walk into their hotel room and—"

Ben laughed warmly and shook his head. He had an incredible set of teeth, gleaming and perfect. "You think I'd just come in here and shoot you in the face?" He pointed an index finger at Vincenzo's face to demonstrate the event. He kept chuckling, covering his mouth with his hand and shaking his head.

"Who sent you?" Vincenzo said.

Ben winced as if charmed by Vincenzo's stupidity. Then, when Vincenzo's own expression didn't change, Ben said, "Look, nobody wants to censor you, but you must know that the US has a PR problem right now, generally, and more specifically in Latin America, and if you're going to make it your personal quest to further undermine our image in that region, we'd like to know. If so, it's no problem. Go for it. But we would like to know. And I want you to understand the kinds of things that might be in the pipeline for you in different scenarios. Like, I gather you're interested in working at Lehman Brothers," he said and pointed toward Midtown, "and that can happen. The others, too, Tellus and so on."

Vincenzo pursed his lips at Ben and nodded. It seemed a bit difficult to imagine that this person could have any sway over whether Lehman made him an offer.

"You don't believe me?" Ben said, reading his face.

"No, no, I do." There remained the ominous question of how Ben knew that Vincenzo was considering those jobs in the first place. And if he was capable of reading e-mails, of finding his hotel room, could he not pressure the heads of organizations, even ones as powerful as Lehman Brothers?

"Have you read my e-mails?" Vincenzo said, hoping to reinforce his insistence on a strict no-subtext diet in this conversation.

Ben uncrossed his leg and then crossed the other leg, presenting another argyle sock, another square-toed shoe. As if he hadn't heard, he said, "If you're helpful, your visa will be extended indefinitely. If you apply for a green card, you'll get one." It had not occurred to Vincenzo before that this was how it could be done, too. No guns and no high-tech gadgets needed. James Bond didn't stand a chance against people like this. "Your daughter's here, I'm sure you'll want more than sixty days per year in the country. If you were to want to be very helpful, as in, forthcoming with help, I can see how the rewards would grow in scope."

Vincenzo had known people over the years who'd claimed to have had encounters like this, but there'd always been a kind of air of the improbable, a gauzy note of hyperbole. Now he saw how it was, and how it wasn't. And it was hazy, yes. It was absurd, and maybe that was part of the plan, just to make it seem sufficiently unlikely. A man entered your hotel room and knew slightly more than should be possible; he encouraged you to approach things in a somewhat different way. He presented a menu of rewards and penalties, all relatively modest, maybe, but meaningful enough to you to make a world of difference.

Vincenzo, curious about the stick that'd accompany these carrots, said, "And what if I were to tell my friend at the *Washington Post* about you?"

As if annoyed by this foolishness, Ben glanced away and shook his head firmly. "He's not going to write about this. That said, for the sake of argument, I'd see it as a very hostile way for you to behave. I wouldn't want to talk to you anymore. Your life would become immediately annoying: US visa out, problems with credit cards, rumors—I don't know, that kind of thing. It's easy for us, and we find it is effective. My boss once said"—Ben affected a gravelly New York drawl—"'If you ever meet someone who seems too fucking unlucky, some dickhead who's got his own personal rain cloud on the sunniest day in June, chances are he pissed us off.'"

Vincenzo nodded, but he couldn't tell how much exaggeration was at work here; the whole equation was tainted by possibly suspect variables. Maybe that was the point. Maybe once this conversation was over, no matter what he did, nothing would happen to his life. Somehow, that seemed unlikely.

"This is unfortunate," Vincenzo said.

"Could be worse." Ben pointed his index finger at Vincenzo again and smiled.

Vincenzo didn't respond.

Ben winked, stood up, extended his hand again, but Vincenzo didn't shake it. Eventually Ben shrugged, retrieved the hand. "I'll see you soon. Have a nice trip," he said, pulling a handkerchief from his pocket; he used the handkerchief to open the door, and then pushed it back in his pocket, before walking down the hallway in the opposite direction of the elevators.

Vincenzo got up and stepped out, watched Ben enter the stairwell at the end of the hall, again using his handkerchief to grip the doorknob.

Then he went back into his room and closed his door and bolted it. Looking around his room, he took a deep breath. He looked at the light fixture in the ceiling, at the mirror, the phone. He looked at the bedside lamps. There was no camera, not that he saw. Then again, he didn't even know where to look, what to look for.

=

"How's New York, by the way?" Walter said on the phone later that day.

"Fine," Vincenzo said as he contemplated whether someone in some maze of basement cubicles in Langley was listening in.

"Don't become a grumpy retiree—it's the geriatric equivalent to the sullen teenager. Teenagers and retirees have it made, everyone in between is fucked. We're the ones who should be complaining."

"Grumpy? That's absurd. And who's old? Aren't you older than me by two years?"

"It's the other way around, you've held a steady two-year lead on me since we met."

"Well, I'm in New York expanding my horizons."

"How?"

He crossed his ankles, thought of those argyle socks, said, "I am staying at the W Hotel, flirting with the receptionists— I am visited by menacing CIA agents and I meet powerful investment bankers and still I find time to buy meals for my daughter's boyfriend, a playwright who does not have a chin—this isn't grumpy at all. I have a new eight-foot-long rainbow scarf—"

"CIA agents?" Walter said.

"I was joking," Vincenzo said. Then again, maybe they weren't listening? All good tyrants know that the threat itself, if convincing enough, should do the job of correcting errant behavior. The CIA didn't need to *actually* listen to people's phone calls, it just had to imply that it was listening and the people would dutifully go about censoring themselves.

There was silence on the phone because evidently Walter had not been appeased by Vincenzo's response. The self-preserving thing to do, the sensible thing, Vincenzo appreciated, would be to head back to Bethesda and lay low for a couple of months. He could then pursue modest options once the CIA and whoever else was offended by him were content.

Vincenzo waited a while and then said, "What do you think the snowstorm will do next? I think it will go out to sea, pick up more water, and then come back and hit us with it again. That is what I think."

Walter noisily, slowly, sucked in a breath and then blew it out. He sighed somberly, said, "You okay, Vincenzo?"

"Yes, of course I'm okay. I was joking before. My question is: Are *you* okay? You sound like you're having trouble breathing." Vincenzo didn't want to make a big deal about Ben. After all, they might actually be listening, and Walter did have a habit of transforming his conversations into articles in a very conspicuous newspaper.

Walter grunted. "Did you say you bought an eight-foot rainbow scarf?"

"Yes."

"Jesus. Next thing, you'll be a line cook in that diner where she works."

"Don't pretend to understand. Look, I'm not sure Bolivia is a good idea," Vincenzo said.

Walter paused for a while and then said, "Well, I believe you sent an e-mail to them yesterday saying that it was a good idea and you were looking forward to it."

"Well, I wonder if we could do it quietly, sort of?" Vincenzo had a scenario in mind where, by dimming the volume on the story, he'd satisfy Ben, Lehman, Evo, and Tellus. The only person who would not be happy would be Walter, who'd be the one being muted. "Maybe if I didn't say anything interesting?"

"Defusing the story by being boring?" Walter paused. "Maybe."

Vincenzo heard nothing in Walter's tone, no innuendo at all, and it worried him. If he had to guess, he thought it might mean that Walter was lying, or scheming the situation in some other way that hadn't occurred to Vincenzo yet. He was out of his depth, here.

Then Walter sighed heavily and said, "Look, call me on the bat phone if you want to talk off the record."

Was that code for something? Some kind of way they might avoid the detection of eavesdroppers? Maybe not? "I don't know what you're talking about—I have to go," Vincenzo said and hung up.

=

A good game of chess isn't a war of attrition. It's not about standing a short distance apart and blasting each other to bits. A great player coaxes his opponent into troubling dilemmas less by taking pieces from him than by constricting the number of attractive options available. In the best games, the most artful games, each player has to see an exponentially expanding array of moves ahead. But the options don't really expand exponentially, if you know how to spot trouble brewing. A good player eliminates all the bad moves quickly, spends his time envisioning all the dozens of options branching down a few genuinely good paths; the options bloom and offer fruit, and a player's job is to locate the most attractive of all the branches—the one with the best fruit. Then he explores the next branch, the next, et cetera, until he isolates the most promising branch. But as the game proceeds, the branches gradually become fewer and fewer, their fruit less and less plentiful. The loser is starved subtly, an inch at a time. A player finds that with those branches that remain, he has to travel farther and farther before he can see something worthwhile. There are fewer flowers, virtually no foliage at all. When a player searches all of the available branches and sees nothing blooming, sees no fruit, no petals at all, he gives up—he resigns.

10

THE WORLD'S GREATEST FATHER

Vincenzo stayed in New York for another snowbound week, during which time he did not hear from Ben again, but did see his daughter on three occasions. Also, he went to the Guggenheim, MoMA, ate dinner at Daniel, and saw a movie, all alone. In e-mail and on the phone, he was cautious. Or, if not cautious, he was aware that he might be speaking to a wider audience. Otherwise, he believed he was approaching a kind of equilibrium. And he wasn't always alone: he ate at several great restaurants with people whom he'd known for ages but didn't quite count as friends.

Strangely enough, or to his own surprise, he ended up agreeing to see Jonathan Paris for lunch.

Maybe it was Jonathan's proximity to Vincenzo's undoing, maybe it was Vincenzo's brush with Ben, who seemed somehow tied to Jonathan in Vincenzo's mind, but over lunch Vincenzo found himself speaking in oddly personal terms with the young man. After admitting that he was a widower—Jonathan had merely asked if Vincenzo was there with anyone—there was the usual lull. More mature people often tried to fill the space that followed the widower confession with something, anything, but Jonathan was so out of his depth that he remained mute, stunned by Vincenzo's humanity. That was when Vincenzo, veering off of the lines of their script, said, "I would like to meet women. The Internet, I understand, it has—"

"Sure, I guess there's, like, Match.com and whatever," Jonathan said helpfully. He was still looking at the table. This table-gazing reflex had been going on for a while. "There'll be something for someone your age, too. I don't know what it's called."

"How do you meet women? Is it on the Internet?" Vincenzo asked.

Jonathan laughed uncomfortably and shrugged and glanced up quickly, as if unsure what to do with Vincenzo's bluntness. He looked out the window at a wall. They were at a Thai place near Union Square.

"Or, do you like men? I'm sorry—I just—"

"No, no, I do *not* like men, I like women. But I don't know. How do I meet them? I guess I'm sort of shy—I don't ever go on dates."

"Shy? You stormed the fucking headquarters of the World Bank."

"Yes, I guess, but I don't know how I meet them. I know them already, usually—friends of friends, or something. It's not easy to meet girls." He looked at Vincenzo and Vincenzo saw another little glimpse of that confidence from that day in his office.

"But I definitely don't go on dates with girls who I've never met. If it doesn't arise organically, I don't want to deal with it. It's just too difficult. What about you? You don't date at all?"

Vincenzo shook his head. "I plan to."

"How are you going to meet them?"

"That was my question."

Jonathan nodded resolutely. "I'm not going to go on dates with girls I don't know. Why make it more awkward than it has to be?"

"Why?" Vincenzo repeated. "Maybe *desperation*?" He smiled mischievously and Jonathan smiled too, but hollowly.

Later in that meal, in another somewhat memorable moment, Jonathan confided that he was terrified of failure, which was not surprising in itself, but it was comforting to hear him admit it. Evidently, he'd spent the previous day with a bullhorn, whipping an audience of hundreds into a fury in front of the United Nations, and yet he was afraid he wasn't doing enough with his life. What would Jonathan think of Leonora, whose current aspirations involved finding a better way to store the margarine at the diner where she worked?

When Vincenzo asked Jonathan to define failure, he embarked on a diatribe, cataloging an exotic collection of ways in which a person could experience failure before concluding, at last, after a momentous pause, "Insignificance—I think that's it. You want to leave your mark on the world. You want to be of value."

"Maybe you should have children?" Vincenzo said. "I think that is the most simple way to take care of that feeling."

"You have kids?"

"I have a daughter."

"Oh yeah, I remember. Oberlin?"

"Yes."

"What does she think about all this?"

"She's pleased, more or less."

"She hated that you worked at the Bank?"

Vincenzo shook his head. "She didn't *hate* it. It became an inconvenient feature of her own biography."

Jonathan tilted his head in a certain way, down to the left, which Vincenzo was starting to recognize as the gesture he made when he felt he had a good line of attack. "You didn't just do it to make her happy, did you?"

Vincenzo squinted. "The thing—my scandal?"

"Yeah, you weren't just trying to appease your kid, were you?"

"No," he said, shaking his head slowly. "I hope not."

"*Jesus.*"

"No, there were many reasons," he said. It was striking: he didn't remember Leonora being part of the decision, but now it seemed clear that she was.

Jonathan's face remained frozen in astonishment, something like horror. Then, at last, the expression broke off and he smiled, laughed a little, shaking his head. "Yikes," he said.

Then Jonathan said, "I guess that's the thing about having kids—they almost inevitably end up hating you. Seems miserable. Why do that to yourself?"

"You don't hate your parents, do you?"

"No, I guess I don't, but it's—you know—it's not easy."

"But life is difficult," Vincenzo ventured. "The best things are *very* difficult." He knew that idea wouldn't quite resonate with Jonathan, who had that Ivy League attitude that assumed further waves of greatness were blossoming out on the watery horizon, then approaching hard and fast. He was the kind of person who, in his midtwenties, bullied his way into the office of one of the World Bank's vice presidents, and then presumed to give that vice president a lecture. The kind of person who had been informed, from the moment that he first spoke, that he was "incredible" and "gifted"—even if he was just drawing a circle a bit prematurely. When he was young and impressionable, many people had, no doubt, assured him that he could achieve *anything* he set his mind to, and then, as he breached adulthood, this myth still rang true for him; it rang loudly, deafeningly, this extraordinary notion that he could achieve anything he set his mind to.

"Parenthood is difficult, but it's kind of fun, sometimes, and you do it because it's important," Vincenzo explained. "Don't you like doing things that are important?"

Jonathan nodded, his mouth bunched up contemplatively, and said that this sort of made sense to him. It wasn't enough to make him run out and impregnate someone, but he seemed to accept that there was something there. "You know, parenthood does sort of appeal," he said. "It's not where I am right now though, it's a different kind of project."

Vincenzo snorted. "Yes, it's a different kind of project." Now, he was starting to regret agreeing to this lunch. Somehow, he had hoped to see some new information here, some flash of insight into his own decision that day, but this wasn't helping.

=

After lunch, Vincenzo ambled into the Barnes & Noble on Union Square and found a copy of W. S. Merwin's translation of *Purgatorio*. He'd read a glowing review in the *Financial Times*. Among English-speaking Dante aficionados, it was the first meaningful advance in decades, maybe more.

When he originally matriculated at the University of Milan, at eighteen, Vincenzo slogged—with increasing discomfort—through Petrarch, Cecco Angiolieri, Dante, Boccaccio, and Machiavelli. In the early winter, when he was starting to be sure that he'd made a serious mistake, he met the legendary and legendarily tetchy economist Federico Caffè at a bookstore where Vincenzo worked nights. Caffè was in Milan giving a series of lectures at Bocconi and Vincenzo, immediately taken with him, went to several of these lectures. Soon, Vincenzo was submitting his application to the Massachusetts Institute of Technology, which Caffè had recommended to him, brusquely telling him that there was nowhere else to study economics, not even Roma Tre, where he taught.

He thought about it for a month but, despite thorough contemplation, found himself still facing a choice between two absolute unknowns. Still, he applied to MIT, as if to test the hypothesis, and when they accepted him he viewed it as a sign. By the time the first flowers were budding on the azaleas, Vincenzo had dropped out of Milan, forfeiting all of his exams, and accepted their invitation to study in Cambridge, Massachusetts.

—

Dante and Machiavelli were each concerned principally with the political machinations of their times. The Italian Renaissance was bookended by the two—a poet at the start, a philosopher at the end, both Florentines, both men whose minds were not lost in any abstract clouds, but were stuck intractably in the thick mud of politics. Dante spent much of the *Commedia* flaying and trumpeting the villains and heroes of his political era, while Machiavelli did much the same in his plays; even his philosophical works were designed to appease the ascendant regimes (as those powers changed, so—subtly—did his philosophies). Both men chased the favor of the leaders in Florence and both missed the mark completely, with ruinous results for their lives.

But Vincenzo had trouble sustaining even the slightest interest in Dante. The decision to allow his lack of interest in Dante and Dante's peers to rearrange his plan was, in a way, the first truly pivotal decision of his life. It was made blindly, madly, with no sense of what it might mean for him.

Of the *Commedia*'s three sections, only *Purgatorio* was, for young Vincenzo, of anything resembling an abiding interest. *Paradiso* and *Inferno* were unreadable—so morally neat, so didactic and certain: the horrendous being treated horrendously and the righteous being rewarded. Vincenzo, already an eager atheist by the time he encountered the *Commedia* at seventeen, was especially off-put by the savage medieval logic and the gleeful sadism.

At least, on the mountain of Purgatory, souls were in a more complicated position. These venial sinners suffered only a partial loss of grace. The only of the three books set on earth proper, it offered a glimpse of people as flawed as the reader and, for that matter, the writer.

All of those undergoing their purgation had to overcome an absurd and arbitrary punishment to locate the solution to the problem of their sin. The sin would be abstract, indelible, and unmoving, but the punishment clear, finite. In the end, the victims would find salvation in escape from their present circumstances, from literally climbing the mountain toward heaven.

The lesson, weighed out properly, was nothing more than a florid insanity, chaotic as the coastline. Saints were tossed into heaven on a series of misplaced whims. Paradise was geography. To hear the heavenly trumpets sounding, you should arrange your body skyward and commence marching. The lesson was that God was capricious and unthinking and that salvation could be located only by force, by unthinking exertion, by way of celestial topography, by walking uphill.

And, yes, Vincenzo thought, maybe that was it, after all. At a loss for other explanations: why not.

$$=$$

On his last morning in New York, Vincenzo sat on the futon sofa in Leonora and Sam's minuscule one-bedroom walk-up in Brooklyn while she brewed coffee. She'd cleaned up in preparation for his arrival; the smell of stale cigarette smoke was still palpable, if mingling noxiously with Ajax and chlorine. There was a squeaky-clean ashtray on a side table. Sitting with Sam, Vincenzo labored to keep the conversation focused on snow. The snow had melted and then there had been more, but it wasn't as heavy. This dialogue was difficult to sustain.

"I wonder if it will ever melt," Vincenzo said.

"Totally, I know what you mean."

"Some of it seems to have hardened into these iceberg-like protrusions that are, I think, attached, or *welded* to the pavement, or something. I feel I am walking on slippery rock formations."

Sam nodded somberly, revealing no appreciation of Vincenzo's charming banter. "Maybe I'm just used to it, because I'm from . . ." and Sam went on for a little while, but Vincenzo was not quite there.

At the next pause, he said, "In Italy, we had no snow."

Sam nodded again, as before, very methodical.

Vincenzo glanced at the door to the kitchen, where Leonora was supposedly making coffee. What he wanted to do was grab her and explain what a waste of space Sam was, to kick Sam out of that apartment right away; he'd tell her what a waste of time her job was, and tell her that she should come with him to Bolivia. Come with him to Italy when he went to repair the house. This had been the problem for several years: he wanted, desperately, for Leonora to step into the role of pseudo wife—a platonic wife who was half daughter, half wife, half sister, and half friend.

But Leonora was avoiding him and had been ever since their conversation at Saks. Instead, he had Sam. When Vincenzo finally let the conversation wander away from urban ice floes, Sam put forward a challenging combination of puffed-up confidence and deference. No doubt, Sam's understanding of his identity was jumbled by circumstances, too. Sam seemed as if he wanted to impress him, but instead of being flagrantly obeisant or withdrawn (either of which would have been perfectly fine, under the circumstances), he forced himself forward brashly.

"You relieved to be done with the Bank?" he asked, adopting an amazingly overfamiliar posture in one of the early salvos.

"Relieved? No. I think I made the right decision, but I'm not *relieved*. It's actually very unsettling." Vincenzo was distinctly aware that Leonora, in the kitchen, was only a few feet away and absolutely within hearing range.

There was an excruciating pause and then Sam spoke again, saying, "Leo told me you're thinking of working for a nonprofit." *Leo?* Vincenzo didn't like that at all. "That's what I'd do if I were you."

"I'll keep that in mind." He heard Leonora clear her throat as she poured the boiling water from the kettle into the French press.

"It was a think tank. I think," Sam said. Then, maybe unsettled by his embarrassment, he added, "It sounds interesting?" Doubtlessly, he had wanted this to be a declaration, but it misfired and came off like a question.

"They call themselves think tanks, but thinking is many times removed from their main priority. It could be stupendous—especially if I were given autonomy. That would be wonderful. And it would be great to focus on issues, instead of working around internal politics. It would be nice to give my most honest opinions oxygen. But these think tanks each have their own stable of projects and their own prejudices, they all have their own biases, so they will each want me to stay on the story that they have." He wondered why Leonora was being so quiet, why she wasn't coming through. What did she think?

"Why not just retire?" Sam said.

"Because I'm fifty-four." Vincenzo stared at him incredulously until Sam nodded and looked away, and from his shrinking expression it was clear he had been caught off guard by the severity in Vincenzo's voice. Everyone, it seemed, was having a hard time controlling their innuendo. Then Sam, implying that maybe he had not actually understood why he'd just been spanked, pressed the point, saying, "But you have that house in Italy?"

Leonora returned then with the coffees and shot a wide-eyed look at Sam, indicating that he should shut the hell up about her father being ripe for retirement. She no doubt remembered what happened the last time she'd suggested Vincenzo go to Piedmont and clean house. Then again, maybe it wasn't self-serving: Maybe she and this person Sam really wanted him to keep himself occupied with that house? That it was, probably, the nicest vacation house in their collective grasp, however, did give their persistence an unfortunate implication.

Vincenzo said, "It seems like the only thing people want to do with me now is talk about my plans. It is as if people are picking over my bones, you know, before I'm—" He left it there.

"Don't be dramatic, Dad," she said and tucked an escaped lock of hair behind her ear. She'd been just about that tense since he'd lashed out at her, and that was understandable.

"Let's talk about your plans," Vincenzo said. "What do you have planned, Sam?" he said.

Leonora wilted slightly. But Sam, to his credit, didn't flinch. He said, "I'm writing plays for now and working a stupid day job at AOL. Is that good enough?"

Vincenzo liked that, a lot. He liked the growling life in it, the bluntness. In it, he saw that Sam, in his enthusiasm to be perceived a certain way, had hopefully sold himself short—that he was, actually, capable of being defiant and bright.

"If it's good enough for Leonora," Vincenzo said, "it's definitely good enough for me." Vincenzo turned to Leonora, who was turning red with something—anger or embarrassment. She didn't realize he sincerely liked Sam's response, of course, and how could she? Ultimately, he wasn't sure why he was so furious with her, but he was, and it was getting worse. Ever since Thanksgiving, he'd been incrementally angrier with her with almost every interaction. Or, maybe it went back further than that?

Outside, later, after a surprisingly delicious vegan lunch, the three trudged along the snowy path that cut across Mc-Carren Park, listening to their own crunching feet. Leonora had brought a hiking pole, and was stabbing the snow as they went. By now, Vincenzo was quite sure that he was being unfair to Sam, but that, either way, Sam was not up to par. The sky was clear and the sun set the snow crystals alight so that the whole snowy field sparkled blindingly, all the more so when a strong gust kicked up dusty ice particles in mini-tornadoes. Leonora offered her sunglasses but Vincenzo declined. Of course, he shouldn't be so angry with her, but he couldn't help himself. It was a peculiar state of mind for him, this angriness. He'd felt that way often when young, with his mother, and with his siblings, and even with Cristina, in their early years, but he'd relaxed in his middle years, or so he'd thought.

"Jesus, it's freezing," Sam said and stopped walking, took a cigarette out of his jacket.

Leonora and Vincenzo stopped while Sam tried to light up in the gusting wind.

"Have you started smoking again, too?" Vincenzo asked her, squinting at the harsh air.

"No," she shot back. And then, after a second, she stared at him searchingly, and said, "Would you hate me?"

He shook his head and looked at Sam, who had managed to get a small flame going, enough to light the lip of his cigarette. "You can smoke if you want to," he said.

She stared at him briefly, assessing his sincerity. Then she shook her head. "No, I don't smoke." She and Sam exchanged a look.

"You really don't have to lie to me," Vincenzo said.

"Why would I lie to you?" she said.

"Because I'm your father." He grinned at her.

She returned his smile, delivering it just as emptily, and they both laughed a little. Then she lifted her hiking pole and pointed it at him as if it were a fencing blade. "*En garde*," she said. But it wasn't a challenge, it was a distraction.

"Mercy," he said, "you killed me."

"That was easy," she said, and he wanted to hug her, to tackle her with affection, but it would be too odd. So he waved them onward. And the three of them set off again, the wind and snow lashing their exposed faces.

=

When they came to the United States, Vincenzo and Cristina had both been isolated, but Cristina, unemployed and friendless, had been more so. Then Leonora was born and Cristina adored the infant too much, or so Vincenzo had thought at the time. The baby screeched nonstop and forever needed a new diaper, or more milk, or more sleep. The cycle was relentless: diaper, feed, cry, diaper, feed, cry, and it didn't improve for almost a year. And because Leonora's late-night wailing was too much for Vincenzo, and because they had four bedrooms in their house, he took to sleeping upstairs in the sweaty second-floor master bedroom (this was before they had their central air-conditioning installed), while Leonora and Cristina were downstairs, where it was cooler.

And while Vincenzo adored looking at his young daughter and she smiled at him, too—a sunburst of a smile that ignited circuits in new sectors of his soul—and he felt warmer around her than he did around anyone else, including Cristina, time was a harsh mistress. Time strained them until there was a good fissure and it was clear that Leonora was Cristina's baby. Diaper, feed, cry—it was really up to Cristina, since Vincenzo was forever at work. Leonora was fascinated with her father, inescapably, had a daughter's crush on him. But the rest, the deeper needs, all of that became locked deep within the path between Leonora and Cristina.

One Sunday morning, when Leonora was three, he entered the kitchen and found the two of them whispering and laughing. As soon as he entered they fell silent and looked away, stifling their laughter. There was another world, evidently, one he could not access, and it was marvelous and alive and it took place in rooms in which he was not. That was when he realized that he'd lost his wife to his daughter, in a sense, and lost his daughter to his wife.

There would be no second child, because his sex life with Cristina didn't recover in time. They talked about having more children, but life had a way of intervening and sex, once ignored for long enough, ceased to interest either of them. After a while, she may as well have been a sibling. They did have occasional periods of intimacy, usually during vacations when life's patterns were toppled, but they were too intermittent. The rest of the time their life was placid enough. Like any bad habit, it ceased to be a question at some point. He went elsewhere, had affairs that sometimes lasted a few months, but the women were rarely invested because it was clear he had no intention of leaving his wife. His trysts were discreet and she never learned of them. She might have had affairs, too; it was likely that she did, in fact, and he had known when they had probably happened, but he never asked. Better not to know. There came a point when a fight could be spotted from the first step of a conversation and both parties chose not to fight, they surrendered at once, because what was left to accomplish? The muck remained unturned.

Finally, when Leonora went to college, Cristina and Vincenzo started to rediscover each other as human beings. At first, it was awkward, but he found he liked her more once Leonora was not in the house—he had been steadily, if mildly, annoyed by the way she fawned over Leonora, and it was a relief to see Cristina without that distracting issue in the way. They started going on dates again, going to the theater, eating dinner at nice restaurants, alone. At some point, they started making love again, and it was far more exciting and erotic than he'd remembered it being. She had changed while he wasn't paying attention; she'd grown confident and wickedly funny. He fell in love with her again and she, he thought, even sort of fell in love with him again. It was a less energetic kind of love, less exhausting, too. Eye contact, which had all but vanished between them, returned; an absence discovered only by the rediscovery.

They started taking holidays in deliberately arbitrary places, places they had never been to before—Scotland, Thailand, Russia. When they disagreed, now, they seemed more able to laugh and argue at the same time. They bought the house in Italy with the thought that its restoration would be a project that they'd work on for a few weeks a year, at least, maybe more, into their dotage.

This was all taking shape when, one day in the late winter, when it was horribly cold and overcast, he returned to his office after an exhausting meeting with a boorish delegate from Germany and found a message from a police officer on his voice mail. The officer said that he had something important to talk about and asked Vincenzo to call him back immediately. It was clear from the man's tone that he had awful news to impart. It was going to be something unimaginably awful.

"This is Palmer," the voice said. It was a hoarse voice, a shambling voice, laden with a DC drawl.

"Officer Palmer?" Vincenzo said, not wanting his dread to come through.

"Yes. Is this Vin—" The officer halted, evidently trying to remember his name.

"Vincenzo D'Orsi."

"Right," he said. "Um . . . I'm—"

"I wanted—" Vincenzo blurted, and then paused because the sentence had nowhere to go; he'd just wanted to shove a wedge into that space. And there, in the moment he'd opened, Vincenzo knew acutely, if obliquely, that this would mark the end of a generous run of good fortune, one that he should have done more to appreciate, even though people never appreciate such things. It *had* been long. Still, in that way, Vincenzo burrowed into the moment he'd bought, but then he found it didn't contain him and time was already up and Officer Palmer was speaking, and so Vincenzo reluctantly surrendered his consciousness to the information at hand.

=

After New York, Vincenzo spent a week at home in Bethesda. By then, the limelight had moved along, more or less. There'd been no word from Ben, either. Walter had relaxed about that question, too, and hadn't mentioned their awkward conversation the day of Ben's visit.

On Christmas Eve, he and Walter roasted a chicken and ate it with a loaf of good bread, sitting in his basement and watching *The Sopranos*, a TV show that Walter rhapsodized about as if it were *Hamlet*, but about which Vincenzo couldn't muster much enthusiasm. At one point, when the lead character, a bloated ogre in a bathrobe, confided to his psychiatrist about his difficult daughter, Walter chirped, "Look, it's you!"

Vincenzo obliged with a smile. The frequency of these digs from Walter seemed to come and go like the tides, a byproduct of the gravitational pull of Walter's waxing and waning sense of self-worth.

Later, they played two florid games of chess, and Walter, too addled to go home afterward, decided to sleep on the sofa in the basement and watch more television.

The next morning, Christmas morning, they ate bowls of cereal and drank espresso.

"You okay?" Walter said, and it was clear he was serious.

Vincenzo nodded. "Did you sleep okay last night?"

"Fine, thank you." In spite of the vein on his face, a murmur of lightning in a distant cloud, Walter was not someone who ever seemed lonely. Even though he almost never dated, he didn't appear troubled by his solitude. It was a charade, Vincenzo knew. After the dishes were washed, Vincenzo handed Walter the keys to the house and got in a cab bound for National Airport. Walter would spend the day with his brother's family in Baltimore before catching up with him in La Paz a couple of days later.

≡

The word "insignificance" had been lodged in his skin like a splinter since Jonathan had spoken of it in New York. It repeated several times a day, the pain of a minor wound that demanded to be recognized. And what a word it was! An oxymoron, or at least a snake eating its tail: a signifier for a thing without significance. And even if that was too literal a reading, significance would have to be a substitute for other more viscerally potent notions, like power, that failed to entice once you understood them. But, still, the splinter stayed.

Were he to take measure of such things, Vincenzo might notice that he had managed the largest aid organization's policies in a very needy continent, which surely indicated a kind of significance. And by that measure he'd annihilated his own significance, but fortunately life wasn't really about such things.

Machiavelli, in his wisdom, was not a fame seeker at all, and had been perfectly content to remain in the shadows. Zeroing in on the functional value of a thing, he would have seen no value in "significance," per se. The question of influence was more timeless, it seemed to Vincenzo. The question being: Who pulls the strings and why? By that measure, the idea of them going to Bolivia was really about forwarding Walter's career, maybe, giving legs to his already leggy story about Vincenzo's scandal. And Colin's recommendation that Vincenzo join him at Lehman was just about advancing Colin's position: calling in reinforcements. Leonora wanted him to renovate the house in Italy, so that, he supposed, he would be far away, and occupied, and maybe even, though it was an uncharitable thought, setting up a wonderful vacation home. She wanted him to like Sam so that this aspect of her life would be easy, too. And what about Vincenzo himself? What was he gaming for? To fill the void he'd helped create in his life. Find some new significance. But he considered his own moves so far: the rash adoption of mutually assured destruction tactics with Hamilton, his pulling the trigger on that situation, the way he courted totally incompatible professional suitors afterward. What kind of ploy was this? He was playing on instinct, and though it seemed a ludicrous series of moves, he knew it was sound.

=

Vincenzo's itinerary had him at a Marriott by the airport in Miami on Christmas night. After settling into his room, he returned Leonora's phone call. A dog barked in the background, but she sounded pleased, altogether. Of course, he had no idea whether she was having fun or not or whether she actually liked those people or not—it appeared that she'd never confide in him that way, or not anymore, if she ever did. It was all niceties, now. He might as well be talking to one of his siblings in Milan.

Later, he took his copy of *Purgatorio* and went to the hotel bar, hopeful that there'd be a group of stranded travelers making a party out of thin air, but he saw that there was only one other man there, another middle-aged guy with not much hair, so he took a stool far away from him and ordered a hamburger from the bartender.

The only of the three books set on terra firma, *Purgatorio* was also the only space that inhabitants were passing through. They were, as in life, just visiting, free from the confines of infinity, blissful or otherwise.

The following morning, he showed up at Miami International Airport three hours early and made it to the gate for his flight to Bolivia with plenty of time to spare.

He sat down and checked his e-mail. The avalanche of correspondence that had followed his scandal was over. After erasing the junk, he closed his computer.

A family: two parents with their newborn in the bank of seats directly opposite him. The derelict father tapped away on his laptop while his wife fed the son, who fussed and cried constantly. The feeding was interminable—it lasted an hour, at least. The baby cried through much of it, but the mother kept pushing her breast on him and eventually he'd give in.

Vincenzo took a brief nap and when he awoke the infant was shrieking and spitting up copiously all over himself while the novice mother tried, in vain, to soothe him, and the father (now wearing headphones) continued with his computer.

Not able to watch any more, Vincenzo got up and went to a different seat.

Some hours later, after the plane had taken off, Vincenzo, up in business class, and trying to get to sleep, heard the baby crying again, loudly—they must have been just on the other side of the curtain from him. After ten minutes, unable to stop himself, Vincenzo got up from his seat and, parting the curtain, discovered the mother right there, in the same awkward position she'd been holding in the airport, hunched over the baby, pressing her breast into his face underneath her floral drape. Nearby passengers did their best to hide their distress.

Vincenzo kneeled beside the woman and, speaking Spanish as well as he could, said, "Can I hold the baby?" This was all he could think of—that maybe somehow the baby would calm down if someone else took over. Then maybe he'd fall asleep. This had sometimes happened with Leonora when she was an infant, she would calm down only for him; other times it didn't work that way, but one never knew.

The woman—too frazzled to be off-put by this breach of in-flight protocol, to say nothing of handling-a-stranger's-baby protocol—pulled the baby out from under the drape and he shrieked, crimson-faced, into the cabin.

Vincenzo took him from her gingerly and stood up. He hadn't held a baby in years, couldn't remember the last time. To the mother, he said, "Maybe it wants to suck on something, and if you keep offering your—" he wasn't sure what the word for breast was in Spanish, so he said it in Italian—"*seno*, but it's not hungry?" He shook his head. "I don't know." Bouncing him in his arms, he blew on the baby's face, because his face was so flushed, and then the baby fell silent, blinking at the breeze. Seeing his little face so pinched with distress, Vincenzo thought of—he couldn't help himself—Dante's treatment of the gluttonous in *Purgatorio*: how Dante denied them food but made them smell it. If overfed infants died early in their cots, before they could speak, let alone confess their sins or take communion, would they be heaped up in a corner of that terrace on the mountain in purgatory, while the metallic odor of breast milk floated across their nostrils and they howled, writhing among each other, in an obscene pile? Was that how God, in his wisdom, organized the afterlife?

The woman had tears in her eyes now, her chin was crinkled as she watched her silent baby blinking calmly at Vincenzo.

Vincenzo shook his head; he had not really expected it to work. The baby kept calm as he blew onto his face and then, abruptly, he burped once, loudly, spat up a fountain of undigested breast milk down the front of Vincenzo's sweater. Vincenzo quickly smiled at the mother to assure her that it was okay, and continued rocking the baby, singing *Fate la Nanna, Coscine di Pollo* softly as the baby fell asleep.

Nearby passengers watched as discreetly as possible. It's not every day that a dapper aging gentleman from first class comes back to coach to console a crying baby.

"You must be a very good father," the woman said, a mixture of relief and gratitude emanating from her face.

Very nearly allowing an ironic grin, he looked her in the eye, hoping to see recognition that maybe he hadn't been a good father at all but at least he'd tried, but there was nothing there, nothing but a plain beacon of appreciation. Snorting under his breath, he glanced at her husband, who had removed one earphone and turned to watch drowsily, vaguely curious. Vincenzo shook his head and handed the now sleeping baby back to the woman. He grinned, awash in sorrow, and rubbed the baby's soft furry head before returning to his place behind the curtain.

11

BOLIVIA

As the plane taxied down the runway of La Paz's confusingly
named John F. Kennedy International Airport on the late afternoon of December 26, the stewardess, who smelled so intensely
of soap that it was as if she'd spent the night in a vat of molten
soap bars, turned on the intercom and recited her "Welcome to
Bolivia" speech about how cell phones were fine to use and so
on. She cautioned against standing up too quickly, saying, "If
you feel like you are going to faint, you probably are going to
faint, and you should sit back down." Out the window to his
right, Vincenzo saw a terrain as barren as the moon. The spine
of peaks cut jaggedly along the horizon—the bare mandible of
a shark the size of a continent. In the foreground stood nothing but an endless shrubby expanse—a plateau as desolate and
mean as Siberia.

From reading Bolivian country reports over the years, Vincenzo knew that El Alto, the sprawl surrounding the airport,

had been a withered shantytown as recently as twenty years ago, but now its population exceeded that of La Paz itself.

Walter, who had covered Latin America for a while at the *Post* and had been to La Paz often in the eighties and nineties, had told him that El Alto was home to what was reported to be the largest informal market in the world. "You want a propeller for that Fokker two-seater plane you bought in the sixties? Try El Alto. They have every object imaginable. Well, everything that can be bought for less than five hundred dollars. No one has more than five hundred dollars."

And it was, of course, owing in large part to the ascendance of the lower classes—owing to their organizing in places like El Alto—that someone like Evo Morales, claiming to want to represent their interests, had won the presidency.

After debarking, Vincenzo moved as slowly as possible, not wanting to collapse on anyone. As he shuffled down the stairs to the tarmac like an invalid, he winced at the wind biting his cheeks, and the overall effect, the way his age felt immediately amplified, was unnerving. An hour earlier, he had been at least a moderately capable person. Inside the airport, nurses with wheelchairs and tanks of oxygen waited by the luggage conveyor belt. Bolivia was a place like that, where people collapsed on arrival and had to be tended to by nurses. This seemed ripe with some metaphorical significance, something political, but Vincenzo's brain was not functional enough to seek the witty core. FIFA had decreed that the Bolivian soccer team could not host games in La Paz because it was unfair to their opponents. Chess, likewise, would be all but impossible up there, he supposed. All the other travelers, Vincenzo noticed, appeared dizzy and irritable already, too. It felt like midafternoon after he'd had three glasses of wine at lunch.

Just standing there waiting for his luggage at the too-small luggage belt, he had to inhale deeply once in a while, as if he'd been forgetting to breathe. His brain was ringing with pain, as if a nest of barbed wire were unraveling in his cerebral cortex.

After customs he found a pretty woman in an Adidas jacket, which was zipped straight up to her chin, holding a sign that read: VINCENZO D'ORSI. He'd expected a mustachioed man in a dirty blazer, but she looked like a thirtyish jock. On closer inspection, he saw that her eyes were closed and her mouth open. Could it be? Yes, she was sleeping on her feet.

"*Buenas tardes,*" he said. "*Soy Vincenzo.*"

Her eyes sprung open and she blinked, dazed. "*Sí, sí—por supuesto. Es un placer conocerte,*" she said. She shook his hand and he could tell, looking at her, that she was still not fully awake. "*Soy Lenka. ¿Bueno, tienes más equipaje?*"

He hadn't understood that last part so he just looked at her searchingly.

"This is all of your luggage?" she said in heavily accented English.

"Yes—*sí. Permiso.* I didn't catch your name. *¿Tu nombre?*"

"Lenka. It is better if we talk in English." She spoke well, but clearly had to think to assemble her English sentences.

"*¿Por qué mi español—*" He winced.

"Yes, your Spanish is not good," she explained very plainly. Already, he liked her.

"I'm sorry," he said. This issue—his disastrous Spanish (to say nothing of his Portuguese)—had been of considerable embarrassment to him, at times, for years. People expected English speakers to be unable to speak other languages, but for Vincenzo, an executive at an international organization who spoke English, by some measures, better than most native English speakers, a linguaphile—a person who'd been to Latin America more times than he could count, and who spoke Italian, the cousin, if not sibling, of Spanish and Portuguese, as his first language—it was an abomination. Still, it was so, and most Italians he knew who tried to learn Spanish also struggled. It was just similar enough to seem easy, and so there was a tendency to be cavalier about grammar and vocabulary, but, in fact, an Italian's bad Spanish was at least as incomprehensible as a native English speaker's bad Spanish.

"Thank you for picking me up," he said. "You didn't have to do that."

She shook her head dismissively. He was surprised that she, herself, had come to pick him up. He was surprised that she was so attractive, too—he'd pictured a dowdy middle-aged woman during their e-mail exchange, but Lenka was not that way at all. She was wearing a track jacket, no less. She looked almost like a footballer. This exacerbated his discomfort about the altitude, too—her virility, her linguistic capacity versus his tongue-tiedness, it was painful. Once, he'd been given a prostate exam by an attractive young female doctor, and it'd been a similar experience.

Lenka was leading the way out to her car. He hurried after, dragging his large suitcase and mesmerized by the way her hips popped when she walked. The sun had fallen behind the mountains and was making a dramatic light show in the western sky, where fleecy wisps of clouds burnt an incandescent metallic hue, as if they had been garlanded with gold leaf. She opened the trunk to the old Datsun, and he loaded the large bag inside, then shut the door.

Darkness swooped in. Vincenzo's headache had settled upon a plateau of its own by then, and it would rest there until he gave it a compelling reason to leave. He massaged his temples, but that just activated new regions of pain. The cranial contortions seemed to be tenderizing his brain, though, and he was already hopeful that the pain sensors themselves would be beaten comatose, eventually, and the headache would cease.

Lenka was more than half asleep as they drove, and he didn't quite know what to do about it. He didn't want to be rude, but he also didn't want to die.

At a red light in the midst of El Alto, she started wheezing a light snore. The light turned green and Vincenzo had to shake her lightly. She opened her eyes quickly and blinked, cleared her throat, put the car into gear, and pulled through the intersection.

On the dark and winding highway that emptied from the heights of El Alto into the basin of the city, Lenka seemed, miraculously, to be driving with her eyes closed. She swerved around the lanes so casually and senselessly that all of the other drivers honked and gestured as they passed, but she was too asleep to care. Meanwhile, the night outside was weirdly serene. La Paz's skyline was, even from above, less than magisterial—a long puddle of orangish globes filling the valley. As they descended, the stench of exhaust became palpable.

Vincenzo did his best to rouse Lenka with bursts of animated conversation—relating the story of how he helped that young mother with her infant on the flight, and how he had once seen lightning strike a church in Cuenca in southern Ecuador—but she was lost in a twilight state.

At the crest of a more lucid moment, she grunted and said, "I have not slept in a while."

"I can tell," he said. "Do you have children that keep you awake?"

She shook her head and her eyes fluttered. "I have one son. But he doesn't keep me awake. He is eight."

"Oh really!" He was thrusting at the conversation now, just trying to keep her attention. "So what keeps you up at night?" he asked, aware that it was inappropriate, supposing that perhaps the inaptness would jolt her enough to keep her awake for another minute or two. She didn't answer, but shook her head and blinked at the road and he doubted if there was a more captivating sight than a beautiful woman battling off sleep, fighting to bring herself back to life so that she could be there in that moment.

Later, after he thought the question had evaporated, she said, "My boyfriend is a bad person."

Images of bad men came into his mind: overconfident womanizers, drug addicts—but then he had to accept that he had no idea what she meant. "My daughter has a terrible boyfriend. I thought she might leave him, but now I don't know anymore." This did nothing to rouse her, so he switched directions quickly, saying, "Tell me about your son."

She shrugged, appeared to think about it for a minute, and then said, "He is a flirt. He takes after his father."

"I see. What is his father like?" It was difficult to piece her story together: a son, a bad boyfriend, the son's father—she

also had a cross hanging from her rearview mirror and was almost certainly Catholic.

"His father is a fool. But I like his new wife. We all live
together."

"Really? The two couples and your son?"

She shook her head and explained, wearily, that her boyfriend didn't live with them, but she lived with her ex-husband,
his wife, and various other family members, including her parents. They lived not far from the hotel where Vincenzo would
be staying.

"I would love to meet them," Vincenzo said.

She groaned and shook her head. She rubbed her eye vigorously. There was a problematically long pause as they approached the first traffic light within El Alto. She pulled to
a stop, and before she could fall back asleep, Vincenzo said,
"Would you like me to drive?"

She nodded like a sleepy child, eyes closed. "Yes," she said.
She opened her door and stumbled out into the street and a car
honked at her, almost hit her.

Once he was behind the wheel and had adjusted the mirror,
he looked over at her. "Where do I go?"

"Straight. When you come to a place where the road goes
into a circle, wake me." She turned away from him and curled
up. He took a deep breath. He looked back at her. She really
was pretty. Maybe ten years older than Leonora, maybe less—
it was hard to tell. On her back, he noticed a narrow strip of
exposed caramel skin above the line of her jeans. A dimple in
the small of her back was visible, as was the pink edge of her
panties, which, from what he could tell (extrapolating from the

glimpse), were very utilitarian: cotton, Pepto-Bismol colored, built to last. When he'd tried to think of the kind of woman he'd like to spend time with, the person who had come to mind was not this woman—she was outside of his experience—but he was grateful for her differentness. Living amid such machismo, and being ambitious, presumably, and being fierce and independent, she came off as very sober and sexy at the same time. DC didn't have women like this, to say nothing of Italy. Or, he'd never met someone like this.

He glanced down at the console and noticed that there was no speedometer or odometer. There was just the fuel gauge, its needle collapsed at E. There was nothing else.

Then he took a deep breath and looked in the rearview mirror. A line of cars was slowing to a stop at the light ahead, so he put the car into gear and put the blinker on, pulled out into traffic. The muffler was probably damaged, judging by the way the underside of the car blared.

At the roundabout, he nudged her awake, and she directed him through it, then fell back asleep, leaving with him parting instructions to remain straight for half a mile.

That was how he made it, finally, to the Radisson.

When he pulled up, he didn't wake her.

He approached a stern concierge who was reading something on the computer screen and grimacing thoughtfully. He wore a dark suit and a blue-on-gold tie. Looking up at Vincenzo, he blinked, but did not smile or speak. Vincenzo handed over his passport. While the man looked him up, Vincenzo asked if there was an extra room available for the woman who had picked him up, because she was too tired to make it home.

The concierge paused, looked at him sternly, his head tilted to the side.

"She's asleep in the car right now," Vincenzo said. "I had to drive halfway here from the airport."

"We can get a taxi for her," the man said, and resumed typing in Vincenzo's information.

"Then how would she get her car tomorrow?"

"She could take a taxi back tomorrow."

"Oh, yes, of course. That's a better idea."

"Would you like me to call a taxi?"

Vincenzo, thinking he'd just park her car in the neighborhood, assented. The concierge picked up the phone and dialed.

Back outside, the valet had already unloaded his luggage and stacked it by the door. Vincenzo tapped the passenger's side window of the car, but Lenka didn't stir. He tapped it again. Nothing. He went around to the driver's side and got in. She was snoring, a light snore that sounded only when she exhaled. He shook her gently. She groaned.

"*¿Señorita Lenka?* Excuse me, it's time to wake up." He shook her again, more firmly.

"*¿Y qué pasó?*" she said, coming to. She looked around. "*¿Llegamos?*" She blinked several times and looked back at him. "Are we—" She wiped her eyes.

"I have ordered a taxi for you," he said. "They're going to put your car in the garage overnight." He had a twenty-dollar bill in his hand. He held it out to her. "This is for the taxi tonight, and so you can come back tomorrow and pick up your car."

She looked at the money and then she looked at him and he noticed that she appeared confused, and then affronted. She shook her head. "I'll drive." She got out of the car and shut the door.

He got out, too. "I don't think that would be very safe," he said. "Anyway, they've already called a taxi for you." He held out the bill again.

"You don't have very good manners, do you?"

Startled, he said, "I'm sorry, I thought—"

"That's twenty times the cost of a taxi," she said. He watched as a taxi pulled up behind her and the bellhop motioned in Vincenzo's direction. Lenka shook her head. It was chilly and she crossed her arms, frowned at him sleepily. She was even more attractive when she was grumpy, he thought. "What taxi driver is going to have change for that? Anyway, I don't need your money." She opened the door to her car and was about to get in when the taxi pulled up alongside her car and said something to her. She got out of the car and went over to him, leaned down and talked to him. They talked for a minute.

Vincenzo put the money away. What, he wondered, would have happened if he'd tried to put her up in one of the hotel's two-hundred-dollar-a-night rooms? She'd probably have slapped him in the face.

Once her conversation with the driver was done, he drove away and she came over and looked at Vincenzo wearily.

"I'm sorry I got angry at you," she said. "That was nice, what you offered, and you're right that I'm too sleepy to drive. It's not safe."

She agreed to stay for a coffee and then take a taxi home. She handed her keys to the valet, took her ticket, and they went inside. They sat in the window of the café in his hotel and talked—he drank coca tea and she had *café con crema*. She was magnificent, and he wondered whether there was a chance that she might overlook his frailties: his baldness, potbelly, and overlong beak, to say nothing of his ineptitude with her language and the fact that he was unemployed. That she had a boyfriend did not help his case, he knew. He asked about the boyfriend and she just shook her head, as if thinking about something else.

"Is he from here, too?" Vincenzo pressed.

She kept shaking her head, and then said, "Do you know anything about hedge funds?"

"Yes, I do. Does he work for a hedge fund?"

She shook her head some more. "Not really. But why would a hedge fund want to invest in Bolivia?"

"It wouldn't. Well, maybe, in passing, for corporate or sovereign debt. Or maybe with one of the larger companies outside of Bolivia that has a significant interest in Bolivian gas or minerals. It is just not a very substantial economy."

"This is what I hear from people. But don't we have something to offer?"

"Of course. Bolivia has a lot to offer. There's just not much money here."

"And money is everything?"

He shrugged. "No. It can be helpful, but it depends on what you're trying to do."

She had a sip of her coffee. "What are you trying to do?"

"Money is not part of it." But this wasn't true for a variety of reasons, mainly because money had everything to do with his former job, and also because his own monetary situation—the lack of financial pressure—surely informed his decisions.

"That is good to hear. Why did you say you wanted to come to Bolivia?"

He sighed. "I'm not sure that I did want to come here."

"Then why come?"

The truth, that he had nowhere else to be, that he didn't know quite why he did many things these days—he didn't want to say that to her, not yet.

After a while she nodded. Neither one of them spoke. She seemed to be waiting for something and maybe he did, too. Eventually, he said, "Should we call you a taxi?"

"I'll just walk—I have a friend nearby."

Wondering if she meant her boyfriend, he said, "I'll walk you."

She smiled at him sympathetically, and said, "Then I'd have to walk you back here." He smiled, somewhat, and she said, "I'll be back here tomorrow morning for my car. We can have breakfast if you want and then I will explain what the plan is. Evo wants to meet tomorrow. He's going to be busy afterward for a couple days, and I am going out of town, too. The reporter comes tomorrow afternoon, yes?"

"Walter? Yes, that is my understanding."

"Evo wants to meet you both. The party is next Wednesday, so you have time to explore the city. I will go, but will be back in La Paz on Monday. Okay?"

"I'm sorry if I offended you earlier."

She put her hand on his shoulder, leaned in, and kissed him on the cheek and he held steady—it was all he could do to resist the urge to pull her to him and kiss her on the mouth, to grope her with two hands. She patted his jaw lightly. He almost kissed her hand, but stopped himself there. "Sleep well, Mr. D'Orsi," she said.

"I won't," he replied.

She gave him a simple smile, free of any decipherable innuendo—one more gesture for him to adore—and then she turned and left. And as he watched her go his heart sank, fearful that he was already mishandling this, too.

=

In his room that night, Vincenzo showered and then flipped through the dreadful television channels. It was all badly dubbed cowboy movies from the seventies, or bizarre Bolivian game shows—half advertisement, half entertainment—on brightly colored sets covered in the logo of some dish soap. Otherwise, there was one slick telenovela set on a farm in the 1800s, and there were the obligatory mirthless newscasts from the BBC or CNN. He turned it off, remembered Lenka sleeping in the car, the sight of the top of her pink panties and how that color had contrasted with the flawless skin on her back. He tried to put his mind elsewhere, but the headache was no better and he felt exhausted now, too, the kind of weariness he associated with the flu. He glanced at the books he'd brought along: Stiglitz's *The Roaring Nineties* and his new copy of *Purgatorio*, but neither would hold his attention. Lenka's skin had been light brown and he had noticed the downy hairs on her forearm, the wrinkles at her knuckles, and how her earring holes drooped from too many rings and too much gravity over too much time. On her chin she had the strangest birthmark, like a splash of inverse freckles. And her dark eyes emitted, even in that sleepy stupor, such ferocious intelligence that, when he thought back on meeting her, he could see that that was what had done it. She must have had that effect on all men, he supposed, and it stung him already. Her boyfriend was—but how could he be jealous already? Well, he was. Or—it wasn't jealousy, exactly. To be jealous you must possess, there needs to be a claim. This was *envy*. It was covetousness.

When Dante and Virgil made their way to the second terrace on the mountain of purgatory, envy, he remembered, they found the inhabitants whose eyes had been sewn shut. There, Dante had a difficult time—having already worried through the first terrace, where he confronted his own pride. Now he had to recognize, with dread, his own weakness for envy. Yet, succumbing once again, he placed himself sixth among the poets he found there, above Ovid and Lucan. Like so much of purgatory, the sin was slippery; it sneaked in, even with the vigilant. The pride and the envy, in all of these cases, came from a desire to measure one's worth, upon death. A measuring of the value, the imprint, of what had elapsed.

$$=$$

Before dropping off to sleep that night, Vincenzo checked his e-mail once more. There were a dozen new messages, mostly junk. But there, among the dross, he spotted one from Hamilton. He wanted to delete it outright, but couldn't bring himself to. Instead, he opened it, hoping to find within it someone else sharing in this experience—some variation on the flinty but

strangely warm camaraderie that can occur between two men
jilted by the same woman.

> Vincenzo,
> As you probably heard, I'm stepping down "voluntarily"
> in the next month or so. And against the advice of my
> wife, and having already had one too many glasses of
> vodka, I've decided to write to you and see what you
> think about all this shit that you heaped onto our plates.
> Do you have any regrets? I'm dying to know.
> In any case, I want you to know that I will never forget
> what you've done to my life.
> —Will Hamilton

It could not have been more unsatisfying and he immediately
wished he hadn't read it. But he had, so he replied, writing:

> Happy to hear you're being pushed out, too. No regrets
> here.
> —V

Then he closed the browser and shut down his computer.
He put on his pajamas and brushed his teeth. Sitting up in
bed, he looked around the ugly little room and felt surprisingly
great. Elated, even. Could he really take pleasure in vandalizing
another man's life? Yes, it appeared so.

12

PHANTOMS

After his morning shower, while dressing, Vincenzo noticed an envelope had been pushed under his door.

He opened it and found a handwritten note on hotel stationery:

> Vincenzo!
> I was passing by and just wanted to stop in and see how you're enjoying La Paz.
> Your old friend,
> Ben

Vincenzo's mind flickered on and off as he reread the note; then the knowledge of this spread in him, staining everything it touched. The wretched feeling souring within him, he shuffled over to the phone and called down to the front desk and asked, despite his reluctance, to speak to the person who'd taken the note.

When asked to describe who left the note, the woman on the phone told him there had been a black man, a foreigner.

Vincenzo thanked her and hung up.

≡

Alone at his breakfast table, Vincenzo swallowed three paracetamol and then stared drowsily at a woman who looked ineffably, uncannily, like Cristina. But "like" would not be sufficient. She was nearly identical and *nearly* didn't do the issue service, either. Doing his best to not seem like he was staring, he watched her as she stood near the bar. From her beige pantsuit and gold name tag, the burgundy kerchief erupting from her neck, the polite posture of her shoulders, he surmised that she was some kind of manager at the hotel. He was tempted to ask the waiter about her, but decided against it. There'd been other doppelgängers before, none quite so convincing, but he'd seen many. Once, in a three-star hotel in Florence, several months after her death, he'd seen one nearly this convincing, also during breakfast. This wasn't the sort of thing you talked to waiters about, of course. No more than you harassed the front desk about the CIA agent who was leaving you jaunty notes, or confessed your lust/love to the PR person who'd invited you to her country. These were all just specters, he assured himself, shady phenomena haunting the periphery of his life, each too improbable to hold much weight, really. Too improbable until they were sitting directly opposite him, that was.

The waiter refilled his glass of water and asked what he wanted.

Vincenzo sighed, picked up the menu, and scanned. He got the idea. It was hotel breakfast, a genre notable mainly for its non-variety, so he just ordered coffee, fried eggs, potatoes, and fruit. There was a buffet option that he'd smelled but not viewed; as a rule he never went for the buffet, not unless the hotel was *genuinely* five-star. Non-five-star buffets were mostly hideous: hollandaise the texture of a melted Barbie doll, a faint essence of butane gas in the desiccated potatoes, scrambled eggs the color and consistency of foam packing material. The way the industrial metal trays hovered, slightly, in their baths of warm water. This hotel was nice enough to have a polished stone lobby, but *not* nice enough to have a vast floral arrangement in that lobby. It was bathrobes and slippers nice, but not pricey fixtures in the bathrooms nice—the breakfast buffet was not advisable.

When the waiter returned with his coffee, Vincenzo gazed at him, a mostly gray-haired gentleman with a face that appeared to have been buffed to a high polish; the hair, too, was unusually shiny, so it looked as if he'd dunked his head in shellac. "*¿Qué es su nombre?*" Vincenzo said and gestured at the woman.

"*¿La señora? Se llama Luz Elena Guerriera,*" the man said. He was a stern person, grim as the concierge from last night, the inner tips of his whitish eyebrows slammed gravely into the center of his forehead.

"*¿Es Italiana?*"

"*No, no—Boliviana.*" The severe eyebrows didn't budge. "*Gerente de servicios alimentos y bebidas por el hotel.*"

Vincenzo nodded, having not entirely understood that last part (she was something of something and drinks for the hotel, he approximated), but he did capture that she was Bolivian, not Italian, and that her name was Luz Elena. Could he go over and talk to her? No, of course not. What would he say? *This might sound morbid, but you remind me of my dead wife, and I was wondering if you wanted to go on a date?*

No. Preferably not.

There were, of course, some differences between her and Cristina. She had the same sunken cheeks beneath dramatically, nearly haughtily, high cheekbones, the steeply arched eyebrows, like she was perpetually suspicious of the quality of what stood before her. The hair was almost identical, thick and wavy and umber, worn at the most unremarkable length possible: some vague area just past the shoulders. This woman had slightly more frizz and her bangs held themselves somehow differently—it was not a thing that could be described, but he was certain of the difference. Her body, likewise, *was* Cristina, if Cristina shaded a few centimeters one way or another—Cristina had been very lucky and had never really grown fat or haggard like many women did. Luz Elena, the doppelgänger, was slightly shorter, he guessed, maybe an inch or so, and a fraction more slender. Of all the doubles, she was by far the closest. The others, often glimpsed out of the corner of his eye, were mirages that vanished with proximity. Sometimes, he had to cross a street and chase the woman down to get a close enough look to dispel the impression. This was different, though. This woman was not Cristina, obviously, but she was so close, even after another look, that he didn't know what to do, but felt *something* had to be done. She looked at him, no doubt aware that he'd been staring at her, on and off, since he'd sat down, so he looked away.

Lenka entered eventually, twenty minutes late, a stack of newspapers under her arm. She was planning on taking stock of the news, it seemed. Vincenzo had already finished his breakfast and the empty plates had been carted away. She smiled immediately, warmly, and marched toward him, and he felt his heart lift idiotically to meet her. He stood up and extended his hand, but she slapped it away and kissed him on the cheek, dropped her newspapers down on the table.

"You hungry?" he said, hoping that she didn't see that he was blushing.

She nodded and beckoned the waiter. "Sorry I'm late." She fixed Vincenzo with a deliberate gaze and said, "I had a very late night."

"Your boyfriend again?" he said—feeling almost goaded into it, but wishing he'd kept his mouth shut.

She exhaled steadily, staring down at the menu with an expression he couldn't read. After a moment, she said, "Thank you for last night. That was very kind of you."

"It's the least I could do. Any news about Evo?" He gestured at the newspapers.

She rolled her eyes. "Yes. There is a lot of news."

Then the waiter came and she rattled off her order to him so quickly that Vincenzo didn't understand anything of what she had said. Once she was done speaking, she looked at him. "You want something?"

"No thanks," he said and patted his belly. "I'm on a diet."

She smiled at him and shook her head, as if he were crazy for thinking he needed a diet, and then she waved the waiter away and began to detail the plan for the next few days.

Once she had picked Walter up from the airport and he had checked in, she would come back and get Vincenzo and take the two of them over to Evo's office, where they would briefly meet the president-elect. Then she and Evo would leave for a couple of days. He and Walter would entertain themselves and then, on Friday, there would be a party at the National Museum, at which Vincenzo would give a half-hour speech. Hundreds of people would be there. A car would pick them up and take them to the event. Evo and possibly one of his ministers would make a speech first, and then Vincenzo would talk, and he should brace himself for significant media attention. Not stopping for a beat, she asked if he wanted to make his speech in Italian or English, because if he wanted Italian she could try to arrange for a translator, but it would be more difficult than English.

"I can do English."

"Good. English is easier, we should do English. Right now, there is many international press in La Paz, because of the elections."

Vincenzo frowned, thinking of what Colin would say. Briefly, he thought about Hamilton, too, his bitter e-mail— how he would feel about having his name brought back into the news. He said, "I am not going to be granting any more interviews, if that's okay."

She shook her head, gazed at him in frustration. "No, that's not okay. Why do you want to do that?"

"It's too much attention on me. I am not used to it. And I don't want this thing to become the defining event of my life. This is—" There was an opportunity to make this a moment of personal connection, but he couldn't manage to bring himself to direct the innuendo.

A small smile broke on her lips. "I think it's a little too late for that, Vincenzo," she said, and put down the first newspaper and picked up the second, but simply laid it on her lap. "The event is going to be covered by the press, one way or another. If you refuse to talk to them, they will only think that you are being strange."

"I'll think about it," he said.

She sighed heavily and looked away, at nothing.

There was no more business between them, really, so they sat there saying nothing and staring at each other for a moment. There was a captivating combination of confidence and doubt in her face, as if she were still a little disoriented by the violent and sudden ascendency of her chosen candidate, but she was acclimating to the new altitude, almost. "How do you like your hotel?" she asked, clearly just wanting to fill the silence.

He glanced over at the doppelgänger, who was talking to a chef whose white jacket was incredibly filthy. "It's nice."

"I'm sorry about last night," she said again.

"It's fine. I'm sorry for being a little presuming. Was I—" He stopped and tried to think of how to frame it, and then he said, "I was very clumsy."

She tilted her head at him and said, "How do you like life after the World Bank?"

Seeing that the waiter was approaching with her food, he shrugged. The waiter, moving exceptionally fast, set her plate down with one hand and then poured more coffee into their cups.

She transferred her newspapers to the floor beneath her chair. Vincenzo wondered if the arrival of her food had distracted her enough that her question had died and they could move along, but she looked back at him and, picking up her knife and fork, said, "Well—your new life?"

"It's—" He smiled and gestured at the room. He shrugged.

"This is it?" she interpreted, nodding vigorously as if she understood. She took a bite of her breakfast. "When you made your decision last month, did you know what would happen?"

"I still don't know what will happen," he said.

Noticeably pleased, she had a sip of coffee.

He went on: "Life has big exciting parts—intersections—where you have to make a choice and you do, you have to, but you never know how it'll work out. You take a turn off one road because continuing in the same direction seems intolerable. Maybe the new road will be worse, maybe it'll be better—you don't know."

"Yes, that is my experience," she said. "I did not know that Evo would win this election, in fact it did not look likely. Still, I am happy with this. What about you, are you happy?" She put her knife and fork down.

He shrugged. "I turned onto this road because it seemed necessary to make the turn. You have a son and a boyfriend and an ex-husband who you live with, and you are the press liaison to one of the most famous politicians in Latin America. This is just what you wanted?" The doppelgänger marched through the dining room and, as she passed, made the briefest eye contact with him, offering a quarter smile.

"The situation with that boyfriend—it was a mistake. He was a liar. I should have known that. My husband was a mistake, too, but at least he gave me Ernesto, who is my favorite person. And I like him, my ex-husband. I hate him and I like him."

"I felt that way about my wife."

"You are also divorced?"

He hesitated, impaled on the moment, then nodded. He had developed this unfortunate habit of lying to avoid the explaining about Cristina.

When he didn't say anything else, she said, "I picked Evo because of who he is."

He continued nodding for a while, still lost in the previous step in their interaction. Then, finally, he said, "But you still don't know what will happen. What if he's a terrible president?"

"He won't be," she said.

He wanted to say, *Don't fool yourself: you have no idea what kind of president he'll be,* but of course he wasn't going to say that. He'd been married long enough to see the futility of arguments on the basis of principle. There were routes: he could point to the fact that virtually all of Evo's predecessors had turned out to be corrupt or inept and that the vast majority of them had been ousted by their angry citizens; or he could remind her that the country had averaged more than one revolution per year since its 1825 independence. But what would be the point? He'd just be making another prediction, insulting her in another way.

So he nodded as if he agreed completely and he let that subject die, too. Was this how courtship worked: Did you dodge mines until the commitment was solid enough that you could exchange maps detailing the whereabouts of all the remaining mines?

During the ensuing silence, he had a sip of coffee and looked around the room, but Luz Elena was nowhere to be found.

≡

Vincenzo spent the rest of the morning eating paracetamol, drinking coca tea, and walking around an adjacent neighborhood called Sopocachi, which was where Lenka apparently lived. It seemed to be home to the city's middle class, such as it was. Stopping at a bakery for a *salteña* and *café con leche*, he noticed that the headache had temporarily vanished. Soon, however, it was back, so he went to his room to lie down. He drank more coca tea, per the recommendation of the concierge, and tried to push on toward the third terrace of *Purgatorio*, but couldn't manage to focus on the words. He watched *BBC World News* instead.

He awoke from his nap to the sound of the telephone ringing. From the digital clock on the nightstand he saw it was three thirty. He answered. It was Lenka, downstairs. It was time to go meet the president. Vincenzo quickly put on a tie and blazer, straightened his hair. Downstairs, Lenka was waiting beside her Datsun with her mobile phone at her ear.

Steering halfheartedly as she drove up the main avenue bisecting the city, she remained mainly engrossed in her phone call. From what he could understand, she was talking to her boyfriend about the fact that she and Evo were leaving town today, and she couldn't see him for a while. "*Tenemos reuniones ahora, y despues vamos directamente al aeropuerto. Pero te llamo prontito, mi amor,*" she said.

When she hung up, Vincenzo said, "Your boyfriend?"

She didn't say anything for a moment, and then she glanced at him with her wickedly smart eyes and said, "He is a liar and a shit. We are not going out anymore."

He nodded steadily, very cool, although he adored her now, almost overwhelmingly so. Her self-assurance and muscular social style. That she could be coolly dangerous, too, was indescribably alluring. It seemed that she'd been talking rather sweetly with the boyfriend/ex-boyfriend a few minutes before, which didn't quite connect with her suggestion that they'd broken up, but Vincenzo thought better of asking her to clarify. Was this how people dated now? Everything was civil, even hatred. The terms of a contentious breakup were hammered out in dulcet tones: "Pumpkin, I don't think we should see each other anymore because you're a foul slag and an idiot—I hope that's okay."

She said nothing else on the matter but her silence let him know that she was bothered. Maybe her oddly and inappropriately mirthful tone had other, more complicated sources. Maybe she, too, was just badly heartbroken and trying to get on with things, leaping through the Kübler-Ross gauntlet.

They veered into a denser downtown area and pulled up outside another hotel—a gaudier place—mirrored windows, fluorescent-lit placard declaring its name: the Presidente Hotel.

"Let me get him," Vincenzo said.

"Hurry," she said, and picked up her cell phone again, put a hand to her forehead, and called someone.

Vincenzo encountered Walter in the lobby and the two men hugged.

"The flight?" Vincenzo asked, surprised by how relieved he was to see Walter.

Walter shrugged and glanced at his wristwatch. "Don't we have an appointment with our biggest fan?"

"Our chariot is outside. It's that woman Lenka."

"Of the e-mails?"

"Of the e-mails," Vincenzo said as he led the way toward the doors. "How is this hotel?"

"It's resolutely mediocre, but I know it well. I've stayed here one or two million times."

"The altitude? Is it . . ."

"Nah, I'm immune to such things!"

"Ha! Of course you are. My brain is cooked." Vincenzo opened the door to the backseat for him. "When we play chess you'll have to give me a handicap."

"Ha!" Walter said and got into the car.

Lenka drove them four blocks and then steered onto the sidewalk outside an anonymous-looking office and pulled up the parking break. That would, apparently, be her parking space.

$=$

They found Evo Morales in a large and bland office at the back of the building, not far above the sidewalk. The windows looked out on the narrow street jammed with cars, the opposing walls riddled with graffiti and Evo's own campaign posters. It was uncanny to sit there, facing the man whose grinning face was repeated, like some epic Warhol painting, on the wall outside his own window.

Evo, with his bizarrely enormous head, encased in its thick helmet of hair, was on the phone, his computer screen at an angle, displaying a blank Word document. He laughed into the phone and Vincenzo looked out the window at all the other Evos, the smiling Evos, all promising *Adelante*—forward progress. The Evo in front of them said, "*¡Te amo! ¡Te amo! ¡Pero tengo que irme!*" into his phone. He listened while the other person talked and was maybe amused, but also visibly eager to cut the conversation off. Clearly new to politics, he hadn't figured out how to organize his facial expression, permanently, into a mask of something dull and enticing. Eventually, he slammed the phone down and sighed loudly.

"*¡Familia!*" he said and stood up—he'd been on the phone with his family, apparently; but, as Vincenzo understood it, Evo was a bachelor.

Evo shook both men's hands and started talking to them quickly in Spanish, until Lenka cut him off and informed him that they had to speak English, because neither man was any good with Spanish.

Evo sat down again and switched to English, though his English was halting and unsteady, full of unnatural pauses. But it made sense, at least.

"Thank you for coming to Bolivia," he said.

"Thank you for having us," Walter said.

Evo held forth, speaking in broad terms, as politicians like to do before they take office: he talked about correcting imbalances, he was confident and vague. Each idea was lovelier than the previous. It reminded Vincenzo of Jonathan Paris, with his talk about how the World Bank should focus on doing right by the helpless and majestic trees in tropical forests. There was a sense even that history had ordained these events because history knew best and was excited about this proper agenda—the righting of old wrongs, the punishing of the wicked, and so on. Having seen some of these issues from the messy interior, Vincenzo was not as confident that history had a plan, or that the trees and the poor were best served by any of the ideas Evo had to offer. Admittedly, he didn't have any especially useful suggestions of his own, but he was quite sure that a general simplification of the issues wasn't going to help.

The central problem, the one voters tended to struggle with, was the idea that people or things were *supposed* to be a certain way. No one—not Jonathan Paris or Evo Morales, William Hamilton or Paul Wolfowitz—seemed able to cope with the stark reality, the abject arbitrariness and stupidity of the world, that life was an insult to everyone's plans.

Evo, though, for the time being, was nowhere near that messy reality.

Sitting there in front of this man, Vincenzo found that he didn't look at all like any politician he'd ever met. Politicians, from his experience, regardless of their nationality or race, were physically potent in a way: a presence that demanded attention. Evo, however, was not like that—he looked exhausted and suspicious.

Addressing Vincenzo, he said, "For Bolivia, you have done a great service. It is a sacrifice you have made—and with the help of this journalist." Then he turned his big face to Walter and Walter smiled his vacant smile, the one he presented when his mind was calculating something else. Then Walter jotted something in his pad, a strangely unnerving accessory, that pad.

While his pen was still moving, Walter cleared his throat, looked up, and said, "I would like to do a more complete interview with you while I'm here."

"Yes, of course!" Evo laughed. It was a hearty laugh, a bodily event, but surprisingly forced—he laughed like a person without much of a sense of humor.

Lenka shook her head as she laughed along with him. She seemed determined to bolster the unconvincing jollity, but Walter and Vincenzo just smiled.

When he'd stopped laughing, Evo looked at her and she glanced at her watch. "*Cuatro minutos*," she muttered and Evo relaxed and looked back at the men, as if they had all the time in the world. Lenka stood up and walked out of the room.

"When are you going to expropriate the gas?" Vincenzo said. Walter grunted, quietly, clearly displeased that Vincenzo had asked that.

"I'm going to do what is best for the Bolivian people. The gas is our primary export, our great national treasure, but we don't see . . ." The points unfurled in this way, very pro forma, all delivered with the kind of mechanical certainty that public figures often develop after being compelled to recite the same lines again and again for months.

When the recitation was over, Vincenzo said, "But what would you do if the international community withdraws support?"

"Fortunately, you have helped us to draw attention to this threat. Because of the thing that you two men did, those people will be more reluctant to punish Bolivia for being an independent country."

"But what if it happens later?" Vincenzo said.

Lenka ducked in and nodded at Evo, who acknowledged her, but stayed, saying, "I will find support elsewhere." Vincenzo sensed that he thought Brazil or Venezuela or others could fill any void left by irate wealthy aid-providers. The paradigm had changed, he was saying. Vincenzo was not convinced it had changed that much.

Evo stood up and apologized for having to leave early.

Vincenzo said, "What if these other places don't give you the kind of support you need?"

Evo smiled innocently, amused, and shook his head. "We will see!" But beneath his smile there was a palpable fury, a river of rage, and while that rage might be understandable, Vincenzo sensed it would steer his governing style, too. Evo *appeared* to be a principled leader because he *was* a principled leader, and he was a principled leader because he was so furious that he could not be anything other than honest.

$$=$$

The persistent question with Machiavelli, when Vincenzo read him in university, seemed to be whether he was a realist, or whether such self-interest is tantamount to a kind of malice. The question resonated throughout Vincenzo's subsequent studies of economics, which also presented its logic as pure and impartial, absolutely rational. Rousseau, meanwhile, thought *The Prince* a work of satire. Giving credence to this argument, Machiavelli wrote it in Italian, not Latin, so his intended readership was presumably not elite princes, but commoners. Still, while Machiavelli's writing persona changed throughout his life, and he was not always so cunning, his view of the human being was always hard.

Sadly, for him, all of his own rigorous scheming was for naught. He managed, with some difficulty, to ingratiate himself to the republican Soderini who ruled Florence, but the Soderini were ousted by the Medici in 1512, so he was imprisoned and brutally tortured. After years in exile, he returned to Florence and, with time, managed to win favor with the Medici. He rose within their ranks as a playwright—this was when he wrote *The Prince*, though it wasn't published until after his death. Then, in 1527, the Medici were ousted and Machiavelli found himself out of favor with the new leadership. He died without title or station, a man who'd spent his life chasing power, but never quite touching it. No master practitioner of the dark arts, he was most distinctive for his bad luck—for always finding himself on the losing side of history's terrifying swing.

Unfortunately for Machiavelli, and his latter-day disciples, people's behavior isn't ever as predictable as other natural phenomena, like gravity.

Dante, meanwhile, in his own grand exercise of meretricious classification, decoded the human problem by sorting everyone into cleanly organized strata of sins and punishments. To one man, there was absolutely no morality. To the other, there was nothing but morality.

As a reluctant student of these men's thinking during his late adolescence, Vincenzo came to find their simplifications and misunderstandings purely aggravating. Economics alone, of the social sciences, seemed to have a legitimate claim on the scientific method in its study of human behavior. GDP could at least be measured, unlike Oedipal urges, or a certain culture's tendency toward cruelty. The heart, the impulse, was arbitrary and faith-based, a phantom of a phantom, whereas logic and statistics were concrete and could, at least, be trusted to be accurate.

≡

Twenty minutes later, when Walter and Vincenzo walked into the lobby at Walter's crass hotel, Walter said, "Next time leave the questions to me."

"What would you have asked?" Vincenzo said as they walked toward the elevators.

"I wouldn't have smacked him in our first meet and greet, to begin with. These guys, you need to coax them out." When Walter talked, Vincenzo could see that he was quite different while on the job than when they were nattering around. Having never encountered this other Walter, the professional Walter, Vincenzo found the contrast between the two jarring.

Upstairs, at the bar, they played two games of speed chess, but had to give up after that because it was only making Vincenzo's headache worse, and because he'd made all available mistakes by now. Everything abominable had been done. They were defying medical advice and drinking Oban, which Vincenzo had been surprised to find on the bar menu.

Vincenzo looked around at the people there, half expecting to see Ben among them, but he was nowhere to be seen. Still, it was disconcerting that Ben had come to Bolivia, too. It was more serious. Barging into someone's hotel room was bad, following them to a different continent and leaving cryptic messages for them was more than that. "I don't want to get into the particulars," Vincenzo said, "but I think the US government has taken notice of me."

"Why do you think that?"

Vincenzo shrugged.

"Does this have to do with that reference you made in New York to the CIA?"

Vincenzo nodded.

"You worried that they're going to put cyanide in your prosecco?"

Vincenzo nodded again. "Maybe not cyanide, but I don't know . . . I could backpedal, of course, could make our interactions here off the record. They seem to want me to either fade away or become an upstanding person again."

Walter sniffed his whisky, cast his eyes at the ceiling, and the vein beside his eye shifted to make room for the crinkled skin. "I have seen some strange things, so I'm reluctant to tell you that you're delusional, but I think you're delusional."

"I'm not delusional. This guy came into my hotel room."

Walter grunted, surprised. Then he shook his head. "Could it be your friends at Lehman, or someone else?"

Vincenzo thought about this. It hadn't occurred to him before that Ben might be working for Lehman. But no, that didn't make sense, at all. Not quite. They didn't *really* want Vincenzo, did they? Not enough to dispatch a ghost to chase him all the way to Bolivia. "That's not it."

"In any case, I don't think you're going to get snipered to-morrow," Walter said. "And, for what it's worth, I do think it's a little late to take a fire extinguisher to the charred bridges behind you."

"If the threats are real, they could cut off my visa."

Walter grimaced. "I could see them doing that. And it would be annoying."

"No, more than annoying—it'd prevent me from seeing my daughter. They could wreck my credit score, audit me—they could attack my way of life."

Walter frowned in thought. "That's probably true."

"Anyway, I would like to be of some use, and I worry that I might have been too hasty in declaring war on the world. Maybe I should just stay here for a while, let things settle down?"

"Stay in Bolivia?" Walter said, pursing his lips. "Are you thinking about that woman?"

"Lenka?"

"Her, yes, you were looking at her in a way."

"So were you."

"Doesn't count, I look at all women that way."

"She had a boyfriend when I arrived yesterday, but they broke up somehow already."

"Good sign." Walter raised an eyebrow.

"No, it's not that—they were talking on the phone earlier like a couple who are still dating. Anyway, she left town with Morales, so—" Vincenzo shrugged, had a sip of his whisky, which burnt as it went down. "I'm worried about you writing a follow-up piece while we're here, because I don't necessarily want to stir this up any more. I don't want to make a scene."

"Here's a hypothetical question: Do you want to save the world or do you want to save yourself?"

"Does it have to be an either/or?"

Walter blinked uncertainly, glanced at his near-empty glass, and, raising it, caught the young bartender's eye and pointed at the emptiness inside. Then he looked Vincenzo in the eye and said, "Pretty much."

In 2002, when Vincenzo and Cristina went to Scotland for two weeks, they stayed at a bed and breakfast on Harris, the smaller of the conjoined islands: Lewis and Harris. Source of Harris tweed, the island was unbelievably small, considering its output of jackets; it was nothing but a grassy postage stamp bobbing in the dark waters of the North Sea. The inn where they stayed had hundreds of whiskies glinting on the walls, and although it was the middle of summer, there were only a handful of other guests. The Scottish bartender recommended Oban, because that was where he was from and his uncle worked at the distillery, and Cristina liked it, so that was what they drank.

There was nothing much to do in Lewis and Harris. They hiked in the hills, watched the wind whip small waves up in little ponds. They visited the standing stones on Lewis. They went to a fly-fishing lesson, but neither one of them had any talent for it. The rain came cold and hard, blown in off obsidian waves. At night, they sat by the fire in the inn and drank tea, or Oban, and read books, played board games (not chess—Cristina was not at all interested in chess). They made love most mornings and every night. Often, they laughed truly and in a way that they hadn't laughed in years, feeling just as alienated as they had when they were first in love, when they were first separated out from the world by their love in that sweltering July in Rome, when they first came to believe that they were special and different. In Scotland, it was partly the gigantic Scots themselves, their guttural and incomprehensible speech, and it was partly the overall solitude. A week later, on the heaving ferry back to the mainland, the gusts were especially violent, but Vincenzo and Cristina remained on the deck, stung by the wind, facing the battered sea, tasting the salty spray.

Now, the taste of Oban scalding his tongue again, Vincenzo listened to Walter, who spoke with confidence, saying, "As I see it, there are probably people in the State Department who consider you a nuisance, but I don't see anyone doing anything about it. They've got a lot on their plate right now."

"Good." In his glass, Vincenzo could still smell the peat-smoke fire at that Scottish hotel. He shook his head, but the heavy memory didn't shift.

"You're spooking yourself out," Walter said. "There are no hidden consequences. Isaac Newton's first law of motion: states of motion have a hard time changing. So, if you're mobile, you'll just keep moving; immobile, you'll stay immobile."

Vincenzo snorted, not quite listening to him anymore. He unfurled the leather chessboard and started separating the pieces again although his headache was sharpening, and he felt drunker than he wanted to. Thinking about what Walter had just said a little more, thinking about it until its meaning coalesced, he finally said, "Who are you to talk?"

"I'm not in your position," Walter said as he started setting himself up as black. "I didn't explode my life."

Vincenzo rolled his eyes. But Walter was swiftly distracted, and stopped setting up the pieces to look around the room at all the other reporters—all of whom, it seemed, knew each other, were drinking and laughing and talking amongst themselves. There were several pretty women among them. It looked, all in all, like great fun, reckless fun, like a convention of witty people who were experts at talking and listening and telling stories. But none of them were as old as Walter, Vincenzo saw. After a pause, Walter turned his mind back to the moment in front of them and finished setting up the chessboard, while Vincenzo gazed at his glass.

13

LOVE IS A CHOICE

The day after Christmas, Vincenzo had hastily fired off a terse message to Leonora saying he'd be out of the country for a while, but hoped she'd enjoy the rest of her stay at Sam's parents' house. There was no point to the message, not that he could tell, and he regretted sending it.

Now he received a reply, which he opened:

Oh, Papito . . .

Thanks (I think) for the message . . . . I don't know what to say really. I know you are flawed and the rest of that, so you don't need to do some demonstration with these odd e-mails. And I know you're angry. God! Of course you are! And I know you feel guilty, too, and I wish you didn't. But what am I going to do about it? I don't want to be mean, but we're in different places,

you know, and I don't know what to say to you. I'm in
nyc and I have a boyfriend who is actually great (despite
what you think!) and he loves me a lot, and you don't
know much about it. You think you know, but really you
don't. You don't even try to know. You are too self-
centered. Why are you that way? Is it just a guy thing?
That's what Sam says—that it's about the male ego. He
defends you. Did you know that?

Anyway, what I think is that I think you've just been
working so hard for so long that you don't know anything else and that's why you're this way. So now you're
in Bolivia. How is that? Are you being treated like some
rockstar-god? Did they have a parade for you? I read
something online that said that some people think you
did a great deed, something really selfless, by ratting out
that guy at the Bank, like it was a big personal sacrifice.
Is that right? I think it might be. But I don't understand
it, to be honest. I wish I did, but I don't. Maybe one day
you'll explain it to me? I hope so. I love you.

—Leonora

It was a difficult message to receive. Vincenzo printed it
out, just as he used to do with important e-mails at work. He
read it several times. When did she become so strange and
wise? He hated to think that she might have been that way
for years and that he hadn't noticed. Could it be so? Yes, of
course it could.

Though he did not intend to show it to Walter, it was bothering him too much, so he handed it over. Walter read the note and nodded, cast his squinting gaze at the ceiling, and drummed three fingers on his chin. "She's great."

"I know this much, but what do I do?"

Walter shrugged. "I have no idea at all. Really, you would know better than me." He glanced down at the note again. "I can't tell whether I regret not having children. I think about it, and pretend to have a theory, but I really don't know."

"You should regret it."

"Maybe—I'm not sure I trust you on this." Walter passed the page back, cleared his throat, picked up the menu, and perused it briefly, groaning under his breath at the awful choices. "I keep wanting to order the trout, but I don't want to get any sicker." Both men had come down with diarrhea the day after they arrived. Their digestive tracts had been a mess since. When they played chess their stomachs seemed to be carrying on a conversation beneath the table, some creaking and groaning dialogue, like whale-speak.

The three days that Lenka and Evo were out of La Paz had been otherwise unremarkable. Walter and Vincenzo had wandered the city, which was not at all beautiful in the same way that most big cities in emerging economies were not beautiful. Haphazardly erected shanties clung to the mountains around the city. Everything was mainly made of concrete. Aging buildings seemed to pile onto one another on the steep grade—nothing looked like it had been built in the last ten years and nothing looked like it had been built more than fifty years ago. Everything was just old enough to be dated, and dilapidated. Mostly, Vincenzo relaxed. Walter had work to do. And it remained strange to see him work, to see how chiseled his focus was while he pursued a lead; further, to see what he dismissed and what he pursued. Of course he was good at what he did, had to be, but his casual command of this universe was startling. And, in it, Vincenzo saw that he'd been much the same—notably adept at work, reckless and inept elsewhere.

After that first night at the Lookout, the bar on the top floor of the Presidente Hotel, they decided they needed to be much more vigilant about fighting off the altitude sickness. Those whiskies had turned out to be a grave mistake—that tint of intoxication was bullhorned the next morning into an angry hangover the likes of which neither had experienced in at least a decade. The hangover was *literally* painful—an experience, Walter noted, "comparable to un-anesthetized dental surgery." Before the headaches began to recede, the two men's digestive tracts started in, and they decided to take it easy, push fluids, and focus on chess.

On a second visit to the Lookout, they realized they didn't like the crowd, mostly international journalists, who tended to get raucous at odd hours, so they decamped to the much more subdued and tasteful Veritas at the Radisson, where Luz Elena—the doppelgänger—worked nights as the bar manager. Vincenzo had walked directly past her twice since he arrived, usually on his way (via a circuitous route) to the bathroom, and found that her shampoo was different from Cristina's. Her scent was sharper, with a hint of rosemary or pine. Still, somewhat inexplicably, he felt tenderness for her scent—he loved it a little, even if it was foreign.

The night before Lenka was due to return, Vincenzo and Walter played a game at Veritas and Walter trounced him with a surprising adaptation of the King's Indian defense: violence and mayhem were foremost. Afterward, they were talking about chess, and how their games were less formulaic and predictable since Vincenzo had quit his job, when Vincenzo noticed that Walter was staring at her.

"It is eerie, no?" Vincenzo said.

"Does she work here?"

Vincenzo nodded. "Her name is Luz Elena. Every time I see her I want to walk up and introduce myself. I want to say something, tell her about it." Sometimes, he deliberately avoided saying Cristina's name, because when he spoke her name it evoked for him the shape of the vacuum she'd left.

"What would you say to her?"

"I'd tell her about the similarity, I suppose, but it would be too bizarre. I would want to ask her questions, maybe."

"That makes sense. I want to talk to her, too, actually," Walter said.

"Yes. I wonder, for example—I know that people's appearance is determined by the genetic code, so this woman Luz Elena obviously has some portion of her genetic code in common with her, but I wonder if there are other similarities. I want to ask her if she hates beer, if she gets flatulent when she eats chocolate. Is she a late sleeper? Does she have unusually bad menstrual cramps?"

Walter pushed out his lower lip, then said, "Yes, that would be inappropriate." He had a sip of his coca tea and sniffled. "Look, I'm going to call my editor. You reset the board."

While Vincenzo started resetting the table, Walter took out his Blackberry and called his editor and asked if they would spring for him to move to the Radisson. Just listening to half of the conversation, it was clear that they said no. Apparently, the Presidente Hotel was listed as comparable in quality and it cost half as much. And although it wasn't really a big deal, Vincenzo thought that it was better that he no longer had to argue about such things with his superiors. For all of his professional life he, too, had been answering to *someone*. And how strange, then, to be suddenly without anyone to report to, and to be without anyone reporting to him.

When Walter was off the phone, Vincenzo said, "No luck?"

Walter shook his head and looked at the board.

"I don't envy you," Vincenzo said.

Walter shrugged, he put his pawn to D4, and tapped the timer. Vincenzo was not faring particularly well at these slower games anymore. He'd become so accustomed to the rhythm of five- and ten-minute games that even a thirty-minute game threw him off. He simply didn't have the patience for it. His mind was bored by thinking that hard for that long about anything. Vincenzo put his D pawn out to meet Walter's, and Walter immediately moved his pawn to C4, for the Queen's Gambit.

Vincenzo looked up at him. Walter hadn't played the gambit against him in ages, regardless of time constraints. Despite his penchant for vocalizing his inner emotions during conversation, while playing chess Walter was studiously inexpressive.

Glancing up from the board, Walter said, "I don't really envy you, either—the empty hours. It's nice that you've started going to the gym. You were thinking of staying around, flirting with the press liaison?"

Vincenzo took the pawn—why not? The worst that could happen was that he'd lose and he had no problem with losing. "Her boyfriend is probably half my age."

With cold certainty, Walter swept knight to F3 and smacked the timer in a single gesture, then looked back at Vincenzo. "I know it doesn't need to be said, but you're not allowed to make a pass at the doppelgänger. Maybe you don't want to. Either way, it's verboten."

"I wouldn't, of course." Vincenzo blushed, more annoyed than embarrassed. He moved knight to F6, tapped the timer. Walter brought out his queenside knight, tapped the timer. The tapping of the timer was just a habit at this point; at the pace of play they kept now there was really no way that either would run out of time. "Who's paying for your room?" Walter said and had another sip of tea.

"Evo's political party, I suppose. That woman Lenka set it up." Vincenzo brought out his queenside knight, too.

Walter grunted, looked down at the board again, sighed. He brought out a pawn to E3 then shook his head and clucked his tongue in the way he always did once the game began to develop actual complexity—a cue that he needed to turn on the rest of his mind. It was his only tell with chess.

Vincenzo mulled his options. Walter had the momentum already, and Vincenzo would have to fight hard if he wanted to regain the initiative. In all likelihood, he'd lost the initiative until the mid-game. Now, he'd have to win with violence, not guile. He'd hack his way to victory. Either that, or he'd already made his fatal mistake. It had been his second move, probably. The best maneuvers in chess, the ones that ended up in the newspaper, were the ones that showed such deep thought, such a thorough understanding of the strategy of both sides, that the outcome seemed almost inevitable. There was no trickery involved. One player did not step into a "trap" as such. What was magical about those moves was that there was never a way out. One had to reverse the course all the way back, so far back that the pursuit of an explanation for the outcome would be lost there, too.

Which was the fatal flaw buried deep within the architecture of economics: that notion that humans behaved rationally. People may intend to pursue self-interest, may set out to be rational, but they don't even understand their own circumstances, don't know what they want, so, in the end, they chase the winds of whim and are ruled only by blind impulses, finally.

=

The following afternoon, the day before the big event, Vincenzo had his second abortive session at the gym in two days—the altitude made such crusades hilariously unpleasant, and he inevitably found himself wheezing in the armchair near the treadmill within minutes. Breathing was unsatisfying work at that altitude, and panting was even worse. Afterward, he showered and put on the hotel robe and sat at the table in his room trying to write a response to Leonora's e-mail on his laptop. The phone rang. It was Lenka, who had just returned from her trip south with Evo. She was hoping to come by the hotel and check in to see if everything was okay.

He threw his robe onto the floor and spritzed his chest with the Hermès cologne his daughter had given him last Christmas. He grabbed a button-down blue shirt and a black sweater, the brown corduroy slacks. He put on his old black loafers, no socks, and checked himself in the mirror: his face was still red from the morning's exertion, and his eyes looked exhausted, almost jaundiced—there were huge pouches underneath. What was left of his hair was more white than black now. Looking like the late-life Neruda who appeared on dust-jacket photos, he pulled his shoulders back and sucked in his stomach a little, then he turned away and walked to the door.

Lenka walked into the lobby wearing a black dress with heels and makeup.

"Well!" he said, and approached—somewhere in a dark and optimistic corner of his being, he wondered if she had dressed this way for him, but it was unlikely. He kissed her on both cheeks. "What's the occasion? Do you have to work on the weekends?"

"Oh—my clothes?" She shook her head. "I came here from church."

"Of course," he said. Then he said it again, but more enthusiastically: "Of course!"

"What about you, why are you wearing this type of clothes?"

"This?" He looked down at himself and thought of the times his daughter had made fun of him for being incapable of wearing casual clothes. "This is how I dress. You think I am an old man who puts on formal appearances?"

"I would not say that," she said, and grinned.

"Right. Well, maybe I just want to be ready in case I decide to go back to church? I haven't been in years. The confessional—" He was meandering, saying too much. But he would say more, he needed to explain, so he went on, "I don't go anymore. But I did when I was a child. I was confirmed."

"If I did not have my son, I wouldn't always make it, either. But I feel like I have to make an example for him. Right?"

It was generous of her to bail him out like that. "Where should we go?" he said, eager to change the subject.

At her suggestion, they walked down the hill toward the park. Vincenzo's room looked out over it, and it was not much to look at: a little sliver of greenery slicing through the gully of the city. Plants had difficulty at that altitude, too. There was a string of skinny eucalyptus trees and some dry shrubs, scrub oak and the like, some burly juniper, but not much else. From his room upstairs, he could see, on the far side, the United States embassy. They called it "The Bunker" in La Paz, because it looked like a cement block spangled with surveillance cameras.

As they wandered down the hill, he began to dread the walk back up. The farther they went, the more he wondered how he was supposed to do it. Going down was strenuous enough, and he had to slow down.

"I'm sorry, it's—" He shook his head and pointed at the sky.

"Yes, we live in a strange place. We are pressed against the atmosphere. I know foreigners who have been here five and six years and who never adjust to this. Every day they have headaches. It must be horrible. And it is too bad, I think, because it means that we will never have that much tourism."

He looked around at the city, down at the park ahead. The city was not attractive, really, but this was a park that he could see himself walking in, if he moved to La Paz. He could see himself reading the newspaper there on a lazy afternoon. There was a way to like this life, even for an outsider. It just took a little work. They continued their descent.

At last, they arrived and sat on a concrete bench. She handed him a bottle of water and he had a long drink from it.

"You are ready for tomorrow?" she said. "You have your speech?"

"Yes, yes, I have ideas," he said, which was not true. Insofar as he had thought about it, he had thought that it'd be best to say something simple and bland during the speech. He could talk about Bolivia's rich natural resources and the need for good governance and how much he appreciated the invitation—a recitation so sanitized it could be an operating table. "I like it here. I mean, I like being away from everything that has mattered to me for so long. I put so much time into these things. A family. A job. Putting together that life I had. Then it ended, and I—I don't know." He shook his head. "I should shut up?"

"No. Tell me." She had a sip of the water and handed the bottle back to him. He studied the inverse freckles on her chin, her bright eyes with those long eyelashes. He looked at the top of the bottle where her lips had been and he thought about her lips, what it would be like to kiss her, and he could barely contain the rush of desire that this brought up in him.

Taking a deep breath and trying to steady himself, he shook his head, still staring at the top of the water bottle, and said,

"I have nothing to do. I don't want to go back to DC, I am not welcome in New York, and I couldn't imagine going to my house in Italy. I would hate to be in Italy right now. So I think maybe I will stay here for a few months, you know? Why not?"

He looked at her and she smiled. She looked away. "You should stay. You would be a good addition to our city. A great economist. Famous economist! Who knows, maybe Evo will put you into his cabinet!"

Vincenzo laughed at this. "That would be strange, no?"

"He isn't afraid of being strange, you know. I think you are not afraid of this, either."

Vincenzo chuckled, shrugged. "Have you—?" he began, but hesitated. "When was the last time that you restarted your entire life? Have you ever done that?"

She held up an index finger, said, "I have done it once."

"Have you ever thought about doing it again? Just starting over?"

"I have, yes, but I don't want to. There are so many problems with my life, you can't imagine. But I don't want to do something else, or to live somewhere else. My ex-boyfriend is a foreigner, and I am not going to go with him to New York City, which I believe is a nice place to go on holiday, but I have no friends there, I have nothing there. So I will not go there just to be near him."

"But what if you could live anywhere you wanted?" He was getting to a point now.

She looked at him and he knew she could see the point he was getting at, too. She shook her head. "I don't want to be anywhere else. I won't go anywhere else. Even if I could bring my son, and go anywhere in the world, and live as comfortably as someone like you, I would not want to leave this place. I want to stay here and do this."

He understood her point, and he was grateful that she had had the decency to see his point, too, and not to judge him for it. It was not going to be a lewd proposition, and she had probably known that. It would have been beneath her, of course, to go with him. And she was proud, in the straightforward sense of the word: she was proud of her country, and the life she had made for herself. No, she didn't long for an opportunity to settle, quietly, into a bucolic life with any man in the Italian countryside. Still, he held out hope; she had, after all, dated another foreigner, so she surely did not reject foreigners outright.

The sun was starting to set, so they headed back up the hill. They had barely made it out of the park when he became so winded that he had to pause and hold on to a nearby wall. They made it another half block before—feeling as if he would faint—he stopped again and shook his head. He could feel his heart convulsing jerkily in his chest, beating so hard that it was frightening—a muscle at the limit of its capacity. "Jesus. I can't do it," he said, and looked up at her. "I'm sorry," he managed to say. "It's not safe for me." And, still afraid of fainting, he sat down there on the pavement.

"Let me go get my car," she said. "You wait here."

He nodded, the indignity of his situation complete.

She set off, and he leaned up against the concrete wall of someone's house and watched her jog up the hill. Before long, he regained his breath, and began to feel quite relaxed. Little beat-up cars zipped past once in a while. Two men in black fatigues and combat boots, one of them wearing an Uzi, rode past on a dirt bike—the one in the back, the one with the Uzi, was holding on to the other for safety. A mangy yellow dog trotted past, panting.

Eventually, Lenka's car pulled around the corner and began putt-putting down the hill. Vincenzo stood up, and brushed the dust off the bum of his expensive corduroy trousers.

On the drive up the hill, he looked at her profile. She was more majestic when the sun was setting, because it allowed her skin to glow, as it should.

She pulled up under the awning of his hotel and yanked the parking break up.

The bellhop opened the car door, but Vincenzo didn't get out. Instead, he turned to her and said, "If I stay in La Paz afterward, can I take you out to dinner sometime?"

Smiling gently, she shook her head. "Thank you, but no. I don't want to."

"Is it your boyfriend?"

She shook her head again. "No, it's you."

"Fine, that makes sense." He made himself smile at her. Then he got out of the car.

The bellhop had opened the hotel door for him and was standing aside, waiting. Moving slowly, Vincenzo approached the open door, and returned to the crisp lobby. There, he sat in one of the leather armchairs. Ten minutes later, someone approached and asked if he needed anything. He shook his head.

$$=$$

Back in his bathrobe, with the *BBC World News* on the television, he sat in the armchair by the coffee table. After several thwarted drafts, he had abandoned any hope of responding via e-mail to his daughter's missive, and had decided to call her instead. The phone rang four times before she answered.

"Hello?"

"Hello. It's me—Papi."

"Oh! Hi! I didn't recognize the number, sorry. How's Bolivia? What's going on?"

"The altitude is destroying me, but I like it here. I have the party tomorrow." The line was fuzzy, and there was a slight echo, so he could hear himself whispering the words again half a second after he said them, and he could hear that his voice was quite effete after all, and his daughter's imitation was accurate. "How is New York? Are you back in the city, or are you still with Sam's family?"

"We've been back for over a week. The party is tomorrow? A big party in your honor? Wow, I kind of wish I were there. I'd love to see that. The president of Bolivia is throwing a party in your honor. That's crazy, isn't it?"

"Yes. I'm sorry about the letter."

"What?"

"I'm sorry about being so—what was the word you used in that e-mail?"

She sighed, frustrated, maybe. It was hard to read her sighs. "So what happened with that woman who invited you there? Did you guys go on a date?"

"No, no. She is not interested in me, not at all."

"That's too bad."

"No it's not too bad. It's fine."

"Okay," she said.

An intercontinental hiss filled the silence.

"Aren't there dating services," she mused as if they were brainstorming now on how to solve his problem. "I'm sure there's something online. I can look into it if you want."

"Don't do that," he muttered.

"It doesn't have to be cheesy," she said.

He didn't answer. And, after a long enough pause, they both started talking simultaneously. Then they both shut up and waited for the other to continue. It was then that he decided that he would wait indefinitely—he would wait silently for the rest of the day, if he had to. Either way, he would see this through. He got up, pulled a half bottle of white wine from the minibar, grabbed one of the tumblers, and sat back down.

"When do you come back?" she said.

"Come back?" He twisted the cap off and filled the glass. "I don't think I'm coming back. I'm going to sell the house in Italy. I'm going to sell the house in Bethesda."

"*Jesus.* Where are you going to go?"

"I don't know."

"Are you sure you want to sell the house in Italy, Dad? You bought that with Mom. You guys worked on it for two years."

"I am aware. You think I don't know? I will sell it." He had a sip of the wine, which tasted metallic, overly bright. "How's Sam?"

She didn't answer.

"Hello?" he demanded.

"He's fine." There was a long pause. He said nothing, ready to wait out anything she had to offer.

"Why do you hate him?" she eventually asked.

"I don't hate him! I've told you that before, and it's true. Now you have to accept it! I don't hate him! I don't hate him! I don't hate him! What I hate, and I do hate this, is that you are giving yourself to him. He is a fool and it is obvious. But I don't *hate* him. In fact, I like him, maybe. In New York I liked him—but I hate that my daughter, the person I love most in this world, is copulating with this fucking fool and she tells me that she is in love with him!" He stood up and, pacing, relinquished what was left of his control. "And I hate the idea that you would allow someone as boring as that—this idealistic child, who protests against things he doesn't understand, things he cannot understand!—I hate that you give yourself to him! I hate that you want to be with him more than you want to be with me! I am your father! I am your blood! Your *only* family! But you *throw* me aside! *That* is what I fucking hate!"

He drew a deep breath and grasped his forehead, aware that he had gone too far—he paused and waited, resisting the urge to throw the phone into the window.

There was no answer. He could hear himself breathing into the hissing static.

He sat down again. He drained the rest of his glass of wine and refilled it. The inferno inside him started to dim as quickly as it had ignited. "Look I . . ." But he decided against apologizing preemptively, and let the silence stand for a moment. She, too, had good reason to apologize, after all.

At last, he heard a sound—a swiftly inhaled breath, a long shuddered exhale. She inhaled again, more slowly. "Is that all?" she whispered. That voice—that phrase—it cracked straight through a plane of glass that had somehow remained intact inside him. It was the most painful sound he'd heard in years.

"I'm sorry," he said, although it was too late.

There was a fuzzy click on the line when she hung up.

14

SPEECH

While not religious, Vincenzo believed in a kind of cosmic balance. Leonora, for example, had been savaged with loss, and so when, in college, she was in a terrible car accident, she emerged unscathed. The paramedics were astonished. But it made sense.

The person who was driving, a friend of hers, drove into a guardrail while trying to turn the volume up on his stereo, and then his car helicoptered through several lanes of highway, missing various cars, miraculously, any one of which could have killed Leonora, before they slammed into a streetlight. The pole, as chance would have it, struck the driver's side. The driver, named Lee, who was drunk and high on marijuana, died immediately. His body absorbed much of the force of impact, so Leonora felt almost none. The car, slowed considerably now, rolled off down a hill into the woods. Leonora walked out of the crushed car soaked in Lee's blood, but completely unharmed. She sat on the damp leaves and watched the full moon above, listening to the cars whipping past on the freeway nearby. Eventually, she heard the sirens.

Visiting her that weekend, Vincenzo asked if she had realized that Lee had died—this happened a year after her mother died—and she nodded sleepily, staring at her thighs. She was in her bed, her prosthesis leaning against the bedside table. Her eyes were still puffy and red and she looked battered, far older than her real age. She had another month or two of shock and horror left before this, too, became another large piece of trauma lodged into her soul. She was expert enough at the process to know how it worked. Vincenzo didn't say it, because it's not the kind of thing one says to another person, but he was sure this, too, was for the best, somehow.

Looking at her in her dorm room that night and listening to her talk dreamily about what it was like to sit there on those damp leaves, staring up at the full moon and smelling the gasoline . . . and as she spoke, he knew for the first time with absolute certainty that she was already a better person—in every sense—than he, better than he'd ever been, better than he'd ever be.

$$=$$

The following day, at three in the afternoon, nauseated and nearly feverish with some bubbling subterranean terror—a supercharged stage fright or stage fright plus another less definable, but still knife-sharp, queasiness—Vincenzo donned a crisp white shirt, dark-blue suit, and dark tie. In the mirror, he saw an aging man dressed for a funeral. He brushed his teeth (again) and urinated (again)—he'd been drinking coca tea all day long, hoping it would set him straight. It had not. His stomach was tangled, cinched, and saturated with acids. Walter, this working Walter, voracious consumer of facts, had spent the day doing interviews and had called to say he was back at his hotel now, filing a preliminary article. Vincenzo wasn't sure he wanted to see him.

=

Against his better judgment, Vincenzo went down to the hotel bar and ordered a whisky, which he hoped would dim his fear and therefore silence the roiling in his belly. Instead, the first sip was a knife twisting in his stomach. But he kept drinking anyway. From his perch at the hotel bar's corner, the doppelgänger was nowhere to be seen. This was for the best. She was not a calming presence.

Last night, Vincenzo had hastily typed up and printed out a draft of something that approximated a speech, but it was too short and too hazily conceived to be an actual speech; it was rambling and aggressively banal, violently bereft of character. He had two hours before Lenka was going to pick him up. He drained the rest of his whisky and was about to beckon the bill and head upstairs to reread the speech and pace for a while more when a supple-voiced man said, "Can I sit?"

Vincenzo turned and saw Ben motioning at the chair beside him. Groaning, he glanced around the room—no one he recognized. He drew a deep breath, and then nodded. Exhaling slowly, he turned to the bartender and gestured for another whisky.

"You ready for your big night?" Ben said. He was wearing loafers, the kind of boat shoes that the blond boys prowling Georgetown wore in the summer.

Vincenzo shrugged, shook his head.

"Was it hard to write the speech?"

Vincenzo sighed again, not looking at Ben. He rubbed his eyes. Maybe he had the mortar of the speech, but he had not discovered any bricks, yet—or probably it was the other way around and he had the bricks, but nothing to bind them. In any case, time was up, and he had built nothing—time was up and he was drinking whisky, talking to this monster.

"Well, you'll figure something out," Ben said.

Vincenzo snorted. "Can I ask you something?"

"Of course you can."

"Am I unusual?"

Ben peered at him uncertainly.

"Of the people you visit, am I different from the others?" he said.

"Oh, *absolutely*," Ben said, catching his meaning and slapping his back like they were old chums. "Everyone's different from everyone, and you're no exception!" He chuckled. What immaculate teeth! They were gorgeous.

Vincenzo waited for him to settle back down, and then said, "And do you enjoy it?"

"Enjoy it? I love it! What's there not to like?" Ben gestured at Vincenzo and then he gestured at the hotel and he continued with the gesture, as if to include elsewhere, nowhere, everywhere, as if to say, *Look at this world we walk upon, look at the majesty of it—what else could a person hope for!*

Vincenzo declined the opportunity to give a pithy answer. Instead he held Ben firm with his gaze. Maybe this was the purpose of Ben's trip, right here. His whole trip to Bolivia was so that he could sit there, a gleaming enigma, charmingly menacing, beside Vincenzo in the moments before Vincenzo gave his speech. Maybe it was just a lot of intimidation and no matter what he said this would be the last time he saw Ben. On the other hand, maybe Ben would go upstairs and inject a lethal dose of radioactive isotopes into Vincenzo's tube of toothpaste while Vincenzo was away delivering his speech.

Sensing this was his time, his only opportunity, he said: "Will I die unexpectedly, some unforeseen heart condition, if I get up there and fan the flames of this anti-American thing—this, what is it? A shoving war from the south?"

Ben rolled his eyes and smirked. But there it was, this little false note. Something in the flawless smile. The artifice was too much. Ben's every movement felt a little overly studied, the opposite of effortless. Ben said, "Don't get ahead of yourself, Vincenzo—we don't care about this that much." And he kept shaking his head, making skeptical faces, like some cut-rate actor, but it was all too deliberate, too forced, and so much less terrifying as a result.

"You're going to secure me a job at Lehman?" Vincenzo said. This hadn't seemed terribly plausible before and now seemed even less so. Vincenzo knew the kinds of people who ran places like Lehman, and they didn't take orders from junior CIA operatives in comfortable footwear, even if those operatives could magically insinuate themselves into their offices. It was too conspicuous. If Lehman hired every aging economist whom the State Department wanted to shut up, their upper-middle management would be overrun with un-cooperative bureaucrats.

"Lehman is possible. And I know you're interested in Tellus, too—we can set that up. I understand that the Project for the New American Century is also interested in you, but I don't think they've contacted you yet. If you conduct yourself respectfully, the world can be pried open for you."

Puffing out his cheeks, Vincenzo squinted as if contemplating this. But the answer, as with everything, was more complicated. In the Latin Bible of his youth, it was written, *lectio difficilior potior*: the more difficult reading is the stronger. Yes, maybe Ben could carve a swath through a crowd of powerful white people, but he was only as dangerous as his job allowed him to be. And this man, with his iridescent teeth and gloomy shoes, his sensible no-wrinkle shirt, this man was no killer, he was one step away from running the fax machine. If this were a convention, he'd be passing out business cards, looking for an angle. And twenty-five years hence, he'd be just another exhausted, well-traveled bureaucrat in the upper management of some organization or other. Vincenzo would bet his life on it. Since he had to decide how to treat this, had to decide right now, that was his decision. He bet his life on it.

Standing abruptly, he drained his whisky, winced as it landed like fuel on the conflagration in his stomach. Then, gritting his teeth at the pain, he patted Ben on the shoulder, saying, "I'll see you later." And with that he walked back in the direction of the elevators, feeling those eyes on him, but never once hesitating, never once looking back.

≡

In Greek, Thanatos was a minor deity who embodied death itself. Son of Nyx (night) and Erebos (darkness), he was a taker of souls, and a prototype of Lucifer. He dwelled in the under-world. While he lurked mainly in the background of Greek myth, usually in the company of his twin, the god of sleep, his presence—and relevance—has endured through history.

Later, the Romans depicted him as a benevolent winged child, not unlike Cupid, who would swoop in to usher people to peaceful deaths. This temporary gilding of his reputation did not last, however.

To Freudians, Thanatos was the opposite of Eros. And, although Freud himself never used the word "Thanatos," he identified its future concept concisely when he described "a diversion inwards of aggressiveness." Later, Freud amended his assessment and came to see that the aggression in question was more often directed outward, pointed out at the world.

From the same root we get "thanatology," the academic study of death among human beings. We also get the word "euthanasia," for when a person, recognizing that their life has run its course, embraces death gladly.

≡

Vincenzo held Lenka's arm—she was dressed in a limoncello-colored suit, her hair up, her mouth crimson. A guard waved them inside the National Museum, which was composed of several interconnected colonial mansions and whose interior, as a result, was a tight, complicated series of rooms and hallways and antechambers and balconies that overlooked little patios. There were no windows facing out onto the street where the natives would have been. The museum organizers had roughly divided the maze into two sections, the modern and the ancient. The architecture was decidedly Spanish and most of the old art was poorly executed religious iconography. Crude and overly colorful images of a ghostly pale Christ looking down from the cross, dripping crimson from the gash at his side, or his emaciated corpse cradled by voluptuous maidens. Vincenzo caught glimpses of the art as Lenka swept him through the hallways and rooms, all filled with people—there were hundreds of people there. Vincenzo was aware, partially, that some of them were staring at him, but Lenka marched him right along to a small room, a claustrophobia-inducing windowless greenroom, in the modern wing.

Tiny *humitas* filled a platter on a small vestibule. There was a bottle of Bolivian red wine, two bottles of water. A paint-spattered cassette player.

Lenka was harried, had been so since she picked him up. Coordinating such an event was presumably not easy, and she was, after all, new at this. "Do you need anything?" she said.

She was ravishing in her suit and he could barely suppress the desire to kiss her, although she had done such a splendid and diplomatically tactful job of deflecting his overture the previous day. "I—want to thank you for everything," he said.

"No, thank *you*," she said. She nodded. She was in a hurry to leave and tend to business. "You wait here for ten minutes, and I'll come get you when Evo arrives."

"Yes," he said, and then grabbed her hand and pulled her close. He kissed her on the mouth, cupping the back of her head with his hand, her silken hair spilling between his fingers. For a brief moment, a glorious sliver of limbo, the two kissed and he felt no judgment one way or another—no victory and no defeat. He laid his hand on her hip, lightly. She pulled out of the kiss, wiped her mouth, and glanced around the room, as if looking for something. Then she took her lipstick out of her bag and a small handheld mirror, and he watched her reapply it.

The spell was only half broken, and he didn't want to do any more damage, so he said nothing. Once she was done she looked at him, amused, warmly even, approvingly even, and shook her head. "You are a crazy person," she said. She leaned in and kissed him on the cheek and left.

He glanced down at the pages of his speech again, sensing that perhaps it might not sit well with her as it was. It was beyond noncommittal. It was committed to an extended stay in limbo. Maybe Walter was right and Vincenzo needed to stake his flag somewhere, anywhere—and maybe he would come down with Evo and the leftists who adored him? He could tilt the speech in that direction. Picking up the pages, he scanned for a place where he could skew the rhetoric, where he could declare a kind of allegiance to Evo. Did that necessitate him renouncing his work at the Bank, though? This question protruded, because he was not prepared to do that. He found a place in the speech where he could digress about Evo's finer qualities. Pulling a pen from his pocket, he marked it with an arrow. In the margin, he wrote:

TALK ABOUT HOW EVO IS SUPERB HERE. ALSO
MAYBE TALK ABOUT HOW THE BANK SHOULD BE
BETTER.

An extended round of roaring applause outside signaled that
Evo had entered the building. Vincenzo waited, feeling his
blood pressure spike at the impending moment. Finally, the
door opened, but it wasn't Lenka; it was someone in a sport
jacket, a man.

"*Señor D'Orsi*," he said. He was overweight, bald.

"*Sí*," Vincenzo said, wishing that he were better prepared
for this, wishing he had found time to get this right, and wishing, moreover, that life didn't happen so goddamn fast—wishing it didn't come at you like so many flying daggers.

"*Por favor, venga conmigo*," the man said and Vincenzo
did as he was told, following him out into a packed atrium.
He spotted Lenka there amid the throng; she was dispatching
orders to an underling, she was in charge, formidable. Seeing
him, she waved the overweight man away and, taking Vincenzo by the arm, marched him through the crowd. People
stared at them, but she parted them assertively and impatiently.
Glancing around, he noticed huge translucent rectangles were
dangling from cables and within each rectangle sat an array of
bills, no doubt Bolivia's abandoned currencies. Each phase of
currency representing a new fantasy of stability, each an imagined prosperity that eventually died. There were more bills
mounted on the walls.

Lenka brought him into a long, narrow room, which was to
serve as their makeshift auditorium. Evo Morales stood at the

back, grinning and talking with Walter, who was tilted predatorily at him, grinning maniacally.

They all took their seats and the museum's director, whose voice was radio-ready, spoke briefly about Evo and the art on display, about the country's rich history of rebellion. He mentioned the exhibition of money too—"A display that was developed with the help of the World Bank and IMF"—at which the crowd laughed raucously. Vincenzo smiled obligingly. A photographer snapped his picture.

Then the director turned his attention to introducing Evo, lavishing him with praise, going so far as to say he was "the most important and exciting leader this country has had since its independence." Vincenzo wondered if that was true. And, if it was true, he wondered if what he had done was more important than even he understood. History would render its verdict sooner or later, of course, and then his kamikaze could be reassessed.

Evo kept his remarks brief, talking about his gratitude toward Vincenzo for standing up to the imperialist forces of his former employers, for sacrificing himself at their hands. Echoing—deliberately, perhaps—Kennedy's "ask not what your country can do for you" speech, he said that such selflessness was imperative for the Bolivian people, moving forward, as they were facing dire poverty, and only through personal sacrifice could they lift the country.

Evo concluded by thanking Vincenzo for "championing this little country. For too long we have been food for the globalization animal." Finally, he beckoned Vincenzo to the stage.

In his best Spanish, Vincenzo said, "Thank you, President-elect Morales, for inviting me to Bolivia. I have never been before, but I have found the country very beautiful; the people are some of the most lovely people I know. Modest and proud—nothing like us Italians." A smattering of laughter filled the ensuing pause. The lights were bright and shined directly into Vincenzo's eyes when he looked up at the crowd, so he could not see much. Lenka and Walter were off to his left, he knew; Evo was off to his right, at the front. He could see the silhouette of Evo's distinctive head, but little else was clear to him.

Against his better judgment, he decided not to switch to English and, casting his eyes down at the page, he did his best to translate the speech into Spanish, saying: "I worked at the World Bank for a long time, since I was in my twenties, and I enjoyed the work. When I was hired, Robert McNamara was in charge and the World Bank was a different institution. We were smaller, for one thing. But, ahm—" Vincenzo hesitated, as if he'd lost his place. He read on, though there was nothing appealing ahead and now that he was getting the temperature of the room, the antiestablishment tone of the night, he could tell his rote talk about his career at the Bank wasn't going to work, so briefly switching to English, he said, "I'm going to skip ahead." He flipped to the next page of notes.

Then, thinking better of trying to do an impromptu translation of his speech, he said, "I will read the rest in English, if that's okay."

The crowd was painfully silent.

"It's, um—fine, here: the World Bank was conceived in 1944 by the Allies, because they needed—" He paused again because this was not of any use, either.

He wiped sweat from his forehead. "Sorry," he said. He skipped ahead, and read, "The future of the Bank is—" But he gave up right there, blushing, as this travesty came into focus— and said, "I'm sorry, I can't read this."

The crowd chuckled uncomfortably. There was some scattered applause. Vincenzo didn't talk for a while—he wasn't sure what he might say. He should praise Evo, he knew. He was supposed to align himself with the liberals in the room; or, that had been the plan, such as it was.

He wiped more sweat from his forehead and said, "I quit the World Bank because I hated what had become of my life while I worked there." This was true. "It wasn't the job, actually." This, too, was true. The truth was, if not liberating, simpler than trying to concoct some other tilt, some advantageous hue, so he relinquished himself to the truth. After all, he was starting to suppose it was all a wash in the end anyway. And, continuing, he said, "I know that this won't be a popular thing for me to say here, but I think that the World Bank is a good institution. It's more useful than NATO, probably. Everyone who works there, including the president of the World Bank, Paul Wolfowitz, whom I and many of my colleagues expected to hate, means well. Believe it or not, Paul is a good person. And he is a smart person, and he cares about the world more than most people. He works hard. He—well, I don't know. All of my colleagues there worked hard. Me too. I did it for more than two decades."

Some people hissed. Fortunately, most seemed too stunned to react.

"But I worked too hard. I gave too much of myself to this thing—this work. And I came to resent it when my life fell apart. I'm middle-aged now and I—I am very angry. I thought that we should be doing better. And when this man, this representative of the Bush administration, came up to me one morning and asked how 'we' were going to respond if Evo Morales won the election, I was infuriated. I was more than that. I was so upset. I felt—I was not *with him*, this man. I hated him and I hated his boss, George Bush."

There was scattered laughter, applause. He tried to see if Lenka was applauding, but he couldn't locate her in the darkness spread before him. He could see no one, really—just the shapes of them—and he could hear them and smell them, the bodies packed into that space.

"But I'm here to tell you that the World Bank is a big and complicated place," Vincenzo said, as he finally started to relax into the moment. "You know, many of my colleagues . . ." He stopped, realizing that he was about to digress altogether too far, talking about the colleagues he liked and how they hadn't gone to work for investment banks despite the obvious financial incentives. Instead, he got back on topic and said, "I congratulate Evo Morales on his win. I hope he can do more for this country than those who have come before him. His job is very difficult. I wouldn't wish it on *anyone*." No one laughed. Lenka would not have liked that, he realized. "The odds against him making it a full four years are very significant, but I know he means well, too. He is here because he cares about Bolivia. He has said he is going to slash his own salary by half and I believe him. I spoke to Evo a little while ago, a few days ago. We met in his office and he is a very pleasant man and he is sensitive, and I know he means what he says. That should count

for something. I think it should, anyway. I have met quite a
few presidents in Latin America, and most of these men don't
mean what they say, not in the way that he does. He is *real.*"
No one stirred. There was nothing else to say. The president-
elect had flown him down and he had taken the stage, rambled
incoherently, and all but insulted his host, before finally losing
his place once again. It had been a flawless disaster. He'd managed to please no one at all. Before they took the microphone
away, before his platform was erased, he concluded, "I hope—I
hope that doesn't change about Evo. I hope that he can make
a difference. But I must confess that I did not do what I did
because of him."

Vincenzo stepped away from the podium.

The crowd hovered, motionless, uncertain of what to do.
The applause began inside the narrow room and spread out
to the atrium. The applause was rapturous, too enthusiastic
to be sincere. Were they delighted by the awkwardness, or did
the halting and naked honesty somehow overwhelm them with
a more visceral pleasure than they'd planned for? Maybe they
just didn't understand his English. In any case, it was over, the
move—such as it was—had been played. Vincenzo waved at
the audience. He wiped his brow again and walked back toward his seat.

=

Evo laughed too forcefully, unnaturally, while shaking Vincenzo's hand, and asked Vincenzo if he was drunk.

Vincenzo said he was not, but that he hoped to be soon.

Walter's expression, meanwhile, was frozen in a kind of shock that only Walter could experience—equidistant from horror, amusement, and bafflement. Vincenzo hated Walter for being amused at all. It was maddening, and he hated the thought that this, too, had been another dose of material for Walter's dispatches. This look here, this pseudo-amused look from Walter, clawed at him as other people started approaching him; they wanted to shake his hand and speak to him. Miming his way through the conversations, shaking the hands, he looked at the faces, noticing that most of them were laughing or smiling at him like he was a chimpanzee in a top hat. There had been two video cameras, Vincenzo now saw, and the cameramen were chatting animatedly among themselves, while one of them casually reviewed his footage on a small screen. Lenka, locked in somber conversation with several people—maybe press, maybe colleagues—was stranded on the far side of the room, and when Vincenzo finally excused himself from the swarm around him to go see her, he saw her glance at him and he saw her face harden and he knew, right away, that she was not happy. *Of course.* This event had been her idea, in a way, what part of it wasn't his. It had been her responsibility and he had blown it. She, too, had wanted him to perform a certain way, and he had not managed to do so.

"I'm sorry," he said to her when he got near. "I had a speech, but I couldn't—"

"You think this is a joke?" she said.

"No, I don't think this is a joke. I wanted to be honest."

"Honesty was not your problem. You made us look stupid."

He nodded at her and he felt his heart shatter at witnessing one more attractive opportunity lost, another possible future squandered. She turned away and started to walk and talk with someone, a woman, probably an assistant. A photographer came up and started snapping pictures of him, the flash strobing in the corner of his eye as he watched Lenka walk assertively, in her gorgeous limoncello suit, toward the exit.

"¡Señor!" the photographer called to him, waving a hand at him. "¡¿Señor?!"

But Vincenzo wouldn't look away, wouldn't turn to him.

15

THE PURGE

The police officer who had presided over the case called Vincenzo two weeks after Cristina died to say that the man who had been driving the truck that hit her wanted to see him.

"It's an unusual request," the policeman said, "but it happens. Of course, you have no obligation, and you can also just not decide, you know, for as long as you want. Just hang out. I recommend that, actually. Really, if you don't want to do it, don't. I mean it. You've got no responsibility to this guy. He feels terrible, that's the point. It has nothing to do with you."

"I want to meet him," Vincenzo said. "Where?"

The cop set it up. The two would meet at the Starbucks in Tenleytown. The cop described the driver. He said that he was from Nigeria, and that he was brawny, with short hair. "Very dark black skin. Blue-black." From the cop's voice, Vincenzo guessed he was black, too.

Vincenzo had no problem locating him. He was the only black man in that Starbucks.

The man was burly, built like a boxer, but he seemed to be trying to shrink himself into the faux-leather armchair. Vincenzo could see that the man was nervous. Unable to look the man in his yellowy eye, Vincenzo studied his long-fingered hands resting on his lap, clasping each other. The fingers looked surprisingly dainty and thin considering his broad shoulders, his otherwise brawny bearing. For some time, neither said anything.

"What can I do for you?" the man said.

Vincenzo shook his head. For the first time in a while, he didn't feel like weeping at all. Already, he had seen that the first phase of grieving was, in a way, a cataloging of things lost. The shared memories no longer shared, mannerisms never to be seen again, plans obliterated, the films, gardens, medicines, furniture, historical eras discussed—and then, of course, the miniature joys and even the annoyances forever gone, and, one of the more onerous tasks, the list of places and objects and other people who would be marred, or at least tainted, by the life that had been. Now, for the first time, he was able to enjoy a reprieve from that cataloging. He looked out the window. It was raining lightly. It was supposed to snow later.

"When did you come here?" Vincenzo said.

"Washington?"

Vincenzo nodded and glanced at his face, looked away. Apart from a few small pocked scars, the skin on his face was flawless, like some polished volcanic rock.

"Six years."

Still nodding, he said, "And how do you like it?"

The man shook his head. "I am sorry. She—she came—she came—I didn't see her."

"I know that, I know you didn't see her. The police said that—I know it wasn't your fault." Vincenzo wondered if the man was maybe just worried about his job. Maybe he had set up the meeting in the hopes of averting litigation. "Do you have a family?" he said.

"I have a brother and a sister and a wife. I had two sons, but they were sick and died."

Vincenzo nodded. "I'm sorry," he said and nothing else, but he felt sure that the man felt the sincerity. They were both fluent in the language.

"You send money home?" Vincenzo said.

The man nodded.

"That's good. Do you make enough?"

"Yes."

"I work at the World Bank. Did you know that?"

The man shook his head. Vincenzo glanced at his eyes, checking for a reaction, and he did observe a little surprise.

"You work at the World Bank?" the man said.

"Yes. I am a senior economist. I've never been to Nigeria, but I have worked on some Nigerian programs."

The man nodded; now it was his turn to look away. Vincenzo was aware that there had been riots in Nigeria in recent years about the country's debt to aid organizations. Nigeria had been borrowing for decades and had rarely, if ever, been able to repay. Because of corruption, mismanagement in the

Nigerian government, and poorly orchestrated and executed World Bank projects, the debt had not produced many meaningful programs. No one in Nigeria did not know what the World Bank was.

"Can you tell me about her?" the man said, still looking away.

Vincenzo shrugged. "Not really," he said and the thought of her voice, the thought that he would never hear it again, arrived, and with that the sorrow tackled him once again— it came on with savage and terrifying immediacy, a thunderclap. Tears fell out of his eyes instantly and he inhaled deeply, held his breath, afraid to exhale, afraid of the sound that might happen. He stood up, still holding his breath. He nodded energetically as warm tears fell out of his eyes and he gazed at this man, and he wanted to say, "This was a mistake, I have to go now," but he didn't dare and instead just turned toward the door. "I have to—" he managed to croak, pointing at the door.

The man stood up, and nodded, tears shimmering in his eyes, too. "I am sorry," the man said and reached out a hand, but Vincenzo just shook his head, hurrying away.

He ducked outside and exhaled in a garbled gasp, wiping his eyes and walking away, surprised to find himself in a flurry of snowflakes, and he saw, through his burning eyes, how the snowflakes seemed to hesitate in the air like the feathers of a freshly punctured pillow, how the world itself had opened up an envelope of time for him.

=

After his disastrous speech, Vincenzo made his way through the bodies crowding the museum until he could smell the air outside. Hurrying around the corner, he broke out into a jog, running down the hill to the main drag. Loosening his tie and slinging his jacket over his arm, he slowed—his lungs ablaze—and kept walking quickly toward his hotel. Girls holding ice cream cones giggled at the sight of the aging bald man in a suit running down the street, perspiring under the yellow streetlights. The last several blocks, he slowed even more, but his pulse kept hammering in his head, his lungs still shrieked in pain.

Sitting on the edge of his bed, still cooling down after a shower, he heard a knock on his door. Assuming it was Ben wanting to thank him for neutering himself in public, he flung the door open, but, to his disappointment, he found Walter there, holding up a bottle of wine.

Walter sat in the plush armchair, put the bottle of wine down on the glass coffee table. Vincenzo handed him two water glasses and Walter poured.

"Believe it or not, I have heard worse speeches," Walter said, and sighed as he sat there gazing at Vincenzo with an intense expression that he often wore when concerned.

"You have?" Vincenzo thought of the cameras, thought of those videos spreading through the Internet. The responses last time—that stranger who'd sent him flowers, the others. What would they say when they heard that the martyr from the World Bank had bashed erratically through a speech that somehow both declared fidelity to Paul Wolfowitz and announced his respect and admiration for Evo Morales?

"No, I was just trying to be nice." They clinked glasses, sipped. "It almost seems intentional, if you don't mind me saying so." Walter gazed at him again, same as before.

Vincenzo drained his glass, refilled it. Glaring at Walter, he said, "Yes, yes, congratulations, you are impenetrable."

"Impenetrable?"

"Yes! You know that? I think that's why your marriage was so horrible, because you are immune to the world."

Walter blushed, unaccustomed to this, to finding himself in the crosshairs. Then he laughed uneasily, and said, "Thank you, but I thought we were talking about you."

"No, I am finished with talking about me. Let's talk about you." Vincenzo gulped down his second glass, and his stomach convulsed. He felt saliva flood his mouth and took a deep breath, steadied himself against the rising nausea.

"You sound exactly like my ex-wife," Walter said, "accusing me of being carefree, as if it were a crime."

"Carefree? You have a fucking blue vein throbbing beside your eye. You used an empty yogurt container as your breakfast bowl for five months—you're not carefree, you're a wounded duck who believes that he is an eagle!"

Walter's face remained red, but his expression was frozen, locked in some kind of fake amusement. Once he had control of his face again, he rolled his eyes, but Vincenzo could tell that he had landed a devastating blow. Walter shook his head and, collecting himself, said, "Get over it, Vincenzo. Yes, the world did not give you everything you wanted. It gave you *almost* everything, and then it took something away. Tough luck. Look around, it gets worse."

"No! This is it!" Vincenzo replied, aware that he was shout-
ing and that people elsewhere in the hotel might hear. He low-
ered his voice to a hissing whisper. "From now on, for me, it
gets *better*. This is it."

"You think you get to choose? You think you're steering
this ship?"

Vincenzo nodded, shook his head, and nodded again,
his lips pursed. He was ready to punch Walter in the face,
but he wouldn't do that. Not since his father's funeral had he
punched someone, and he wouldn't do it again now. Instead,
he redirected. "You know, that fucking CIA agent showed up
at the hotel earlier?"

"Jesus, really?" Walter leaned in, and, whispering too, said,
"What's he look like?"

"This is off the record, of course."

Walter nodded, grimacing, unable to hide his disappointment. "Sure—go on."

Vincenzo glared at him. "No. Everything I've said to you
since your last piece is off the record. *Everything!*" he yelled.

"Jesus fucking Christ," Walter said. "What is wrong with
you?"

The rage swelled, but Vincenzo resisted the urge to hurl
his glass at the window. He held himself still, dared not move.

"What concept are you protecting?" Walter said. "You
got up there and acted like a deranged person in front of
the world. Videos are, I'm sure, already circulating the Internet. I wouldn't be surprised if you ended up on the *Daily
Show*. The Lehman Brothers are, I promise, not interested
anymore. Tellus, likewise, doesn't want you. You've alienated

everyone in the most public way possible. Why refuse to be on the record with me, now? What do you gain? You'll just damage me."

"I'm ready to live with that. I'm done with this."

"This is not *yours*. You do understand that, right? This isn't about you. You may be done with it, but *it* is not over. This isn't your decision, not anymore."

"That may be true, but it doesn't change anything. It's all unprintable. I want nothing more to do with this thing you are doing."

"Why are you doing this? I set this up and fly down here with you and then, once we're done, you throw me away?"

Vincenzo picked up the bottle of wine and emptied the rest into his glass, put the glass down on the console. "Thanks for the wine." He extended his hand to Walter.

"Am I supposed to shake your hand?"

Vincenzo nodded.

"God, you're a fucking asshole."

Vincenzo nodded again, withdrew his hand. "But at least I'm not a vampire," he muttered, aware that it wasn't fair. But this wouldn't be accomplished by half measures. He opened the door for Walter, stood aside while Walter walked through.

=

Up close, the doppelgänger looked less like Cristina than she did even from a slight distance. When she stared at him there, beside the horrible bar at that horrible hotel, saying nothing, he knew he was looking at someone else altogether.

"You look a lot like someone—my wife," he said, in English.

She smiled, surprised. "I do?" She looked relieved, in the way of a woman who, after being leered at, discovers that the source of her discomfort is happy to speak of his wife.

"Yes," he said. "Very similar—it's very, very, very similar."

"How long have you been married to her?" she said.

The question boomeranged through him, and he let it do that, he let it move. Then he did the math. "Twenty-five years."

"That is incredible," she said. Her voice was nothing like Cristina's. It was higher, ditzy. It was no good.

"Yes."

Now was when he would have kissed her, now was when he almost needed to kiss her, but it wasn't fair, not to him, not to her, not to Cristina, not to—who else? He knew that there were others, too, who would be understandably offended. So he just reached out and took both of her hands in his hands. She looked perplexed, even worried, but he squeezed and released her hands quickly and she smiled at him, confused, sort of, and maybe very sympathetic, too.

"See you around," he said, and turned and walked to the elevators.

—

The question that always seemed most vivid was: How much can you remember of anything? And then the harder question always snuck in, too: Of that which you do remember, how much of it is *true*? These memories, nicely edited and cropped to form by time and our wily minds, do come to look so tidy. Now that the image has been neatly assembled and the lighting adjusted, how are we supposed to embrace this Photoshopped ghost? Eventually, even the most enthusiastic owner has to be suspicious of its provenance.

Cristina's emergent jowls had transfixed him for months, but now he found them scrubbed from his image of her face. Or worse—at other times—they were all he could see. She was vanishing, supplanted by an assembly of gauzy ideas of Cristina. Eventually, you can't even live in the past anymore, because there's nothing left.

After Leonora lost her leg, she wouldn't let them fit her for a prosthesis. For almost two years, she insisted on using crutches, not because she loved being teased or having limited mobility or drawing attention to her loss, but—Vincenzo and Cristina came to believe—because the idea of her functioning well was such an affront to her new understanding of her life. During that first year, she was so terrified of becoming whole again, or being mistaken for whole, that she'd have nightmares about feeling the toes on her right foot again, about her leg returning. Eventually, the dreams went away, and she put her artificial leg on. In a few years, she was even talking about it with people, making jokes about it. The gap became part of her.

And what about that, as a deeper compartment in the slowing, draining bank of a person's being: the attrition of memory. Cristina's smell, once so distinctive, was the concept of a smell. The memory of a memory. Here he found gleaming rafts of nostalgia, wishful thinking bobbing, commingling with tattered slabs of honest memory. Here were abstractions whittled into "facts" by the currents. Like, for example, Cristina's much-ballyhooed intelligence, which he and Leonora had begun to celebrate as if ambitious scholarly sojourns were Cristina's raison d'être. But she wasn't a senior fellow at the Brookings Institution, she was a marketing manager, she was in charge of event planning. Still, every church needs its myths, its miracles, and what else is there to do with such a colossal vacuum, but set about beatifying the spirit? What else is there, but to map her way up the hill to heaven?

$$=$$

Later that night, Vincenzo sat on his bed and waited, expecting something. A visit from the doppelgänger, or Ben, or Walter, or Lenka—a phone call from someone, a moment of clarity, a vision, a cathartic jag, but nothing happened. The air teemed with potential violence and yet calm ruled. The hotel room was still. The television dark. Below, he could hear cars honking and people talking in the street, the barely muted roar of the masses, but that didn't concern him. In the closet, his shirts hung on their hangers, neatly pressed. Beside his bed, the shoes, in their shoetrees, awaited his feet. The two books on his bedside table awaited his reading. The suitcase lay on the ground, gaping at the ceiling, awaiting his need to go somewhere. Nothing moved.

16

FINAL DISPATCHES FROM THE OUTER EDGE OF LIMBO

A month passed.

There had, not surprisingly, been no word from Colin and nothing from Tellus. Ben had not contacted him either. Whomever Ben had represented, they weren't interested anymore. No one was interested. There'd been no word from Lenka. Nothing from Walter except one short e-mail, a week later: *Sorry about the argument. But, just so we're clear, it was your fault.*

Vincenzo replied: *:-)*

Hamilton had not reached out, not since their e-mail exchange. Even Leonora hadn't written. The deluge of e-mails from reporters had stopped altogether. Instead, he woke to messages about elongating his penis and unbelievable deals on airfare to Iceland.

Only Jonathan Paris, of all people, contacted him to ask how it went in Bolivia. Had Jonathan really not read about it? Had he not seen the footage on the Internet? It had been reposted on the *Huffington Post* and, if it had not gone viral, it had certainly torpedoed whatever claim to sanity Vincenzo had before. Yes, perhaps Jonathan, who was not like other people his age, had not seen it.

Vincenzo wrote: *It went as planned. Hope to see you again when I'm next in NY.*

But, in fact, he was already in New York. He'd been in New York for three weeks.

He ate dinner at the far end of the bar in the top-floor restaurant at the W Hotel. There were two bartenders who worked the night shift: Trent, an aspiring graphic designer who was chillingly—exhaustingly—ambitious, and Rachel, who "made paintings," as she put it, in a linguistic contrivance that he hadn't encountered before. Rachel reminded him of Leonora minus the politics, and maybe minus the problem of real and unrecoverable loss, minus that fury. But maybe Rachel was just sanitizing herself for her customers' benefit—maybe the paintings she made were Marxist drivel? He'd asked about her father once, a few days prior, and the question had compelled her to say that her father was dead. With this, unfortunately, he saw that this was probably why she reminded him of Leonora—she *wasn't* missing the loss at all.

"I'm sorry," he'd said.

She shrugged and shook her head, because what else was there to say?

Then, as usual, he drove right past his misgivings, he couldn't help himself, there'd be no scab left unpicked—one way or another, he'd worry the wound until it bled freely again. "How did he die?"

She drew a sharp breath and he could see how much she wished he hadn't asked that. Then, after exhaling, she said, "He killed himself," and presented a tight-lipped smile, bug-eyed—as if shocked by the news herself. As if she wanted to put together a joke to help Vincenzo through the information, but no joke would help. It was a familiar expression—it was the face of maturing but fixed, intractable sorrow.

He knew some things he could say, but those things would just mend the awkwardness on top, so he didn't speak.

=

Another night, he met a talkative drunk man who was a screen-writer and had been flown to New York to meet with some producers who were hiring him to adapt a novel. He talked, tediously, about the details of his work, and then, maybe sensing that the conversation had been lopsided, the man—porcine, with a rake of bushy black hair across his head, Vincenzo had already forgotten his name—asked about him. Specifically, he said, "What about you?"

Vincenzo shrugged and gestured at the space around them vaguely.

"What are you doing here?" the man pressed.

"I like this hotel."

"That's it? You're staying here because you like the hotel?"

Vincenzo nodded, then said, "I don't know."

"What, do you have amnesia?"

Vincenzo laughed a bit too loud and shook his head. "I wish."

"You *wish?*" the screenwriter said, clearly pleased by the unexpectedness of the phrase.

"I used to be an economist," Vincenzo said.

"When?"

"Recently. Now, I'm between things."

"My brother is an accountant, and he insists that . . ." And he went on like that for another ten minutes, just talking about his brother, who was an inept tax accountant. What he said was amusing, but beside the point. Then he asked, "Where do you live?"

Vincenzo had already put his house in Bethesda up for sale. He had put his house in Italy up for sale, too. He'd sold his car back to the dealer. Movers were shuttling his things into a storage unit in Gaithersburg, where they would likely remain, he sensed, for the rest of his life. "It's hard to answer that question," he said. "I'm between places."

The man laughed loudly, and then started talking again.

Looking around, Vincenzo saw the same people—mostly middle-aged men—were there, mostly eating alone. Some were in pairs, coupled with a woman or a man, but not many. Many wore suits, but had removed their ties. Vincenzo was in his mustard corduroys and a burgundy sweater, a white T-shirt underneath. He had the beginnings of a beard. He hadn't had a haircut in a while and didn't anticipate getting one for another month, or two, or more.

And although he had been working on this—on this pulverizing—for only a couple of months, he could see now that the work was mostly done. Wrecking was always easier than construction. There were chunks left, but they wouldn't last long at this rate. It had not seemed like a strategy at first, but of course that was its true cunning. Piloted by intuition, yes, it was a strategy nonetheless.

Now, when he was at a loss to summarize himself—or to describe any aspect of himself, even to enunciate his place of residence—he could see the true end of the mayhem he'd been pursuing. There would not be angels spreading their majestic wings at the conclusion. There had been only this—the space left between where he'd been and where he would emerge again. What he'd had to work with was too badly damaged to be salvaged. He'd had what, in the parlance of insurance adjusters, was referred to as a *total loss*—a designation often viewed as a blessing, counterintuitively, by people ready to wipe clean and start over.

=

The next afternoon, at the diner where Leonora worked, he ordered coffee.

The waitress—another tattooed young lady, about the same age as Leonora, but plump and freckled with wild red hair—brought it to him. He resisted the urge to ask if Leonora would be there soon. Five minutes later, when the waitress next passed him, he flagged her down and asked if Leonora would be working there later. She said no, Leonora had the day off.

The day off? The concept drifted around his mind, opening spaces for itself. What might she do on a day off? Did she and Sam walk Central Park, or meet friends somewhere? He tried to picture it and could see nothing at all. It was beyond the range of his imagination. So he decided he would stay in New York for the foreseeable future. That was step one of his new life.

When the young waitress came back, she said, "How do you know Leo?" Her lower lip was pierced twice, once on either side.

"She's—" he said and then shrugged, thinking better of it. Why make it more difficult than it needed to be? "I'm a friend of the family," he said.

The woman nodded. She was suspicious, he could see, and he was pleased that she felt protective of Leonora, too. "You know, you kind of look like her," she said.

Aware that the ruse was probably up, he said, "Yes, I'm actually her father."

She chuckled, shook her head. "Why'd you lie? That's pretty weird. You didn't want to embarrass her?"

"Yes, I didn't want to embarrass her," he said.

She laughed, and he liked her, liked the intelligence in her manner. She planted a hand on her hip. "She didn't tell me you were in town."

"It's a surprise," he said.

She smiled coquettishly, winked at him. "I promise I won't tell her."

"Thank you," he said, and picked up his coffee, had a sip, grateful for that. He still had time. He had no idea how much time he had. But he had time.

≡

When he entered the gallery in Chinatown, there appeared to be no one there. After a minute, a pasty middle-aged woman, scrawny and haunted, emerged. She wore noisy clogs, maroon-colored; they pounded the floorboards. Her hair, a nest of curls mounded extravagantly on top of her head, was a compellingly unnatural coppery hue. The hair seemed to ignite under the halogens, so that she looked ethereal, some luminous city-dwelling sprite, or ghoul.

"Can I help you?" she said. Her skin was moist, ashen.

"Is Gillian Tilman's video—do you have her—um—her art here? It's a video," he said.

Gillian Tilman was Colin's girlfriend, the video artist. Though Vincenzo had never met her, had never seen any video art at all, to the best of his knowledge, he had wanted to know what she did ever since Colin had described it to him, over lunch in that room on top of the Lehman Brothers building. What Colin did, when it was all said and done, would have probably been the optimal choice for Vincenzo. Vincenzo desperately wanted to see what such a life looked like up close. What else was there, to be with someone like Cynthia? Himself, as a woman—more or less. No, he'd had enough of himself.

The gallery owner sat him down in a small room in the back. There were several simple wooden seats, black curtains boxing him in, a flat-screen television mounted on the wall. She closed the curtain behind her and he sat in the darkness as the large screen awakened.

In the video, a blond and freckled young pixie of a girl, with an aquiline face and a bunched-up mouth, large eyes, licked her lips and had a sip of wine. She readied herself, staring nervously at the camera. A clock in the corner ticked away the time. It was mostly dark in the room and someone could be heard snoring, no doubt Colin. She scratched her forehead, had another sip of wine. She started to appear amused and her mirth grew until she had to stifle a laugh. And all the while she was staring straight out of the screen at Vincenzo, who sat alone in the darkness. Then this elfin little girl had another sip of wine and began to speak:

"Today, I sat here and listened to this car outside and it sounded awful. The engine, I mean. Like, it sounded like it was revving itself to death. You could smell it, even up here. And I gotta say, I loved it. Like, I mean—I *really* loved it. Who was doing that? And, while we're at it"— she stopped to inhale sharply and he saw her expression change subtly, but completely—"I know that there had been another life that I could have had and I don't know whether it would have been better, but I think I would have liked that one, too. Just a couple more turns to the left, or a couple more to the right, and I would have a different life right now."

She had a sip of wine, lit a cigarette. During the pause, the snoring behind her grew louder. A backdrop of digitally animated stars appeared in the darkness of that room and commenced twinkling and turning, moving slowly across the screen, spinning gradually.

She sighed. She looked exhausted, ready to cry.

"Look," she said, "I'm sorry, but I don't care anymore. The car . . . this here, too . . . and you . . . it was . . ." She shook her head. "I shouldn't have done this, either." Then she glanced at the camera and whispered hoarsely: "This was a terrible idea."

But instead of turning it off, she lingered. She sat there for a minute, face scrunched up, staring at nothing. Eventually, she looked back at the camera and said, "I guess that's everything."

The clock in the corner said that the video had been playing for three minutes. Vincenzo reached out and picked up his overcoat, but the camera stayed on her, so he paused, in case there was more. The video kept going. He laid his coat across his lap.

The fake stars continued to twinkle behind her in the bedroom as she sat, smoking cigarette after cigarette, in silence, for the next hour.

When the clock in the corner read 1:04:55, she stubbed out another cigarette and glanced at the camera, and said, "Thanks for sticking around."

Then she reached out, behind the camera, toward the off switch, and he knew that the video was about to end and, in a matter of seconds, the gallery owner would pull open the curtain and ask him if he was still awake, so he tried to dig into the moment as deeply as he could, he tried to stretch it out, to hide, here, on this side of the line, but the video was already over, and he could already hear those clogs on the floor, and he knew it was, all of it, all of it was already over.

ACKNOWLEDGEMENTS

My gratitude to 4Culture, Seattle's Office of Arts and Cultural Affairs, the Corporation of Yaddo, and Seattle Arts and Lectures for their support. Also, especially, the Richard Hugo House, Seattle's writing center, which has given me a second home.

This book would not exist without the support of Jennifer Mountford, who has been my first and best reader for many years.

For advice on technical matters, much gratitude to David Beach, Darren Floyd, Andrea Corcoran, and my sister, Helen. For years, David Shields has been an insightful reader and an invaluable advisor.

My agent, Ayesha Pande, is the most passionate and wise partner a writer could hope for. Likewise, Tony Perez and the wonderful people at Tin House have welcomed me enthusiastically.

Finally, this book owes a substantial debt to the lives and memories of a number of loved ones whom I have outlived; to these extraordinary people—my mother, my grandparents, Farah, Patrick, Eleanor—thank you.